Praise f

"The authentically So _____ ~~yci~~ writes with heart, insight, and a deep understanding of human nature."

– Hank Phillippi Ryan,
Agatha Award-Winning Author of *What You See*

"Boyer delivers a beach read filled with quirky, endearing characters and a masterfully layered mystery, all set in the lush Lowcountry. Don't miss this one!"

– Mary Alice Monroe,
New York Times Bestselling Author of *A Lowcountry Wedding*

"A complicated story that's rich and juicy with plenty of twists and turns. It has lots of peril and romance—something for every cozy mystery fan."

– *New York Journal of Books*

"Has everything you could want in a traditional mystery...I enjoyed every minute of it."

– Charlaine Harris,
New York Times Bestselling Author of *Day Shift*

"Like the other Lowcountry mysteries, there's tons of humor here, but in *Lowcountry Boneyard* there's a dash of darkness, too. A fun and surprisingly thought-provoking read."

– *Mystery Scene Magazine*

"The local foods sound scrumptious and the locale descriptions entice us to be tourists...the PI detail is as convincing as Grafton."

– *Fresh Fiction*

"Boyer delivers big time with a witty mystery that is fun, radiant, and impossible to put down. I love this book!"

– Darynda Jones,
New York Times Bestselling Author

"Southern family eccentricities and manners, a very strongly plotted mystery, and a heroine who must balance her nuptials with a murder investigation ensure that readers will be vastly entertained by this funny and compelling mystery."

– Kings River Life Magazine

"*Lowcountry Bombshell* is that rare combination of suspense, humor, seduction, and mayhem, an absolute must-read not only for mystery enthusiasts but for anyone who loves a fast-paced, well-written story."

– Cassandra King,
Author of *The Same Sweet Girls* and *Moonrise*

"Imaginative, empathetic, genuine, and fun, *Lowcountry Boil* is a lowcountry delight."

– Carolyn Hart,
Author of *What the Cat Saw*

"*Lowcountry Boil* pulls the reader in like the draw of a riptide with a keeps-you-guessing mystery full of romance, family intrigue, and the smell of salt marsh on the Charleston coast."

– Cathy Pickens,
Author of the Southern Fried Mystery Series

"Plenty of secrets, long-simmering feuds, and greedy ventures make for a captivating read...Boyer's chick lit PI debut charmingly showcases South Carolina island culture."

– Library Journal

"This brilliantly executed and well-defined mystery left me mesmerized by all things Southern in one fell swoop... this is the best book yet in this wonderfully charming series."

– Dru's Book Musings

Lowcountry
BOOMERANG

**The Liz Talbot Mystery Series
by Susan M. Boyer**

LOWCOUNTRY BOIL (#1)
LOWCOUNTRY BOMBSHELL (#2)
LOWCOUNTRY BONEYARD (#3)
LOWCOUNTRY BORDELLO (#4)
LOWCOUNTRY BOOK CLUB (#5)
LOWCOUNTRY BONFIRE (#6)
LOWCOUNTRY BOOKSHOP (#7)
LOWCOUNTRY BOOMERANG (#8)
LOWCOUNTRY BOONDOGGLE (#9)

Lowcountry BOOMERANG

A Liz Talbot Mystery

Susan M. Boyer

HENERY PRESS

Copyright

LOWCOUNTRY BOOMERANG
A Liz Talbot Mystery
Part of the Henery Press Mystery Collection

First Edition | September 2019

Henery Press
www.henerypress.com

Trade Paperback ISBN-13: 978-1-63511-543-7
Digital epub ISBN-13: 978-1-63511-544-4
Kindle ISBN-13: 978-1-63511-545-1
Hardcover ISBN-13: 978-1-63511-546-8

Printed in the United States of America

For Jim, always

ACKNOWLEDGMENTS

Heartfelt thanks to...

...each and every reader who has connected with Liz Talbot.

...Jim Boyer, my husband, best friend, and fiercest advocate.

...every member of my fabulous sprawling family for your enthusiastic support.

...Mo Heedles, who appears in this book by virtue of winning a character auction at Bouchercon 2018. I so hope you enjoy your role. Special thanks to Mo's husband, Jim, for being a good sport.

...Margie Sue Frentress, Tanna Mullinax, and Vicki Turpitt, members of the Lowcountry Society, who appear as characters in this book. Special thanks to Margie's twin sister, Marylou Willis, Tanna's husband, Eric, and Vicki's husband, Jim, good sports all.

...Mary Hannah, at 86 Cannon, for your patience with so many questions, and for agreeing to appear in this book as yourself.

...Marcia Migacz, Robin Hillyer Miles, and Pat Werths, whose sharp eyes find my mistakes when I can no longer see them.

...all the members of the Lowcountry Society, for your ongoing enthusiasm and support.

...Susan Busada, my assistant, who handles All the Things with grace.

...Laura Henley, for lovely graphics.

...John Burke, at FSB Associates, for building and maintaining my virtual home.

...Christina Hogrebre at Jane Rotrosen Agency for being the best sounding board around and for your encouragement.

...Kathie Bennett and Susan Zurenda at Magic Time Literary.

...Jill Hendrix, owner of Fiction Addiction bookstore, for your ongoing support. I can't imagine being on this journey without you.

...Kendel Lynn, Art Molinares, and all the folks at Henery Press.

As always, I'm terrified I've forgotten someone. If I have, please know it was unintentional, and in part due to sleep deprivation. I am deeply grateful to everyone who has helped me along this journey.

ONE

The dead are serene, joyful characters. That's been my experience, anyway. Since my best friend, Colleen, came back into my life—thirteen years after her funeral, mind you—the import of this has gradually permeated my brain, giving me a deep-seated sense of peace I hadn't known before. I'm truly grateful for this gift.

That's not to say there aren't still days when Colleen works my very last nerve and I want to throttle her—like the day last September when I was trying to have a civilized conversation with Moon Unit Glendawn at The Cracked Pot over a Cobb salad.

It was the Tuesday after Labor Day. The lunch rush had slowed enough at our island diner that the waitstaff could manage things. Moon Unit, who owned the place, took a seat across from me in the pink gingham-backed booth, something she typically did when she wanted to milk me for gossip, or share some. This was no ordinary day. Moon had called me the night before and said she needed to talk, which was somewhat akin to her telling me she needed to breathe. She was universally acknowledged as our town's Chief Information Officer.

Colleen popped in beside Moon. My guardian spirit wore a green gingham sundress. Her long red curls shimmered with golden highlights. The thick mane draped loose well past her shoulders. Heat and humidity had no effect whatsoever on her since her death. I'd pulled my own hair into a ponytail to get it off my neck. Colleen flashed me an impish grin and propped her elbows on the table. She was up to something, no doubt about it.

I glanced at the ceiling, took a deep cleansing breath.

"Liz? Is this not a good time?" Moon clutched her chest with both hands.

"Of course. It's fine." I grabbed something from thin air. "I was just thinking about Daddy."

Moon twirled a finger through her own ponytail, it a more golden shade of blonde than my multi-toned version. She flashed me a knowing look. "Your poor mamma is a saint walking this earth, and that's all there is to it. Nothing harder to deal with than a sick man. Every little sniffle, they think they're 'bout to die."

"Well, his 'little sniffle' has now turned to bronchitis."

"Bronchitis?" Moon gave me an incredulous look. "He sneezed twice at the pool party week before last."

"You know Daddy. He was running a fever that next night. Wouldn't go to the doctor. Refused to take care of himself. He had a miserable cold within a couple days. By the time Mamma got him over to Warren Harper, it was bronchitis."

"I am so sorry to hear that," said Moon. "Is there anything I can do? I know—I'll whip up a pot of chicken soup and run it by."

"That's sweet of you, really, but Mamma's got a sixteen-quart stock pot full of soup on the stove. She's trying to feed it to all of us to ward off the germs. I told her it's too hot to be eating soup. She's going to end up freezing some of it as it is. Doc Harper wrote Daddy four prescriptions, gave him strict orders to rest in bed, and sent him home with Mamma."

"I hope you know I didn't mean to sound unsympathetic to your daddy's suffering. Bronchitis can be serious business. Even a cold is a misery in this blistering hot weather. It's just...your poor mamma."

"I know." Everyone on this island knew my daddy was a piece of work. "He's turned the corner, we think. But you're right, he's not an easy patient, to say the least. Anyway, how's your family? Everyone doing okay?"

Moon waved a hand dismissively, "They're fine."

"Sonny?" I hadn't talked to Sonny Ravenel since we wrapped up the Drayton case about a week ago. Sonny was a Charleston Police detective. My husband, Nate Andrews, and I were private investigators. Our paths crossed professionally on occasion. Sonny was also my brother, Blake's, best friend. I'd known Sonny forever.

Colleen leaned in.

Moon glanced over her shoulder, like maybe she was verifying no one had sat down behind her. Her eyes slid around the room. She leaned in. "Sonny?" she said casually. "Oh, he's fine."

I scrunched my face at her. Something was off.

"Y'all still dating?" I asked.

"Four months now." Happiness shone from her eyes.

"Sonny and Moon," said Colleen, like she was about to follow it up with sittin' in a tree. "This might stick after all. That's like, totally awesome." Of course, no one but me could hear her. She was in ghost mode, her default setting. Colleen, like me, was a teenager in the nineties. But while I grew out of that, Colleen would forever be seventeen, the age she was when she drank tequila and went swimming in Breach Inlet, which everyone in town knew was suicide, but no one mentioned in polite conversation.

I was thinking how four months was a record for both Sonny and Moon. I smiled back at her. "Y'all sure seem to make each other happy."

She kept smiling, tucked a nonexistent stray lock of hair behind her ear. Then she glanced around again.

"Spit it out already," said Colleen.

I waited for Moon to speak her piece. She called this meeting.

"It's just..." She licked her lips, took a breath. Her shoulders rose and fell.

Moon tilted her head. "You know how when you *really* know someone, you can read between the lines?"

"Sure," I said.

"I'm almost positive Sonny intended for me to tell you this. But he'd never, ever admit that. I've got to figure out a way to tell you, without tellin' you."

"Tell me what, exactly?"

"Well, you know about Trina Lynn Causby, of course." Moon shook her head. "Just heartbreaking."

"Did Sonny catch that case?" Trina Lynn Causby was Troy Causby's oldest sister. My sister, Merry, had an unfortunate lapse in judgement and dated Troy Causby for a while, but that was a whole nother story.

Moon nodded. "Mmm-hmm. Him and his new partner."

"Sonny has a new partner?" I caught myself furrowing my brow and responded instantly to Mamma's voice in my head admonishing me about wrinkles. I smoothed the skin between my eyebrows.

"Didn't I mention that?" Colleen's eyes glinted mischievously.

"Detective Jenkins," said Moon.

I pondered that. I'd met Detective Jeremy Jenkins a time or two. He was a decent enough guy. Seemed like a good detective. He probably wasn't my biggest fan, but still. "Reassignments aren't all that uncommon."

"That's what Sonny said," said Moon. "But Detective Jenkins—Jeremy—he's one of those that's a stickler for policies, protocol, procedures—all such as that."

"This'll be trouble," said Colleen. "Hey, don't forget my ham biscuits. You didn't order them when you ordered your salad." One of the benefits of being departed was that Colleen never had to count calories. She did have to materialize to eat, something she couldn't do in public. I ordered enough takeout with my meals to make folks wonder if maybe I suffered from an eating disorder.

I said, "So there's something about the Trina Lynn Causby case Sonny wants me to know, but he and I can't have coffee and discuss it. Why doesn't he just call me?"

Moon studied something over my shoulder. "I'm not a hundred percent certain? But I think he doesn't want to have to lie to his partner. And he knows Jenkins wouldn't cotton to discussing an active case with a PI."

"Maybe especially this PI."

"Maybe so," Moon winced. "Or a local small-town police chief."

Sonny couldn't get Blake to tell me, so Moon Unit was up. My brother was the Stella Maris chief of police. Something seriously unusual was going on here. Sonny had a burner phone specifically to talk to Blake when he technically couldn't. "Trina Lynn was shot in Philadelphia Alley Sunday night. The news made it sound like a robbery gone bad. Do they already have a suspect?"

"*So* not what happened," said Colleen.

What do you know about this? I threw the thought at her. Usually she could read my mind, which was how I communicated with her when other folks were around so they didn't have me carted off to the nervous hospital.

"I know it was cold-blooded murder, but that's all the information I've been given at this point," said Colleen. "The fact that I know that much means there's a connection to this island."

Colleen's afterlife mission was serving as the guardian spirit of Stella Maris, our island home just north of Isle of Palms, South Carolina.

"I think they might...have a suspect in mind. More iced tea?" Moon picked up the pitcher and filled my glass. "By the way, have you seen Darius Baker since he moved back home?"

"Darius Baker?" The question seemed completely random. I drew a blank.

Colleen burst out in her signature bray-snort guffaw. "When you draw your chin back like that and squinch your face up, you remind me of your Uncle Cecil."

Hush up. Mamma's youngest brother Cecil took a Greyhound to Florida a few years back. The last we heard he'd started his own church somewhere near Orlando. He sent Mamma a postcard once with a picture of him, shaved bald, cloaked in a white robe, standing in front of a statue of Mary that wept blood. He had an albino boa constrictor draped across his shoulders as big around as a cat. I guess no one told Cecil that the snakes handled in religious services were generally the venomous kind. We didn't discuss Uncle Cecil. It upset Mamma.

Moon examined her manicure.

"What does Darius Baker have to do with Trina Lynn being robbed and murdered?" I asked.

Moon shrugged, looked innocent.

"No," I said, "I haven't seen Darius Baker since he moved home. He's only been here a week. The moving trucks have barely unloaded his furniture at the Devlin homeplace. And it's not like Darius and I were ever close friends or anything. He's four years older than us. By the time you and I were at Stella Maris High, he was already on his way to Hollywood. I hadn't planned on taking him a casserole. Have you?"

"Me?" Moon raised her eyebrows. "Why no, I haven't seen him. I hadn't even thought about a casserole. Do you think we should take him a casserole?"

"No. No, I do not." I searched my brain for anything I knew about Darius Baker. "He did date Trina Lynn in high school, but good grief—that was more than twenty years ago."

"Did you ever hear anything about him maybe being rough with her?" asked Moon.

Colleen stared at Moon. "They think Darius killed Trina Lynn."

"Wait," I said. "What? I always thought he was like the court jester of his class. He wrapped the principal's car in a ton of cellophane so he couldn't drive to school the last day of final exams."

"I don't think they actually proved that was him," said Moon.

"He and a couple of his buddies rearranged everyone's Christmas yard decorations so that the reindeer were being frisky with each other. Mamma had a fit over that one."

"That was back before everyone had cameras in their doorbells, so no one was actually apprehended," said Moon.

"But everyone in town knew Darius was behind it," I said.

"Well, that was the rumor," said Moon.

"He was a clown," I said.

"Umm." Moon shrugged, made a face that said she conceded the point. "A very handsome clown."

"He was a football player," I said. "I seem to remember he had a reputation for being a bit of a tough guy...never backed down from a fight. But I never heard he hit Trina Lynn."

"It was probably just talk," said Moon. "Everyone said she broke Darius's heart and that's why he left like he did, with barely a word to anyone."

"She kicked him to the curb," said Colleen. "I remember that much."

"But again, Moon," I said. "That was more than twenty years ago. They both moved on a long time ago."

"It's interesting they both ended up on television, isn't it?" asked Moon.

"I suppose," I said, "but there's no connection at all. Trina Lynn was an investigative reporter at WCSC. She was a local celebrity, sure. But Darius...Darius is a household name. I doubt they've seen each other since the day he left town."

"I wonder if that's true," mused Moon. She gave me this encouraging look, like maybe she was steering me down the right track.

"Sonny thinks after all this time Darius was jealous of some boyfriend of Trina's or something?" I was highly skeptical of this notion.

"I'm sure I wouldn't know," said Moon.

"And a week after he moves home, he tracks her to Philadelphia Alley and shoots her?"

"There's that Cecil look again," said Colleen. "Kinda like a turtle. I always thought Cecil looked like a turtle after he shaved his head."

While Moon stared into space, I cut Colleen a warning look.

"You know," said Moon, "I don't think he's been home a single solitary time since he left. His poor mamma left not long after he did. I'm kinda surprised, to tell you the truth, that he came back here."

"There's no place like home." I shrugged. "It's remote enough. I guess I can see the appeal for a semi-retired celebrity. Plus, he was always close to his aunt Nell. She and Bill practically raised Darius." Nell Cooper, née Baker, Blake's dispatcher and administrative assistant, was Darius's aunt. Her younger brother, Marcus, had a wild streak a mile wide, and an out-of-wedlock baby with Jasmine King. By all accounts, Jasmine tried to be a good mother, but she was only seventeen when Darius was born, and Marcus didn't stick around.

"Hmmpf. They sure were good to him," said Moon. "If you ask me, he coulda made life a lot easier for them. He must be right up there with Oprah in the earnings department."

"I wouldn't go that far. Why do Sonny and his partner suspect Darius?" I asked.

"That's not entirely accurate?" Moon wore a pained look.

I tilted my head, looked at her sideways. "Am I going to have to guess every single bit of this story you're not telling me?"

"Uh-huh." She nodded, a pleased look on her face, as if she was proud of a slow student.

"Hell's Bells, Moon. Can't you just tell me, in strictest confidence, of course, what it is you think Sonny wants me to know? I won't breathe a single word of it. Although, if he wants me to know anyway—never mind. Just tell me for Pete's sake."

"I can't do that." Moon reached across the table and grabbed my hands. Her large eyes pleaded with me to understand. She vibrated with tension. How much had the strain of not talking raised her blood pressure? "I'm so sorry."

"All right. Fine." I stabbed my fork at my Cobb salad. "So, Jeremy Jenkins suspects Darius, but Sonny's not on board? Or is someone pressuring both of them?"

Moon beamed, nodded quickly.

"Was Darius in Charleston Sunday night, around the time Trina was killed?" I asked.

"That's my understanding," said Moon.

"Was he with anyone?" I asked.

"*Exactly*." Moon made a rolling motion with her hands, the way people do when you're on the right track in charades. "*Some*one..."

"He was with Trina Lynn?" I asked.

Moon clapped twice and pointed at me.

"Where? Where was he with Trina? What time?"

"Well...maybe you should ask Darius about all of that?" Moon had a hopeful look on her face.

"Moon. The man is a celebrity. He probably has bodyguards. I can't just waltz over there and interrogate him regarding the murder of his high school girlfriend." When Darius left for Hollywood, he probably had dreams of being the next Eddie Murphy. He'd had a decent run as a standup comic, but his big break didn't come until he landed the role on *Main Street USA*, a reality TV show where he visited a different small town each week, eating at local restaurants, visiting festivals, and interviewing old men swapping lies at the hardware store. He'd filmed ten seasons before retiring. He was also the brand ambassador for Best Dang Drawers, a high-dollar line of men's underwear.

"Sure you can." Moon nodded emphatically. "And you'd better hurry."

Colleen stared at Moon Unit.

What's going on in there? Can you read her mind?

"Sonny and Jeremy Jenkins are on the 1:30 ferry from Isle of Palms," said Colleen. "They have an appointment with Blake at 2:15."

The only reason I could think of that both Sonny and Jeremy Jenkins would have an official appointment with Blake was they were coming to make an arrest. There's no other reason they'd involve Blake in their case. Darius had been gone too long for Blake to have background information they needed.

I stood, grabbed my tote. "I need my check, Moon."

"It's on the house," she said. "Go."

"Don't forget my ham biscuits," said Colleen.

"Don't forget your ham biscuits." Moon jumped up, ran behind the counter and grabbed a takeout bag from under the hot lights on the pass-through bar to the kitchen. "Here you go."

"Thanks." I took the bag from her and headed for the door.

"Liz?"

I stopped, pivoted back towards her. Moon's face was washed in uncertainty. "Just in case I misunderstood...please don't mention anything I said unless you absolutely have to, okay? I don't want to mess this thing up...me and Sonny, I mean."

I grinned, shook my head. "Moon, I honestly can't recall you telling me a solitary thing."

TWO

From the outside, the home Stuart and Kate Devlin had built and raised two sons in looked the same as it always had. Two stories of white painted wood sat atop twin garages, with a central staircase sweeping up from the brick walkway to the wraparound porch. On each front corner, the porch jutted out into twin square porch rooms that might have been turrets were they round and on a Victorian home. The house and all its porches were topped with an array of shiny silver roofs. The woodwork was stained dark, the architectural details nautical. I had rarely been back inside the house since the night Kate Devlin died in front of me. At the bottom of the steps, I steeled myself, squared my shoulders, and climbed to the porch.

"He's here alone." Colleen was behind me, her voice right in my ear.

"*Gah*! Are you trying to give me an early heart attack?"

"As if," said Colleen. "I'd have to train a new POC. That'd be a pain. I figure your heart's pretty healthy, as much as you run."

I was Colleen's only Point of Contact right up until Nate and I got married. Now we shared that mixed blessing. I shook my head, rolled my eyes. "Go finish your ham biscuits." She'd been in the back seat, out of sight, munching away when I got out of the car.

"Mmm-kay," she said in a singsong voice that notified me how

I was going to regret that suggestion.

The door swung open. "Can I help you?" Darius Baker looked around, his face screwed up in a confused look. Dressed in a designer warmup suit, he was tall, fit, and completely bald, his smooth skin the color of Belgian milk chocolate. "Thought I heard you talking to somebody out here. You by ya'self?"

Colleen laughed and faded away.

"I am. Mr. Baker?"

"That's me."

I held out a hand. "I'm Liz Talbot. You probably don't remember me."

"Blake Talbot's little sister?"

I smiled. "That's right."

He nodded, grinned. His teeth were brilliant white, perfect celebrity teeth. "You the one my cousin Clay was always sweet on."

I half laughed, shook my head. It was common knowledge Clay'd had a crush on me in high school, but he'd never asked me out. "Was he?"

"Girl, if you didn't know that, you was the only one. I heard you was smart, so I'm thinking you know that's the truth. What can I help you with?"

The way he spoke was some hybrid blend of down home Southern black laced with an occasional touch of Hollywood. It was relatable. It was his brand, the down-to-earth way he spoke on television to people across the country. I had no doubt that he could dial it up or down at will, just like I could my own Southern drawl.

"I'm hoping I can help you," I said.

"Is that right? Well, don't stand here on the porch, come on in and tell me all about it." He opened the door wide, stepped back, and gestured elaborately with his left arm.

"You've redecorated," I said. The house was nearly unrecognizable inside, and I was grateful for that.

"Uh-huh. The, ah, interior designer did all a that. Updated it.

Just a nip here and a tuck there. Can I get you something to drink? I got a pitcher a iced tea in the kitchen. Fresh made."

"Sure, that sounds great."

"Right this way."

I followed him down the hall to the back of the house. It looked like Chip and Joanna Gaines had been hired and given an unlimited budget. The kitchen and dining room were now all one room with two dining areas, as well as a u-shaped row of high-back counter stools. Everything was white on white, except for the black marble counter tops, dark wood floors, and stainless-steel appliances.

"Your decorator did an excellent job." Whoever it was had worked fast. There'd been a swarm of workers on the property for the past two weeks, but I was nevertheless amazed at how much the place had changed.

"Thank ya." He handed me a glass of tea. "Grab a stool." He settled into one on the corner and motioned me towards one across from him.

"Welcome home." I smiled.

"Thanks," he said. "There's no place like home. Every small town I been to made me homesick for this place. It's special."

"It is that," I said.

"My spirit's at rest here, ya know what I mean?"

"I do. I feel exactly the same way."

"Now tell me," he said. "What kinda help do I need?"

"Mr. Baker—"

"Enough a that. Call me Darius. You're making me feel old up in here."

I nodded. "Darius. First, I should tell you I'm a private investigator."

"Oh, damn. This don't sound like good news."

"Honestly, it's not. You're aware that Trina Lynn Causby was killed Sunday night in Charleston?"

He looked down at his glass of iced tea, drew a deep breath. "Yeah. I know about that."

"When's the last time you saw her?" I asked.

He raised his head, his eyes wary. "I had dinner with her Sunday night in Charleston. We went to Hall's Chophouse. Why do you ask?"

"Is there any reason you can think of that the police might suspect you are responsible for her death?"

"*Me?*"

I nodded.

"I jus' got back into town, remember? I knew Trina in high school. We dated. First girl I ever loved. You might remember about that. 'Course, livin' in Mt. Pleasant, she went to Wando, so maybe not. But back then, all a East Cooper was a lot smaller place. But Sunday night is the first time I seen that girl in more than twenty years. We hadn't had time to get that mad at each other yet."

"I understand. And I know this sounds crazy—"

"You right about that, now. This conversation is a waste a damn time. I know I mighta had a certain reputation when I was in high school, but hell, none of us are what we were in high school, now are we?"

"Of course not."

"You mighta heard...I made somethin' of myself."

"I know, of course. It's just—"

"And on top a that, I got myself three ex-wives—every one of 'em healthy as they can be. If I was ever gonna shoot a woman, it woulda been number two. Mean girl. Mmm-mm. But not a one of 'em ever been shot. Let me tell you something. They live well. I take good care of the women who hate my guts. Not that Trina did. It wasn't like that. Naw. Unh-uh." He shook his head vigorously.

"So you and Trina didn't have a disagreement Sunday night?"

His eyes got big and round, his expression resembling that of a possum staring down a freight train. "Well, now, I didn't say that, exactly."

"What did you argue about, exactly?"

"We might have remembered certain things a little differently. I mighta said some stupid things..."

I raised my eyebrows, inquiring.

"Something along the lines of like maybe she threw me out like the damn trash 'cause I had dreams she was too immature to understand at the time. I mighta been all, 'How do ya like me now?' Like maybe I was showing her or something. Maybe she didn't take all a that too well."

Go figure. "How did she react?"

He shrugged, looked innocent. "Trina, she was a lady. I coulda said all that to some other woman, and they mighta been broke shit all over that restaurant. But Trina kept her cool. I mean, she let me know how I was an idiot and all a that. But she didn't get loud or nothing."

"Did anyone overhear the argument?"

"Well, uh...they could have." He rubbed a spot above his right ear, like maybe he was smoothing his nonexistent hair.

"What time did you leave the restaurant?" I asked.

"It was about ten minutes 'til ten. Things had calmed down. We had a nice dinner. But she said she had to meet someone. A source for a story she'd been working on."

"Do you know where?"

"Naw, she didn't say."

"Do you know who?"

"Unh-uh. Naw."

"Do you have any idea what story it was related to?"

He shook his head. "She was all tight-lipped about it.

"Have you spoken to the police?"

"Yeah, couple detectives came by yesterday. Sonny Ravenel. You know him?"

I nodded. "Sure."

"Him and his partner. Asked me about all a this. But they weren't thinking like I had anything to do with hurting Trina."

"Did they say that?"

"Not in so many words. But what kinda sense would that make?" He was getting louder, agitated. "We didn't even barely know each other anymore. People don't go killing strangers. Well, I guess some folks do, but I'm not a damn psychopath."

"Of course you're not." I used my calming voice.

"I'm Mr. *Main Street USA*."

"Congratulations on all of your success." I offered him my sunniest smile.

He seemed slightly mollified. "You said you could help me. Tell me exactly how that is."

I sighed. "I have reason to believe you *are* a person of interest in the Charleston Police Department's investigation. In fact, I think they may consider you their primary suspect."

"Say what?"

"And if I'm right—"

"That's just crazy right there."

"Okay, but listen to me, please."

He eyed me for a minute. "I'm listening."

"Do you have a local attorney?"

"Yeah, uh-huh. That was the first thing I did when I got home after twenty-one years, was hire myself a lawyer just in case somebody I knew got killed and I happened to look guilty. Who does that?"

"I'll take that as a no."

"I got contract lawyers and divorce lawyers, but they all in California. The only local lawyer I got is the one from when I bought this house."

"You need a criminal attorney. A good one. A local one. Charleston judges aren't all that fond of attorneys from off." I pulled one of Fraser Rutledge's cards from my purse and laid it on the counter in front of him. "He's one of the best. If it comes to it, call him."

"I don't need no damn hoity-toity Broad Street lawyer." Darius slid the card back towards me on the counter. "No thank you. This here is crazy, like I told you."

I didn't pick it up. "My partner and I often work with Rutledge and Radcliffe—Fraser's firm. The Charleston Police won't make an arrest until they can make a case. At that point, you'll need investigators to run down alternative theories of the crime for your defense attorney to present to the jury."

"*Jury.*" He drew back, an incredulous look on his face. Then he nodded. "Okay. Okay. I see what this is about."

"What do you mean?"

"Local boy makes good on TV. Has endorsement contracts. Comes home, buys hisself a big ass house right on the beach. Remodels. Puts in a pool. He's obviously rolling in some serious dough. You want to be on my payroll."

"I assure you, I have plenty to keep me busy. I don't need your money." This wasn't strictly true. Nate and I needed a steady stream of paying clients to keep up the beautiful but aging beach house my Gram left me. But we stayed busy enough. "I'm here as a favor to a friend."

"And just who might that be?"

The doorbell rang.

We both looked down the hall.

He raised his eyebrows, shrugged. "I'm not expecting company this afternoon," he said. "'Course I wasn't expecting you either. Whatever they selling, I don't need. Where were we?"

"I was explaining how you need to call Fraser Rutledge lickety-split," I said.

"And just like I was telling you—"

The doorbell rang again, three times in rapid succession.

"Now that's just plain rude." He glared towards the door. "And

I wouldn't have expected that here, ya know what I mean? Folks here was always the kind that call before they just show up on your front porch, hammering on your doorbell. What is this world coming to? If folks here done lost they manners, I don't even know what to think. That's disappointing. Mmm mmm mmm." He pressed his lips together, shook his head.

A fist banged on the door. "Darius Baker? Charleston Police. Open the door."

"Oh, shit." Darius's voice went high-pitched. His face reflected astonishment.

I slid the card back to him.

"Listen to me," I said. "Go quietly. Do not say. One. Single. Word. Except 'Lawyer.' Do you understand me?"

"Oh yeah. I understand you just fine. I'm being railroaded on this here thing so someone can look good closing a high-profile case fast."

"I don't think that's it, truly."

More banging on the front door. "Darius Baker. We know you're in there."

Sonny's voice. He knew I was in here too. He knew the white Ford Escape parked out front was mine. Blake would be with him. This was Stella Maris, and out of Sonny's jurisdiction.

"Answer the door," I said. "I'll call Fraser Rutledge and have him meet you at the jail."

"Uh, this here is privileged communication, right?"

"Provided Fraser Rutledge is your attorney. My firm is on retainer with his."

"Well, see, I might have left out a li'l part of that story I was telling you just now."

"Fill me in. Quick."

"Remember how I said I had three ex-wives?"

"All healthy—yes."

"The truth is, I mighta understated that number by one."

"And?"

"A hundred years ago, Trina Lynn was actually my first wife. If that was even legal. It shouldn't a been. We were way too young."

"That's a pretty big omission. Did you leave anything else out?"

He reached up, rubbed his smooth head with both hands. "Oh, Lord."

"I can't help you unless you tell me absolutely everything."

He said something, his voice soft, wounded.

More banging on the door.

"What did you say?"

"I said we had a child." His voice was coated in misery.

"When?"

"I was already gone. Trina, she put the child—a li'l boy—up for adoption."

"How is that not common knowledge in this town?"

"I got no damn idea. I didn't know myself until recently."

The doorbell rang three times in succession. "Darius DeAndre Baker. This is your Aunt Nell. You get yourself out here right this very minute."

Of course. Nell knew everything that happened at the Stella Maris Police Department. She ran the place, regardless of who was chief. No way would she have stayed behind while Sonny and Blake came to arrest Darius.

"Aw naw." Darius strode towards the door and I followed.

He flung it open. "Aunt Nell?"

Nell Avalee Baker Cooper, a full-figured black woman, wore a tailored pink suit, heels, and pearls. Her salon blowout drooped a bit from the humidity. She planted her hands on her hips and bowed up, ready to strike. She clutched a dangerously large Coach carryall that matched her suit in her right hand. "Stand back, Sonny Ravenel. You can have him when I'm finished with him. He's not going anywhere."

Sonny took a step back. "Yes, ma'am." His eyes met mine.

I knew Sonny well enough to know he was relieved to see me. Moon had been right.

Blake stood off to one side. Jeremy Jenkins must've gone around back.

I stole a glance at Blake.

He nodded ever so slightly, looked away. The fact that he said nothing told me all I needed to know. He was happy to see me too.

"What is this I hear, Darius?" Nell asked. "You've barely been home five minutes and you're in trouble with the law already."

"Now, Aunt Nell—"

"Don't you 'Now, Aunt Nell' me. I want the truth out of you. Right now. Did you hurt Trina Lynn?"

"Of course not. Aunt Nell, you know me better than that. You know I ain't hurt nobody, 'specially not a woman. Most 'specially not Trina Lynn."

She stared him down, took his measure. "No, I don't think you did. So you go along with Sonny now." She swiveled her head towards Sonny. "He won't let a soul harm a solitary hair—"

She spun back to Darius, took in his smooth head. "Sonny's not going to allow anybody to hurt you. Isn't that right, Sonny?"

"No, ma'am," said Sonny.

"I beg your pardon?" Nell's tone threatened to call down a plague.

"I mean yes, ma'am," said Sonny. "Nell, all due respect. You know better than to think I'd let anything bad happen to Darius."

She jerked her head back to Darius. It crossed my mind how she was in serious danger of giving herself whiplash. "You keep your mouth shut tight, you hear me?"

"Yes, ma'am."

"I will see about getting you a good lawyer," said Nell.

"I've already got me a lawyer."

"This is no job for one of your slick Hollywood mouthpieces."

"I got me a local attorney—a good one. Now, Aunt Nell, don't you go worrying yourself. This here is all a big misunderstanding. We gonna get it straightened right out. I even got my own investigator." He looked over his shoulder at me.

Nell raised an eyebrow at me. "Mmm-hmm. I see that."

Jeremy Jenkins climbed the last step to the porch. "Why am I not surprised?" Tall, with broad shoulders, if he hadn't had such a nasty look on his face, he would've been handsome.

"Sonny," I said, "Detective Jenkins. Mr. Baker is represented by Rutledge and Radcliffe. Mr. Rutledge will meet y'all at the jail."

Jeremy muttered something under his breath.

"All right then," said Sonny. "Let's head in that direction, why don't we? Darius Baker, you are under arrest for the murder of Trina Lynn Causby. You have the right to remain silent—"

"And you see that you do that very thing," said Nell.

"I will, Aunt Nell. Everything's gonna be all right."

Nell looked heavenward and raised her hands. "Lord Jesus, look after Darius. Keep him safe from harm. Help us find the truth about what happened to poor Trina Lynn, Lord. We know the truth will set Darius free. Amen."

Nell looked at me hard. "I'll expect to hear from you directly."

"Yes, ma'am," I said. "Of course."

THREE

I loved my new Escape, but missed the happy green color of the one we'd recently traded. White showed every speck of dirt and dust. But white and silver were the most common car colors in the country. Private investigators needed to blend in. As soon as I was in the car and the air conditioning cooled things down, I called Fraser Rutledge and outlined Darius's situation.

"Very well, *Miz* Talbot." Fraser never let an opportunity escape to express his disapproval of the fact I hadn't taken Nate's last name. "I will meet with Mr. Baker and then ascertain how quickly we can get before a circuit court judge on the matter of a bond. I gather that you and Mr. Andrews will begin investigative work forthwith."

Our contract with Rutledge and Radcliffe for a recent case was open-ended, allowing us to begin work on behalf of any of Fraser's clients without executing a new agreement. While Darius hadn't technically hired us—signed our contract for services—Fraser had. Any client of Rutledge and Radcliffe's was a client of ours as soon as we did work on the client's behalf at Fraser's request, or that of his partner, Eli Radcliffe.

"Nate is still finalizing the pretrial work for Lucas v. Lucas," I said. "I can get started right away on Mr. Baker's case." Nate and I had planned to take some time off as soon as he finished the Lucas case and enjoy the beach, catch up on our reading. That would now have to wait.

"I was given to understand the two of you had wrapped up Lucas, Miz Talbot."

"*Mr.* Rutledge, you might recall our conversation on Thursday? We were sitting right in front of your desk when we mentioned there was a loose end or two, and that Nate was going to follow up on those."

"Precisely. That was Thursday. Today is Tuesday, and the sun which the good Lord hung in the sky has set and risen again five times in the interim. I dislike loose ends, Miz Talbot. The Lucases go to court next week."

"Which is why Nate is still focused on the Lucas case, and I will get started on the Baker/Causby matter."

"No one speaks to the media except me."

The media. Sweet baby Moses in a basket. Stella Maris was about to be invaded. "Of course. Will you be stashing Mr. Baker in a hotel under an assumed name?"

"Not at this time. Let us have a multitude of unruly reporters trampling through his yard and taping spots in front of Mr. Baker's home for the time being. We cannot have him appear to go into hiding. Optics, Miz Talbot. We start thinking about our jury pool and what they see and hear right now. Perhaps the logistics involved in travel to Stella Maris may prove a deterrent to the fourth estate after the first week."

"I'll alert the local authorities." Blake would no doubt rather Darius stayed in a yurt on the moon than Stella Maris under the circumstances.

"Very well. I will see you and Mr. Andrews tomorrow morning at 9:00 in my office." He ended the call.

"High-handed boor." Fraser Alston Rutledge III, Esquire, challenged my sunny disposition. While we'd steadfastly refused to become the in-house investigators for Rutledge and Radcliffe, preferring to retain our autonomy, Fraser had managed to arrange things to suit himself through trickery. He sent us a steady stream of work and paid us twenty percent above our standard rate. I thought of it as an aggravation tax. And here I was sending him a client, ensuring we'd be working with him yet again. I drew a deep sigh. We had bills to pay.

I dialed Blake.

"Do you have any idea what's going on with Sonny?" I asked when he answered.

"I was there, remember?"

"Blake Talbot, don't you dare play innocent with me."

"I don't know anything you don't know," said Blake. "Sonny's not talking to me about Darius Baker except in front of his partner. All very official. But hey. The guy has a new partner. He's going to be loyal to him. That's just natural. But what I would like to know is exactly how and why you ended up at Darius's house before I did."

"And here I thought you looked happy to see me."

"I didn't say I wasn't," said Blake. "But I am curious how you came to be there."

"I can't say."

"You mean you won't."

"I have client confidentiality to consider," I said.

"Darius call you?" Blake sounded skeptical. "I can't imagine how he even knew you were a PI."

"Whatever. Look, I talked to Fraser. He's letting Darius come home after he's released. No hiding him away. So get ready for the onslaught."

"Are you freakin' kidding me?"

"Afraid not."

He muttered a lengthy string of words Mamma would've disapproved of. "I better go tell Nell and Bill. You know those yahoos are going to harass them."

"Later."

I sat there in Darius's driveway pondering my next steps.

By habit, I worked cases starting with the people closest to the victim, then moving out in widening circles until I found the culprit. I needed to speak to the people who knew Trina Lynn best, or at least the longest. This was bound to be difficult. Our families had history. Troy Causby had been involved in a case of mine a few years back, the one in which my Gram had been killed. I opened an app on my iPhone and looked up the number, then took a deep breath and dialed Billy Ray and Georgia Causby's home.

"Hello?" A woman answered on the fifth ring. Her voice betrayed that she'd been crying.

"Mrs. Causby?"

"Who's calling?" Her tone was polite, but nevertheless put me on notice that she would suffer no fools. My mamma had taught me that exact tone.

"This is Liz Talbot."

"What do *you* want?" This woman was younger. Not Georgia Causby. Probably Trina's sister. She might harbor ill will towards me, though she had no just cause whatsoever.

"Laura Beth?"

"We are grieving. You have a lot of nerve calling here."

Another woman spoke to her. Laura Beth must've put her hand over the phone. There was muffled arguing. After a moment, she yelled, "Fine. Fine."

"Hello, this is Georgia Causby. What can I help you with?"

"Mrs. Causby, this is Liz Talbot. I'm terribly sorry for your loss."

"That's kind of you." Her voice was stiff. "Again. What can I help you with?"

"I'm investigating what happened to Trina Lynn."

"Why on earth would you of all people be doing that?"

"Because I was hired to."

"By who?"

"I'm working for an attorney in Charleston. He wants only to get to the bottom of what happened." This was the truth, just not the whole truth.

"Aren't the police doing that?"

"Let's just say we want to make sure they don't miss anything. Police officers are often stretched thin these days."

She was quiet for a moment. "I don't hold you responsible for what happened to Troy. But you are a reminder, you understand me?"

"Yes ma'am. I do."

"On the other hand, I'm grateful to your family for not making things hard with Sara Catherine."

"Of course." Sara Catherine was Troy Causby's daughter. She was also my cousin Marci's child. As Mamma would say, Marci and Troy had been called elsewhere. Billy Ray and Georgia Causby had adopted Sara Catherine. "Mrs. Causby, would you please talk to me? In person? I know it's a lot to ask right now. But I promise you, I only want to help."

"You'd best come on now, before Billy Ray gets home."

"Thank you." I glanced at the clock. "I can make the 3:00 ferry. That should put me at your house around four. Will that work?"

"As long as you're gone by five it will."

"I'll see you soon."

I did a mental inventory of my freezer, then zipped over to Mamma and Daddy's house.

"Mamma?" I called out softly as I walked in the front door. I wasn't sure if Daddy would be asleep or not.

"We're in here," she called from the family room.

Chumley, Daddy's basset hound, woofed a greeting.

I stepped down the hall and stopped short at the doorway. Daddy was in his recliner, wrapped in a robe and a blanket, with a heated wrap across his shoulders. Chumley spilled out of his lap. The table beside him was covered with pill bottles, Vicks VapoRub,

Halls Mentho-Lyptus, and all such as that. A humidifier delivered a steady cloud of moisture to the air. An episode of *Main Street USA* played on the TV above the fireplace. Daddy muted the TV.

Mamma was curled up on the end of the buttery yellow sofa working a crossword puzzle. "Don't get too close to your father. He caught this mess from somebody. It must be contagious. I've had my flu shot and my pneumonia shot."

"The hound can tell I feel bad." Daddy stroked Chumley's back. "Every time I sit down he crawls up in my lap like this. Your Mamma won't let him in the bed."

"Him or me." Mamma's gaze returned to her crossword. "Your choice."

"Are you feeling any better, Daddy?"

"I'm fine," he said. "I've never seen such a fuss over a cold."

"You say that," said Mamma. "But the very second I stop making a fuss, you imagine your fever's gone up."

"What are you talking about, Carolyn?"

Mamma shook her head.

"Mamma, are you sure you need that humidifier? The humidity level outside is over eighty percent."

"Your father says he needs it," she said, like she knew exactly how ridiculous that was.

"When's the last time you took my temperature?" Daddy asked. "We're supposed to call the doctor if it goes over 102."

"Frank, I just took your temperature ten minutes ago and you know it." Mamma looked at me. "What are you up to, sweetheart? You want a bowl of chicken noodle soup?"

"No, thank you, Mamma. How's your freezer inventory?"

"Overflowing. What do you need?"

"A casserole...maybe your chicken noodle casserole? I haven't had time to cook recently."

"Of course. You taking it over to Darius?"

"No, but it's for his benefit."

"Liz, darlin', I'm afraid I don't understand you." Mamma sighed. "But there's nothing unusual there, is it? Help yourself."

I reached down and gave her a hug. "Thanks, Mamma. I'm taking it to the Causbys."

"Better take one home for supper. You can't feed a husband salads every night," said Mamma.

Daddy went into a coughing fit. When he got control of it, he looked at me like he'd bit into a lemon. "The Causbys? What in the world do you want to carry food over there for?"

"I'm hoping to generate a little good will. I need to talk to Georgia."

"You've got no business with those Causbys," said Daddy.

"I do today, Daddy."

"Take your gun."

"Seriously? You think Georgia means me harm?"

"I wouldn't put it past her." Restless, he lowered the leg rest on the recliner and eased Chumley to the floor.

"What are you fixin' to do?" asked Mamma.

"I'm tired of sitting still. I'm just stretching my legs."

"You're supposed to rest," said Mamma.

"I've been resting for a week now. I'm not tired of anything but sitting still. I'm going to fix myself a glass of iced tea, which I'm perfectly capable of doing. Would you like one?"

Mamma stared at him. "I think your fever might genuinely be up. In thirty-eight years of marriage, I don't think you've ever brought me something to drink unless I was hospitalized. Let me get the thermometer." She laid down her crossword puzzle, started to stand.

"For the love of Pete. Would you sit still, Carolyn? I'll be right back."

Daddy strode towards the kitchen and I followed him.

I went to Mamma's walk-in pantry and started digging through the deep freezer against the back wall. Every dish was wrapped in Saran wrap and foil and labeled with freezer tape. I found a stack of chicken casserole under the beef stroganoff. I snagged a dish of the stroganoff to take home. When I shut the freezer and turned, Daddy was standing inside the pantry.

I jumped. "Daddy, you scared me. What are you doing?"

"Shhh." He pulled the pantry door closed.

"I worry about that poor little girl," he said.

"Daddy. You know that Troy and his grandfather aside, the Causbys are decent people. I'm sure Sara Catherine is well cared for."

"I'm not so sure of that. Just...check on things, would you? If there's anything she needs..."

"You think Billy Ray and Georgia would accept money from you? Even if they needed it, they wouldn't. And it's not like they're impoverished."

"I know that. But it takes a lot to raise a child these days."

I eyed him suspiciously. "Why are we in the pantry with the door closed?"

"This is a sore topic with your mamma."

Sara Catherine's mother, my cousin Marci, was Daddy's dead sister Sharon's only child. We were the only blood family Sara Catherine had on her mamma's side. Her daddy, Troy Causby, had a dark history with my sister, Merry, in addition to his involvement in the events surrounding Gram's death. Mamma had been in favor of fighting for custody of Sara Catherine. A pragmatist, Daddy knew that grandparents outranked a great uncle and aunt. He'd held firm on not getting into a legal wrangle with the Causbys. What Daddy didn't say was that Mamma was impatient with waiting for grandchildren. He knew I couldn't help with that.

"I'm not sure what you want me to do here," I said.

"Just check on the child while you're there, would you?"

"Of course." I'd planned to do that anyway. "So you're not really afraid Georgia will try to take me out?"

"Probably not. But it's best to be careful. You need to borrow a gun?"

"No thanks, Daddy. You know I carry a Sig 9."

The door to the pantry swung open. Mamma stood there, hands on her hips, her head cocked to one side. "What is going on in my pantry?"

"I was just helping Tutie here find a casserole," said Daddy innocently.

"Like you even know where the freezer is," said Mamma.

Daddy pointed to the appliance in question. "Damn thing's right there where it always is."

Mamma stared him down.

"You know, I'm feeling a bit dizzy," said Daddy. "I'd better go sit back down. Carolyn, could I get that glass of iced tea? Or maybe something warm would be better. How about a cup of hot tea with some honey in it?" He slipped past Mamma.

"I've got to run," I said.

"Here, take Georgia the reheating directions." Mamma stepped over to the kitchen desk, flipped through a recipe box and handed me an index card.

She craned her neck to make sure Daddy was safely out of earshot.

"Check on Sara Catherine for me, will you?" she asked.

"Of course, Mamma."

I hugged Mamma bye and got out of there lickety-split.

FOUR

Billy Ray and Georgia Causby lived in the Old Village of Mt. Pleasant, a couple blocks off Charleston Harbor, not far from Shem Creek. The historic neighborhood, with its canopy of stately live oaks and eclectic mix of homes, never failed to charm me. I parked in the street, in front of the white picket fence with azaleas spilling over, so as not to block access to the garage—and not be blocked in by Billy Ray should he come home while I was still there.

It wasn't that I was afraid of Billy Ray Causby. He had a reputation as a man's man, a shrimper by trade who hunted, fished, and played poker with the guys on the weekends. But he was also known to attend church regularly and volunteer with Habitat for Humanity. I kept tabs on the Causbys. Troy and his grandfather, Hayden, aside, the Causbys were hard-working, God-fearing, upstanding citizens. But grieving folks sometimes lashed out at whoever was handy. I needed to be able to make a quick exit if necessary.

The house was some version of a Cape Cod, white, with large, three-window dormers and a wide front porch. The landscaping was mature and lush. A row of hydrangeas with large blue globes lined the left-hand side of the yard. It was a nice home, large enough for the couple and the four children they'd raised, but not an especially flashy one. It probably hadn't been updated since the nineties. In recent years, however, real estate prices in that part of Mt. Pleasant had risen so dramatically it was probably a two-million-dollar home. In some cases, families who'd lived in the Old Village for generations struggled to afford taxes, insurance, and maintenance. Did the Causbys struggle?

Before I got out of the car, I swapped out my crossbody bag for a medium-sized satchel—one that would accommodate my Sig 9. Then I opened the Voice Memos app on my phone. "Georgia Causby. Interview at her home."

I noted the date and time, then slid the phone upside-down with the microphone at the top into the exterior pocket of my black and taupe Kate Spade bag.

My skin prickled as I approached the front door. Was someone watching me? Who all was here? I pressed the doorbell, hoping that Laura Beth had gone home to her husband and children. Where was Sawyer, the Causbys' oldest son?

The wooden door swung in. Georgia Causby regarded me through the glass storm door for a few moments, seemed to size me up. We'd never officially met. But she knew who I was, and I her. She was close to Mamma's age, maybe a few years older. But pain had etched deep lines in Georgia's face. Her platinum blonde hair was chin-length, with a fringe of bangs across her forehead. In jeans and a loose blouse with a tank underneath and tennis shoes, her body had a soft, comfortable look to it. Her eyes were wounded, but glassy. Had the doctor given her something?

She unlocked the storm door and pushed it open. "You may as well come in. You're here."

"Thank you for seeing me. I hope you can use this. It's chicken noodle casserole. The directions are on the card on top." I handed her the dish and walked inside.

"Thank you. That was thoughtful of you." She closed the storm door, but left the wooden door ajar.

"Have a seat in the living room." She gestured to the room to the right off the foyer, then followed me in.

I took a seat on the far end of a striped sofa.

She sat in a wingback across the room from me and set the dish on a small side table. Her gaze drifted, not settling on anything in particular.

"Is Laura Beth still here?" I asked.

"No. She took Sara Catherine over to play with her children for a while."

I nodded. "I can talk to her later."

She swiveled her head, looked at me directly. "Why would you talk to Sara Catherine? She's only three years old, for heaven's sake."

"I meant Laura Beth."

"Oh. Of course." She relaxed. "Well, I doubt you'll get far with that."

No doubt she was right. I offered her a wry smile and switched channels. "Trina Lynn was a force for the underdog around here," I said. "She'll be missed. I didn't know her, but I always appreciated how she tried to help folks. The last story I saw of hers was about a financial shortfall in the school district."

Georgia pulled a wad of Kleenex out of a side pocket on her shirt. "Trina Lynn always fancied herself an avenger of sorts, I guess."

"I imagine that could be dangerous. Do you think she crossed someone who didn't take it well?"

"That occurred to me. If it wasn't some random evil, then I guess that's the most likely thing." In her lap, her hands squeezed the wad of tissue as if it were a stress ball.

"Do you know of anyone who she was afraid of?"

"No. Trina knew I thought she took chances. She didn't talk to me about her work. She knew it worried me."

"Was she seeing anyone?"

Georgia hesitated. "I told the police this. I can't see how it matters now. She was dating Grey Hamilton."

"The news anchor at WCSC?"

"That's right. It was against the station's policy, so they kept it quiet. But they'd been seeing each other for nearly a year."

"Any trouble there?"

"No. Grey treated her like a china doll. He adores her." She teared up. "Adored her."

"Any old boyfriends who were maybe unhappy about her relationship with Grey?"

"Not that I know of. Auggie might know."

"Auggie?"

"Her cameraman. August Lockwood. He and Trina were very close."

"Were they ever romantically involved?"

"I wouldn't have been surprised if she'd told me they were seeing each other. But she said he was her best friend." I wondered how he classified their relationship.

"Sometimes celebrities have stalkers. Anyone ever bother Trina?"

"Oh, she heard from her share of crazies. She said they were all harmless. The station would have all that."

"Right...I know this will seem out of left field, but do you know if Trina had spoken to Darius Baker recently?"

She raised an eyebrow at me. "You mean was I aware she had dinner with him on the evening she was killed? Yes. The police told me that."

"But Trina didn't tell you?"

"No. She would've known I wouldn't've been too happy to hear about that."

"You don't care for Darius?"

"All I know of Darius Baker is that my daughter dated him in high school, and he broke her heart. She was happy with Grey. I wouldn't have wanted her to mess things up."

"I heard Trina broke Darius's heart."

Georgia lifted a shoulder. "I guess you might say they broke each other's hearts. He was hell-bent for Hollywood. She didn't want any part of that. She had her reasons. But she didn't want to hold him back. So she broke up with him, but it like to a killed her. All that was such a long time ago."

I debated how far to push her today. I didn't want to upset her, but I might not have another opportunity to talk with her. Her family certainly wasn't in favor of it. "Did Trina's reasons for not wanting to go to Hollywood involve a child?"

Georgia looked like she'd been struck. She stood. "It's time for you to leave." Her voice slurred. She was definitely medicated.

"I'm terribly sorry. I didn't mean to upset you."

"You listen to me, Liz Talbot. No good will come from dragging my poor daughter's dirty laundry from two decades ago out and airing it in public. That will only serve to tarnish her memory. It has absolutely nothing to do with her death."

"Are you certain of that?" I kept my seat, kept my voice even.

"Of course. That child was adopted as an infant. How do you even know about that?"

"Darius told me."

"Why, after all this time, would he do such a thing?"

"Because I made him tell me everything about Trina that he knew."

"You made him tell you?" She threw me a sarcastic look, like maybe she thought perhaps I overestimated my persuasive powers.

"Mrs. Causby, what was Trina and Darius's relationship like?"

"Why are you asking me about something that happened in high school? This is a ridiculous waste of time."

"Was he ever violent with her that you know of?" I asked. "Please. This could be important."

She glanced at the ceiling, huffed. "Well...No, not really. Right before graduation they had a big fight. Trina, she could have a temper too. They'd been at a bonfire over on Stella Maris. Lot of the kids in their class were there. He grabbed her arm and she jerked away from him and fell down. She had a bruise afterward. Some of the kids told it that he'd pushed her, but she said that wasn't true. Billy Ray, he would've killed him if he'd believed that."

"How did you and Mr. Causby feel about Trina Lynn dating Darius?"

"What? You mean because he's black?" she asked.

"Yes."

She sat back down, crossed her legs. "It was a different time, you understand? Folks didn't do that back then as much. It was a bigger deal. We wanted what was best for Trina Lynn."

"And you didn't think Darius was what was best?"

"No," she said simply. "And I won't apologize for that. Darius was a nice enough boy. He was always funny—he could always make you laugh. But who could have known how well he'd do? We thought it was unlikely he'd go to college. And he didn't, did he? His good fortune...that's like a lightning strike. Against tremendous odds. We didn't want Trina Lynn to be serious about any boy. We wanted her to get her education. But if she was going to date, and let's face it, of course she was going to date, we wanted her to see someone with prospects. What parent doesn't want that for their children?"

"Do you have any reason at all to think Darius would hurt Trina after all this time?" I asked.

She shook her head, cast another glance at the ceiling. "I can't imagine that..." She lowered her gaze to mine and held it. "Although, I suppose if he found out about the child...it's possible he flew into a violent rage. It just seems farfetched to me. I'd sooner believe it had to do with a story she was working on."

"Mrs. Causby, I'm just verifying some background information here. Has Trina Lynn ever been married?"

"No. She was focused on her career." She didn't blink or look away.

"Did the police ask you about Darius?" I asked.

"Why, yes. But I told them the same thing I told you. They dated in high school. Whatever was between them was ancient history. They had dinner together. So what?"

I had all I was going to get from her except her reaction. "You don't know, do you? I would've thought they'd have notified you."

"Notified me of what?"

"The Charleston Police Department arrested Darius earlier this afternoon."

"What?" Her hand fluttered to her neck.

"They think he killed Trina."

She stared at the floor, seemed to be calculating things.

She looked up, frowned hard at me. "You're working for him, aren't you?"

"I told you, Mrs. Causby. I'm working for an attorney in Charleston."

"*His* attorney."

"Yes ma'am."

"Get out of my house."

FIVE

I turned into our driveway and rolled down the oyster shell and gravel lane towards the circle drive in front of the sprawling yellow beach house Gram had left me. The charming amalgamation of several architectural styles perched atop a four-car garage to protect it from storm surges. Trimmed with teak and topped with a metal roof, the entire house was wrapped in a series of connected porches. It was far too much house for two people, but many of my happiest childhood memories were made here. I could never part with it.

Rhett, my golden retriever, came running out to greet me with a ball.

"Hey, buddy." I patted him on the side and scratched behind his ears.

He dropped the ball at my feet.

"All right, hang on a minute." I grabbed a nitrile glove from the back of the Escape. I adored my dog but had an aversion to slobbery balls.

He barked his impatience with my trivial neurosis.

We played fetch until the heat got the best of me. The late afternoon sun was still hot enough to scorch a person.

"It's too hot out here right now. Let's play some more later, okay boy?"

He grinned a sloppy grin, his tongue hanging out, panting. When I didn't pick up the ball again, he barked at it once, then picked it up. He was one of the most agreeable men in my life.

I patted him on the head, and then headed inside. Rhett followed me up the front steps and down the hall. He scampered into the mudroom for a drink of water while I stopped in the kitchen. After disposing of my glove, I scrubbed my hands with hot soapy water and slathered on a thick layer of hand sanitizer. While the oven preheated, I ran back out to the car and retrieved Mamma's beef stroganoff from the cooler I kept in the back seat. Once it was in the oven, I grabbed a Cheerwine from the refrigerator, poured it over a glass of ice, and added a straw. Then I headed down the hall to my office.

Nate and I operated our agency out of our home. We'd thought about getting office space, mostly for security reasons, but more often than not we met clients in their homes or at Fraser's office. Most of them came from Charleston, Mount Pleasant, Johns Island, and the surrounding area. It wasn't particularly convenient for our clients to take the ferry to Stella Maris.

The sunny room off the foyer made the perfect center of operations for Talbot and Andrews Investigations. Once Gram's oversized living room, it accommodated three separate zones: my office area, consisting of a desk, chair, and two visitors' chairs; a reading nook with two comfy leather club chairs in front of the fireplace; and a conversation space in front of the wall of windows looking out over the front porch.

Only recently had I given in and parted with Gram's massive green velvet sofa and tropical print wingbacks. She'd had those pieces for years, and though they held sentimental value, they'd gotten lumpy and the springs poked us in places. The week before, Ethan Allen delivered a deep, sand-colored sectional and four swivel club chairs. We'd floated the sofa in the front corner, with twin sofa tables behind each section, leaving an L-shaped walkway behind. This positioned the sofa diagonally across from the corner of the room where we kept our case boards. One club chair sat to the right, with the other three pushed back along the window where they could easily be pulled in to form a square. In front of the sofa, we placed a large, square leather ottoman. Soft turquoise and cream pillows and throws made the area cozy. Nate and I worked together in this room most of the time, though he had an office upstairs.

I settled in at my desk, turned on my laptop, and created an electronic case file for Darius Baker. The first thing I did was type up my notes from our chat earlier that afternoon. Because I hadn't known I'd walk out with a client, I hadn't recorded our conversation. I typed everything into our agency's clone of an FBI FD 302, printed it, dated and signed, creating a hard copy file to back up my electronic one. It was important to document every interview, all surveillance, and every piece of evidence. Everything in our case files while working for a defense attorney was work product, and as such, was privileged. But if either of us were called to testify, we'd be subject to cross-examination. Our records had to be unassailable. We dotted our i's and crossed our t's.

While it was fresh in my memory, I documented my conversation with Georgia as well. I uploaded the Voice Memo from my phone and attached the recording to the electronic file.

Next I started my list of questions. So far, I was most curious about two things. What on earth was going on with Sonny and his partner? It was unprecedented for Sonny to support my involvement in one of his investigations. Typically, when we worked the same cases, I went to him and pried the few morsels of information I could from him. Stranger still was that he abetted my involvement knowing he'd be making an arrest. I'd gleaned from Moon Unit that her impression was Sonny and Detective Jenkins were being pressured. Were they? By whom? It was clear to me that Sonny was not in favor of arresting Darius, and yet he'd done exactly that. Where did Jeremy Jenkins stand?

The second thing that mystified me was how Darius and Trina Lynn had kept a high school marriage secret, let alone a child. Secrets are a hard thing to keep in a small town. Within the palm tree and live oak-lined streets of Stella Maris, everybody loved secrets so much that their first inclination was to share them over iced tea on the front porch, making it next to impossible to hide anything. Darius being an international celebrity and Trina Lynn a local one made it doubly strange.

Regardless of who paid for my time, I always viewed the victim as my ultimate client. Trina Lynn Causby was the first piece of my puzzle. I googled Trina Lynn and clicked on images. There was no shortage of photos online of the intrepid reporter. Petite, with blonde shoulder-length layered hair, she appeared in everything from business suits to jeans to formal gowns to bikinis. In many of the pictures, she was serious, her hazel eyes intense as she covered violent crimes or corruption. In other photos, she was smiling, laughing, dancing with Auggie at a wedding, serving Thanksgiving dinner in a homeless shelter, reading to children at story time in the library. I chose the one of her in a hardhat with a hammer and an apron for nails, standing on a roof with a pile of shingles, grinning from ear to ear. This was how I would think of her. This was the light in the world that had been snuffed out. I printed the photo and attached it to the top of the case board with a magnet.

I pulled information from various public and subscription databases to create an electronic profile. Because I knew the family, and because Trina Lynn had lived most of her life in Charleston County, much of her history was an open book to me. She was born March 3, 1976, at Medical University Hospital—what MUSC Medical Center was called at the time—the second child of Billy Ray and Georgia Morgan Causby.

I hadn't known her, but I knew of her. In high school, she was a peppy blonde cheerleader, an all-American girl-next-door type.

I'd lost track of her after she graduated until she showed up on camera at WCSC. Her online bio stated that she'd attended Trident Tech and then later College of Charleston, majoring in communications. She had a reputation for relentlessly pursuing stories where folks were somehow being taken advantage of. A part of me hated digging into her personal life, but it had to be done if I were to help bring her killer to justice. Motives for murder were most often personal.

Trina Lynn had no criminal record and no civil judgements. According to the Charleston County real property database, she owned a condo in Mt. Pleasant. A mortgage was recorded, but there were no liens. She appeared to pay her bills on time.

It wasn't hard to find her marriage license to Darius Baker. Anyone who'd cared to look could've found it. They were married right here in Charleston County, on Valentine's Day in 1994. That would've been their senior year in high school. I checked Darius's birthdate. They were both seventeen when they married, summer babies who wouldn't turn eighteen until after they'd graduated. I mulled that. Had Trina Lynn been pregnant when they got married? Darius had said he didn't know about the child until recently, so why had they married in February?

Darius might be right about it not being legal. In South Carolina, you could get married at sixteen, younger if a pregnancy was involved, but you had to have an affidavit of parental consent. Absent that, you had to be eighteen to legally marry.

Maybe Darius could've talked his mother into signing such a document. But based on my conversation with Georgia, there was no way she or Billy Ray had done that. They wanted Trina Lynn to get her education. They weren't enthusiastic about Trina dating Darius, much less marrying him. Then again, if she'd been pregnant at the time, that would've changed the calculus. But Georgia was believable when she said Trina had never been married.

In any case, no parental affidavits were attached to the

marriage license in any of the electronic records. I made myself a note to follow up with Darius, and make a trip downtown to the probate court if necessary.

I searched my subscription databases for a birth certificate for a child born between 1994 and 1995 with Trina and Darius as parents, but wasn't surprised to find nothing. In cases of adoption, generally, the birth parents' names were replaced on the birth certificate with the adoptive parents', and the original birth record was sealed. I made note of the year's gap between Trina's high school graduation and when she started classes at Trident Tech. How and when had Darius found out he had a son?

Darius was the next piece of my puzzle. I started an electronic profile on my client, querying the same sources I had for Trina Lynn. I took only a cursory look at his website, which appeared to have been put together by a high-dollar PR firm. It had everything from his official bio to information on his foundation, which generously supported children's educational and welfare programs.

I could have spent days combing through Google hits on Darius. There was so much information available on him it was overwhelming. Some of it was no doubt true, but he also had as many articles in the tabloids as Jennifer Aniston. I assumed the story about alien abduction while filming an episode in Nebraska was false. If the case drug on, I'd come back to the mountain of nonsense on the internet.

Born on June 14, 1976, to Marcus Clive Baker and Jasmine Shaniqua King, also at Medical University Hospital, Darius DeAndre Baker had a rough start in life. His father was eighteen and had recently graduated high school. He left town shortly after Darius was born. I hadn't heard anyone mention him in years.

Jasmine, Darius's mother, was only a junior when she had to drop out of school. She'd worked as a waitress at the diner but wasn't able to support herself and Darius. They'd both lived with Nell and Bill Cooper off and on. Jasmine left town around the same time Darius left for Hollywood. None of this was news, but I had to document it, some of it from memory.

However humble his beginnings, Darius had recently retired from a lucrative television career at the ripe old age of thirty-nine. He had no criminal record, and no civil actions. The latter surprised me a bit. Public figures were often subjected to frivolous lawsuits. He'd paid cash for the Devlin house and owned it through the Baker Family Trust. Interesting. The other beneficiaries of the Baker Family Trust were Nell, Bill, and Clay Cooper. Did they know that?

The software I used to build my profiles automatically searched for information on relatives whose names I entered. By the time I'd finished with Darius's basic information, I could see that Marcus Baker was living in Boca Raton. He'd moved there in 2012, owned a house he paid half a million in cash for, and had no debts. The last employment history he had was in 2012 at a Walmart in Jackson, Mississippi. Either he'd won the lottery, or Darius had tracked him down and set him up.

Jasmine King had similarly retired from a career as a hairdresser in 2012 and paid cash for a $2.5 million home in Laguna Beach, California. Darius appeared to be taking good care of both his parents, but I would verify that with him.

Darius's ex-wives were spread across the country: one in Los Angeles, one in New York, and one in Chicago. Was it possible one or more of them still carried a torch for him? Had they seen Trina Lynn as competition, if not for Darius's attention, then maybe for his money? It seemed a stretch, but in the interest of being thorough, I would need to verify if any of them had been in town Sunday evening.

Hell's bells. By all indications, Darius had been truthful when he said they all lived well. None of them had remarried. Any of them could have hired someone to kill Trina. I saved profiles for Arianna English (#1, Los Angeles), Vivianne Whitley (#2, Chicago), and Lily McAdams, (#3, New York). Darius and Lily had only been divorced for a little more than a year.

The sound of tires on oyster shells and gravel announced that Nate was home. Rhett barked once from the kitchen. By the time I made it to the front door, Rhett had raced through the doggy door in the mudroom, down the steps, through the garage, and out the doggy door on the pass-thru garage door. He waited by Nate's brown Explorer.

Nate opened the car door and climbed out. "Well, would you look at this reception." He patted Rhett, then his gaze drifted up the steps to where I stood. "I'm a lucky man."

I watched as he crossed the driveway towards the steps. A single golden curl lay across his forehead. In khakis, a white button-down shirt with the sleeves rolled up, and loafers with no socks, he was impossibly handsome.

A slow smile slid up his tanned face. "How was your day, Slugger?"

As always, my husband's velvety drawl was my undoing. "I missed you."

He pulled me into his arms. "I missed you too." He kissed me slowly to make his point.

I smiled up at him. "My, what a pleasant distraction you are."

"Happy to oblige. Was there something in particular you needed distracting from?"

I sighed. "We have a new case."

"And here I was hoping to celebrate putting Lucas to bed and spend some quality time rubbing sunscreen on you."

"All done?"

"I's dotted and t's crossed. Fraser's case is solid as a rock."

I turned and pulled Nate towards the door. "He'll be happy to hear that. We have a meeting with him first thing in the morning."

"I've already given him my report. There's no need to drive into Charleston."

"About the new case."

"And he called you? That's progress, I suppose."

"I called him."

Nate pushed the door closed behind us, looked at me quizzically, then lifted his nose. "What is that heavenly smell?"

"Mamma's beef stroganoff."

"You go by your parents' house again today?"

"I did. Long story. I'll tell you over dinner. Would you open a bottle of wine?" We headed towards the kitchen.

"Certainly. You want to eat outside this evening? It's still hot, but there's a nice breeze."

"Sounds nice."

Nate opened a bottle of Ropiteau French pinot noir and poured two glasses. I tossed together a couple of salads and brought him up to speed on our new client while he gathered placemats, napkins, and cutlery. It took us two trips to get everything outside to the round teak table on the deck. I drew a deep lungful of salt air. Across the row of sentinel dunes, waves danced towards the shore, the remnants of the day's sunlight glinting off the tops.

"Dinner music." I smiled.

"None finer." Nate lifted his glass.

We toasted the evening and dug in.

"You know I didn't marry you for your mamma's cooking," Nate said after his first bite. "But I have to say, it is a delicious fringe benefit. Not that you're not a fine cook in your own right."

"She's worried I don't feed you right."

"I'd weigh three hundred pounds if we ate like this every night." He sipped his wine. "So you think someone pressured Sonny and his new partner to arrest Darius?"

"That's all I can figure," I said. "The question is who and why. Clearly he thinks there's more to be investigated."

"It'd sure be nice to know what they have tying Darius to the crime."

"I hope Fraser will be able to find that out sooner rather than later. Eventually they'll have to tell him—discovery and all that, of course. But I'd rather know what we're up against now."

"Smart of you to get Fraser involved. I know he can be a pain in the ass, but...."

"I'd want him on my case if I were arrested."

"I'll bear that in mind."

We turned the conversation to lighter matters while we finished supper, then straightened the kitchen, and took the rest of our wine into the living room. We settled into the center corner of the sofa and propped our feet up.

"Let's wait to start a case board," I said.

"Sounds reasonable," said Nate. "How's your daddy?"

"He's feeling good enough to get into trouble."

"That sounds promising. Let me guess. Another emergency computer virus?"

"Not this time," I said. "He wanted me to see about Sara Catherine while I was at the Causbys." I told Nate about our pantry meeting.

A troubled look crept into Nate's eyes.

"What's wrong?" I asked.

He studied the rim of his glass, traced it with a finger. "How'd you feel about that?"

"I don't know...I'm curious too, I guess. She's family. He means well."

"I'm sure he does. It's just...I'm not sure it's a good idea for you to get between your parents and the Causbys regarding your cousin's child."

"I was just going to check on her. I wasn't going to abscond with her." I couldn't see the problem.

Nate winced. "I can't help but worry that seeing her might stir up things best left alone."

"You mean things related to Marci or things related to

children?"

"Children. I'm fairly confident your cousin poses no further threat to your well-being."

I sighed. "Sweetheart, I can't go the rest of my life avoiding children. Merry and Joe may well adopt after they get back from their wedding trip. Who knows with Blake? If Mamma has her way, he'll marry Poppy or any available female soon and commence giving her grandchildren as well." Severe cases of endometriosis had led to both Merry and me having hysterectomies.

"You're sure you don't want to think about adopting?"

I took a long sip of my wine. "Are you saying you do?"

"I'm saying I'm open to it if that's what you want. I'm also fine if you don't. You know my family relationships aren't what yours are. We're not close. I think that maybe changes how I feel about having children. It's not that I don't want them. But I also like our lives the way they are now. I just don't want you to miss out if a family of our own is important to you."

"Our lives are full. I've given it a lot of thought. Merry and Blake will get us some nieces and nephews to dote on. I don't fret about not having children. Not often, anyway. The thing is, and I know this will sound silly, but I feel like what we do...it's important. I guess I'd say I feel called to do it. Fight for justice and all that. If we were to have children—adopt them, I mean, of course—it would change everything. We take chances I wouldn't take if we had children. And who would we get to babysit while we're on stakeout?"

Colleen popped in, curled into the far corner of the sofa closest to me. "Me, of course."

"Right," I said. "That would work."

"It appears we'll always have a teenager, at any rate." Nate drained his glass.

"Where have you been?" I asked. "I was surprised you didn't show up at Georgia Causby's house."

"Yeah, I wanted to come," said Colleen. "But I needed to stick with Darius."

"You've been with him since he left with Sonny and Jenkins?" I asked.

"Every second," she said. "I had to cover my eyes a few times, like when he changed into his jumpsuit. Where did you think I was?"

"Most of the time I have no idea where you are," I said.

"I'm here when you need me." Her voice held a touch of fake hurt.

"Lookit," I said. "You've had a lot of quality time with him. Plenty of opportunity to poke around in his head. Did he kill Trina Lynn or not?"

"Why would I be protecting him if he killed someone?" she asked.

"Well I just found out you were protecting him," I said. "And that's not an answer."

"I sent you over there to begin with." Her voice held a healthy dose of teenage outrage.

I focused on my breathing, keeping my blood pressure down. "That was mostly Moon Unit. Could I just please, for once, have a yes or a no?"

"No." She raise her chin, looked away.

"No, I can't have a straight answer, or no, he didn't do it?" I asked.

She sighed dramatically. "You take all the fun out of this. No, he did not kill Trina Lynn. And I'm shocked you think I'd be involved if he had."

"Colleen." I gave her a level look. "My initial assumption was that he must be innocent because you were involved. But I am a fan of clarity and simply wanted confirmation. Now. You're sticking awfully close to him. Closer than you typically stick to me even. Do you think he's in danger?"

"No," said Colleen. "I know for a fact he is."

"From who?" I asked.

"I sense multiple threats."

"Wait a minute," I said. "Is Darius in danger while he's in custody or once he's released?"

"Both," she said.

"Where is he right now?" asked Nate.

"He's with Fraser, so he's safe for the moment."

I looked at my watch. "It's nearly 9:00. Why is he just now getting to speak with Fraser?"

Colleen did her best to look innocent. "Somehow, the paperwork got mixed up. He was in the wrong holding cell."

"I take it this was your handiwork. Why?" Nate asked.

"Some of Troy Causby's old buddies are in jail. They know Darius has been arrested for Trina Lynn's murder. They've put the word out. I needed to buy some time, slow things down 'til after supper."

"This has to do with an alternate scenario?" I asked. One of Colleen's gifts was the ability to see alternate outcomes of situations depending on actions taken or not taken.

"Yeah," said Colleen. "But this doesn't keep him safe for long. Make sure Fraser asks for protective custody—solitary confinement—whatever they call it these days. I'm going to stay with him until he's released. But it's better if I can keep a low profile."

"I'm glad you're keeping him safe—thank you," I said. "But I can't help but wonder why you're doing that. Typically, you only protect people who have a direct impact on Stella Maris."

"I guess you answered your own question," said Colleen. "Gotta fly."

SIX

Mercedes Westbrook, Fraser's administrative assistant, showed us into his stately office the next morning at nine sharp. Fraser Alston Rutledge III came from Old Charleston money, his lineage distinguished. But he'd earned his reputation as one of Charleston's best criminal defense attorneys. At forty, he was fit, a nice-looking man, and though he was well-groomed, his style choices were a mix of traditional and outlandish. He wore his brown hair combed back on the sides and gelled on top so that it stood on end. Today's seersucker suit was oyster grey with a red striped bowtie and red suspenders. He was a character, and he looked the part. Fraser looked up from a file on his heirloom quality mahogany desk. "Mr. Andrews. Good work on Lucas."

Nate stopped beside one of the visitors' chairs in front of Fraser's desk, but he hesitated before sitting. "All I did was tie up a few loose ends. You can thank my wife for the solid case you'll be taking to court." His voice was easy, calm. But he met Fraser's gaze and held it.

Fraser looked from Nate to me. "Very well then. Thank you, Miz Talbot." He dropped his customary emphasis on "Miz."

Nate and I took our seats.

"Were you able to get Darius into protective custody?" I asked.

"He is in the protective custody wing at Charleston County

Jail, yes. But let us not delude ourselves that his safety is guaranteed there. It is not unheard of for individuals in protective custody to attack other inmates. I have requested a bond hearing, and I am hopeful that will be held on Friday. With a modicum of luck, Mr. Baker will be home later that day." Fraser Alston Rutledge III liked the sound of his own voice so much that he rarely used contractions. He preferred to use as many words as possible.

"Do you have any information regarding what evidence the police might have against Darius?" Nate asked.

"I am delighted you asked, Mr. Andrews." Fraser raised his right hand and lowered his palm to the desk for emphasis. "As it turns out, our fair solicitor was most pleased to tell me that she has an *eyewitness* who saw Mr. Baker discard the murder weapon." He nearly shouted the word "eyewitness," and he got louder from there. The combination of his gold, brown-flecked eyes, his perfectly white teeth, and his spiked hair brought to mind a lion roaring.

"*What?*" Could he possibly be guilty? Could Colleen be wrong? Had that ever happened? My thoughts scrambled back. "That can't be right."

"I sincerely hope you are correct, Miz Talbot," said Fraser. "I detest losing. I took this case at your request. And while I did not specifically ask if our client was innocent, nor is that a requirement of my representation, I do like to know what I am getting into. I surmised he was unjustly charged from your characterization of the matter."

"I believe that to be the case." I originally thought that because I figured Sonny must think he was innocent. *Damnation.* I needed to talk to Sonny. This situation with his new partner was not working for me in the slightest.

"Let's back up, shall we?" Nate said. "Do we know who this witness is?"

"We do not," said Fraser. "We do know it is a tourist who, and this is the part I especially like, asked Mr. Baker for his autograph. Mr. Baker was kind enough to oblige."

"Oh dear God," I said.

"Okay, so it was definitely him the witness saw," said Nate. "No chance it was mistaken identity. But what exactly did he or she see him do?"

"I have not been given these details, Mr. Andrews. That was all Miz Wilson was inclined to share with me at this juncture." Scarlett Wilson was the Ninth Circuit Solicitor. "Though I deduce that since she specifically referred to the murder weapon—she didn't say 'a gun'—a weapon must have been recovered, and it must have been identified as the murder weapon."

"What did Darius have to say about all this?" I asked.

"I spoke with the solicitor after I had spoken with Mr. Baker. I have not had the opportunity to inquire as to his version of this encounter with the tourist."

"What did he tell you about his movements Sunday night?" I asked.

"He said he had dinner with Miz Causby at Hall's Chophouse. The reservation was for 8:00. During the course of dinner, they had an argument. Miz Causby then left for an appointment with a source at approximately ten minutes before 10:00, at which point Mr. Baker decided to take a stroll around our fair city. Alone. He has no alibi for the estimated time of the murder, shortly after 10 p.m. He was on the 11:30 ferry back to Stella Maris."

"Who discovered the victim's body?" asked Nate.

"That would be yet another tourist—wait," he glanced at his notes. "Twin tourists. Margie Sue Frentress and her twin sister, Marylou Willis. They're in town from Paradise, Texas. They're staying at the inn at number two Meeting Street. They happened upon Miz Causby when they cut down Philadelphia Alley on their way back to the inn after dinner at The Peninsula Grill."

"I'll try to see them first thing," I said.

"That would be a very good idea," said Fraser. "I have no idea how long they plan to be in town. I only happened by the knowledge that they discovered the late Miz Causby by virtue of it being reported by Live Five News at five this morning."

"We need to find out who our witness is in the worst way," I said. "If he or she was just in town for Labor Day weekend, they could already have left town."

"That would be correct," said Fraser. "However, in this particular case, budget is not a concern. If you need to book llamas to Machu Picchu, Mr. Baker's retainer will cover it."

"Understood," I said. "The solicitor must believe she can establish motive to a jury. The only reasonable motive I can think of—and I'm not saying he had a motive, just that they are ascribing one to him—is anger. Jealousy, three ex-wives later, isn't plausible."

Fraser nodded. "If, Miz Talbot, the prosecution knows that Mr. Baker just learned that he has a twenty-year-old son, they may well surmise that a woman hiding that kind of information would make a man angry enough to kill. It remains to be seen whether they are in possession of this particular fact or not. Some of my friends in the Charleston Police Department have suddenly lost their spirit of cooperation."

He meant Sonny. Fraser's partner, Eli Rutledge, and Sonny Ravenel were good friends. "We're having the same issue," I said.

Fraser said, "I think it's safe to assume the command staff wants to avoid any appearance of preferential treatment due to Mr. Baker's celebrity status. They are handling this case very carefully."

"The only person I can think of who might have told the police about Darius's son is Georgia Causby, Trina Lynn's mother. I know they spoke to her. She didn't say that she told them about the child. In fact, she practically scoffed at the idea that Darius killed Trina Lynn right up until she found out he'd been arrested. She wanted to keep that baby a secret, not tarnish Trina Lynn's name. It's hard to believe she would've told them."

"But we have to assume they know, unless and until we find out otherwise," said Fraser.

"Agreed," I said. "Did Darius happen to mention how he came to learn that he has a twenty-year-old son? Did Trina tell him?"

"Mr. Baker indicated that he was contacted by the young man in question directly," said Fraser.

"Did the adoption agency release that information?" Nate asked.

"No," said Fraser. "Apparently he ran into trouble there. The laws in South Carolina are complex, evolving, and at times interpreted differently by various agencies. Additionally, as I understand it, his adoptive parents did not want him to pursue a connection with his birth parents. He traced his paternal line through one of those ancestry family tree applications and a DNA test."

I squinted at him. "But Darius would also have to be in the database."

"Mr. Baker is likewise a heritage hobbyist. He had his own DNA tested. There are several tools online that help you connect with relatives. The young man reached out to Mr. Baker, who was naturally skeptical, given his financial position. But these test results are impressive evidence."

"Did Darius tell him who his mother was?" I asked.

"I did not ask him that. I will when next I see him," said Fraser.

Colleen had warned us that Darius was in danger from several fronts. "We need to find out who Darius's son is," I said. "We don't know anything about him. He could be angry that he was given up for adoption."

Nate said, "You're thinking he might have killed Trina Lynn?"

"I think we have to consider the possibility," I said.

"We need to get moving," said Nate.

Fraser stood. "Keep me apprised."

SEVEN

Nate and I had brought both cars to Charleston that morning in case we had to split up. We street parked towards the end of Broad, near the Old Exchange and Provost Dungeon, me in front of Fraser's office, and Nate across the street a half block away. At 9:45 in the morning, it was already too hot to stand on the sidewalk and talk. We climbed into my car, and I started the engine and got the air conditioning going. The first order of business was finding the witness who claimed to have seen Darius discard the murder weapon.

"The only people we can say for certain know who that so-called witness is are Sonny and his partner, the solicitor, and the witness him or herself," I said.

"Right," said Nate. "But I think Sonny has told us by his actions that he can't talk to us. We don't know what his reason is, but we know Sonny. It's a good one."

"Agreed. We shouldn't badger him."

"Do we know anyone in the solicitor's office?" Nate asked.

"I don't. We could maybe come up with a ruse to get close enough to the file to sneak a peek, if we have to. But that will be tricky and time consuming. I have an idea we can try first." I smiled. "It's nearly 10:00. Let's head towards Kudu."

Sonny's habit was to have coffee and a pastry at Kudu Coffee and Craft Beer on Vanderhorst at 10:00 most mornings. Often, under normal circumstances, I met him there.

"I thought we just agreed to leave Sonny alone."

"No," I said. "We agreed not to pressure him to talk to us." I pulled away from the curb.

Nate shook his head.

When we turned right off of King Street onto Vanderhorst, Sonny's black Jeep Grand Cherokee was parked two spots down on the right, in front of the bicycle rack and adjacent to the courtyard at Kudu.

"Bingo," I said.

"No offense, Slugger, but finding him was a no-brainer. Now what's the plan?"

"We need one of the burner phones out of the back. And a couple ball caps." I turned left onto Phillips Street, which ran behind St. Matthews Lutheran Church, but dead-ended at a loading dock for the College of Charleston bookstore. I executed a three-point turn and pulled into a parking space behind a white van, but cheated to the left so I could see around it. A sign on the exterior wall of the adjacent building clearly indicated that the parking space was for College of Charleston service vehicles only, twenty-four seven. We wouldn't be here long.

"Oh, I see what you're up to." Nate hopped out and retrieved one of the burner phones we kept for anonymous calling. He climbed back into the car and handed it to me.

I tapped the top of the phone against my upper lip thoughtfully. "I know all emergency calls to Charleston County Consolidated 911 Center are recorded. I'm not certain calls going to the non-emergency and office lines at Charleston PD aren't taped. I need to find a number that for sure won't be recorded."

Nate tapped his iPhone a few times, typed, and tapped some more. "How about the Victims Services Program? They work with witnesses too."

"Perfect. What's the number?"

He read it out and I typed it in. A woman answered after two rings. "Victim Services, may I help you?"

"Yes, ma'am. I think I must've pressed the wrong button by mistake. I need to get a message to Detective Ravenel."

"I can transfer you—"

"No, please don't do that. I'm afraid you'll lose me, and I'm scared."

"Ma'am if you're in trouble, I can get you help."

"Oh, thank you. I spoke with Detective Ravenel earlier about that nice TV star, Darius Baker?"

"Yes ma'am?"

"I need to speak with him again immediately. I've remembered something else I forgot to tell him. And I think I'm being followed. I'm worried. Could you ask him to come right away?"

"Yes ma'am. I'll get him a message. And I'll stay on the line with you until he gets there. Now what was your name again?"

I ended the call.

Nate nodded, gave me a little grin. "As always, your acting skills are impressive. Worries me sometimes, how good you are at that."

"Oh, *puh-leeze*. That's what I love about you most. You never give me a reason to be anything other than exactly who I am. Let's just hope my performance works." I snagged a scrunchie from my purse, pulled my hair up, and slipped on my navy ball cap with the white palmetto and crescent design on front. We rotated the caps we wore, but this was one of my favorites.

"You think these are necessary?" asked Nate. "Has Sonny seen your new car?"

"Regrettably, yes. Not only that, since he's all about bonding with his new partner, there's a better than even chance Jenkins is there too. We want Sonny to be above a glimmer of reproach. If Jenkins spots us, he might suspect Sonny tipped us off."

"Fair point." Nate put on a faded blue Atlanta Braves cap.

Three minutes later, Sonny's Jeep Cherokee rolled down Vanderhorst past the narrow intersection with Phillips. I pulled out of the parking space and turned left. I was the next car behind him, so I stayed back a ways.

We went through the intersection of St. Philip Street, then made a right on Coming, and passed the Cathedral Church of St. Luke & St. Paul. Five blocks later, Sonny made a left on Cannon Street and we followed.

"This is a bit off the beaten path for most tourists," said Nate.

"This isn't off the beaten path anymore," I said. "The Cannonborough-Elliotborough neighborhood is one of the hottest parts of town."

"Yeah, I get this is where all the cool kids hang out. But most folks from out of town still stay somewhere between King Street and East Bay."

"Perhaps our eyewitness is a bit more adventurous."

"Or Sonny and Jenkins could've stashed their witness," said Nate. "We might not be headed towards their original hotel."

"Maybe."

"You sure he doesn't know we're back here? Could be he's decided to take us on a joyride."

"Sonny could know that. But Jenkins does not. I'm thinking Sonny's okay with us being back here."

"Is Jenkins even with him?"

"I'm betting yes."

Sonny pulled to the curb in front of a brick building in disrepair that appeared to have once been a storefront.

"I can't stop," I said. "Jenkins would surely spot us."

"Go as slow as you can." Nate grabbed a pair of binoculars from the console.

"This must be a stash house." The street was definitely transitional, with some fully restored homes and businesses, and a few that looked on the verge of falling down.

"Not necessarily. I'll circle around."

"Jenkins is with him. They're out of the car. They're headed back in the other direction."

I circled the block and pulled in behind a red Honda half a block away from Sonny, where Smith intersects with Cannon.

"It's gotta be the grey house." We were parked two doors away.

"The one in front of the fire hydrant? Why's that?"

"That's 86 Cannon. It's one of the most popular B&Bs in the city right now." It was a three-story Charleston single house with double porches running down the left side. Painted a soft grey, with shutters in a darker, contrasting shade, the house exuded Southern charm. Stately twin palm trees and lush crepe myrtles with vibrant pink blossoms added to the curb appeal. The house would be easily identifiable in any photograph as uniquely Charleston. "It was built in 1862, but it's been fully restored. The photos on the website are gorgeous."

"Is that right?" His tone was soft, with a hint of a tease.

"I've had it earmarked for a night downtown for a while."

"Interesting." Nate scanned the area. "Still a few fixer-uppers on this street."

"Don't get any ideas. You won't find any bargains." I unfolded a tourist map. "Here."

Nate took one side of the map. We held it up as a screen, but I peeked out from behind one edge and he the other.

"The house only has five bedrooms," I said. "Once they leave, we can surely figure out which guest is the one we're looking for."

"What if they move the witness?"

"Well, at least we'll see what he or she looks like when they come out with Sonny and Jenkins. If they're going to do that, they'll do it now. And we can follow. If the witness doesn't leave with them, I say we check in."

"Why did I know that was where this was headed?"

"Because you're an exceptionally smart man."

"Buttering me up will not get you your way."

"Typically it does." I let a slow grin slide up my face.

"Pretty sure of yourself, aren't you now?" He must've tried hard to sound put out, but I wasn't buying it.

"Well, it is a business expense."

"Now you know good and well I'd bring you here any time you wanted to come. But since we do have a legitimate business need to go inside right now, I guess Darius can pay for this stay anyway."

"I'm going to move up the street a ways," I said. "All we need to do at this point is confirm which house they come out of, and whether they come out with a witness or alone. They'll be suspicious. Jenkins will be looking for us."

"No doubt Sonny will see your hand in this. But he won't call us out. I'd be willing to bet he won't tell his partner he suspects you're behind the prank call that got them over here."

"Doesn't matter. You should've seen the look on Jenkins's face when he saw me at Darius's house. He will come out of that house expecting to find us someplace close by. If he sees us, he'll make a point to move the witness."

"We'd best hide then, hadn't we? Sonny's windows are dark. We might not be able to see if the witness is in the back seat. We need to see who gets into the car. I'll hop out here, cut down Smith and through somebody's backyard. Slip between that building on the corner there and the white house beside it. I'll be able to see from there, but not be seen."

"All right. I'll be in Sugar, the bakeshop a block down the street. The YMCA building next door has a small, but deep parking lot. I can get away with stashing the car there for a few minutes. Just in case Jenkins is doing a car-to-car search."

"Sounds like a plan." He hopped out of the car and crossed the street.

I pulled away from the curb.

There was a line in Sugar, but I didn't mind. I loved browsing all the artfully displayed confections. Thirty minutes later, I had selected our cupcakes from the antique display case and checked out when Nate walked in.

"I got vanilla blueberry, and I got you a double chocolate." I smiled as he held the door for me. "What happened?" I asked once we were outside.

"They came out of that fancy B&B you like. They were looking for us, no doubt. Looked in the window of every car parked close by."

"And the witness?"

"Whoever it is, they're still inside."

"Well, then. Let's go check in, shall we?"

EIGHT

We turned left between the brick columns, one with a gold plaque announcing the address, and rolled down the palm-lined brick driveway with a stripe of impossibly green grass down the middle.

"I'm reasonably certain they're unaccustomed to walk-in guests," said Nate.

"I'm sure you're right," I said. "But it is September, after all. I doubt they're fully booked." Weathermen and statisticians will tell you July is the hottest month in Charleston. Perhaps because we're all heat weary by then, a typical Lowcountry September feels hotter to me. And it's the height of hurricane season.

Behind the house was a cottage I hadn't noticed from the street. It was two stories, painted in what appeared to be the same shade of grey as the shutters of the main house, with white trim, a front porch and a metal roof.

"I'd forgotten that was back here. It's the office, if memory serves," I said. "It's been a while since I checked the place out online, but I believe it's also a staff kitchen."

"I would imagine it's also the owner's quarters," said Nate.

"Now it is," I said. "When the main house was originally built, this was the kitchen house."

Two curly buff cockapoos, one a lighter shade than the other, came bounding out of the multi-purpose kitchen house down a set of steps at the back that led from a doggy door to a small fenced yard. They appeared to be the official welcoming committee. Beyond the fenced yard was a pea gravel parking area that would accommodate ten cars. Just then, ours was the seventh.

"Plates from South Carolina, Georgia, Ohio, and New Hampshire," said Nate. "Newer ones could be rentals, of course."

I parked the car and Nate and I walked back towards the fence to speak to the cockapoos.

"They're adorable." I reached over the fence to pet them. After we'd cooed over them for a few moments, we walked around to the front porch of the kitchen house. Colorful plants spilled out of container gardens by the door. A row of rocking chairs invited us to sit and enjoy the shade.

"Oh, look," I said. "It's got a haint blue ceiling. And a sign on the door."

The bright yellow sign gave notice that reception and the front desk were now located on the first floor of the main house. We made our way across the brick drive and climbed the back steps to the lower piazza of the bed and breakfast.

This porch also had a haint blue ceiling, but here the paneled woodwork lent a more formal air. Closed now, the tall stained wooden door with a transom above at the far end would lead to the front steps. A row of white columns with matching railing between them overlooked the palm-lined brick driveway. Tall hurricane lanterns lined the floor by the rail. A deep-cushioned outdoor sofa sat to one side of the front door, a pair of chairs to the other.

Nate hesitated in front of the door in the middle of the porch.

"We know the owners live out back," I said. "This building isn't their home."

I opened the door slowly. "Hello?"

The wood floors in the foyer had a lovely painted design. To my left, a closed door with a brass number plate was clearly a guest room. In front of me, a stained wooden staircase with a carpet runner rose to a landing where it switched back.

"Hello!" A welcoming call came from the open door to our right. A young woman with light brown hair appeared in the doorway. "Can I help you?"

"Hey." Nate extended his hand with a smile. "I'm Nate Andrews. This is my wife, Liz. I know this is a bit spontaneous, but we wondered if you happened to have a vacancy."

"I'm Mary Hannah," she said. "It's so nice to meet you. How many nights did you want to stay with us?"

"Two," said Nate. "We figured maybe we'd stay 'til Friday if you have availability."

"Sure," said Mary Hannah. "I can offer you number five. It's our third-floor room. I'm afraid it's all I have for both nights."

"Sounds great, thanks," said Nate.

"Come on inside and I'll get you checked in." Mary Hannah led the way into the room from whence she'd come. "This is the salon. It's also our reception area now. We tried it out back, but folks always seem to want to come here first."

A couple I pegged at mid-thirties sat in the center of a cozy deep blue sectional in the front corner. "How lovely," I murmured. And it was. Indigo grass cloth covered the walls. A mirror with an octagonal frame hung above the fireplace, which was flanked by cushioned benches. A desk with a modern office chair and an iMac floated in front of the fireplace. The room was decorated with a mix of traditional and contemporary touches that somehow blended together to create a fresh but authentic style.

"Hey, y'all," I offered the couple on the sofa my sunniest smile. "Sorry to interrupt."

"Oh, you're not interrupting us." The attractive woman with near shoulder-length brunette hair and a lovely smile waved away the notion. "I'm Tanna Mullinax. This is my husband, Eric. We're from Travelers Rest. How about y'all?"

"I'm Liz. This is my husband, Nate. We live on Stella Maris," I said. "We just love spending time downtown."

"Aw, we just went there last year for vacation," said Eric. "My wife loves the B&B on the north end of the island." Eric had brown hair and a horseshoe mustache and one of those smallish beards just around his mouth and chin.

"Sullivan's," I said. "My godmother, Grace Sullivan runs it."

"Small world," said Tanna. "Y'all just checking in?"

"We are," said Nate. "How long are y'all in town for?"

"'Til Saturday," said Eric. "We came down for the week."

They'd been here Sunday night. "Great," I said. "We'll see y'all later on. Maybe have a drink?"

"Sounds good. We were just heading out to do some sightseeing." Tanna stood and Eric followed her cue.

We all said our goodbyes and they headed through the foyer and out the front door.

They'd been downstairs in the salon. That would've been the logical place for Sonny and Jenkins to have spoken with their witness. But they seemed awfully relaxed and open, not exactly what you'd expect in folks who'd just had a surprise visit from local law enforcement.

Mary Hannah had taken her place at the desk chair. "Please, have a seat." She gestured to the sofa Tanna and Eric had recently vacated. In short order Nate filled out the registration form and provided identification and a credit card.

"Do you all need restaurant reservations?" asked Mary Hannah.

"I think we're all set on that," said Nate.

We weren't, of course, but we needed to see where the day took us.

Mary Hannah poured us each a glass of champagne. "I think we're all set then. Let me give you a tour of the house."

We picked up our glasses and followed her back into the foyer.

"There are two bedrooms on the first floor," said Mary

Hannah. "One is accessed off the porch, and the other is here." She gestured to the door across the hall from the salon.

She led us up the stairs. "The second floor has the same layout, but above the salon is the kitchen. Breakfast is served in here each morning, and here's where you come for wine and cheese at five, though most folks take theirs out onto the piazza."

Mary Hannah stepped into the kitchen and moved out of the way so we could follow. With white walls, cabinets painted a muted shade of teal, and marble countertops, the kitchen was light and airy. It wasn't a full kitchen, but more a breakfast room and serving space, with five cafe-sized tables along the wall. At that hour, I wasn't surprised to find the kitchen empty. It was 11:30 a.m.— nearly lunchtime.

We continued to the third floor, where Mary Hannah showed us the library, a cozy room with exposed beams decorated in bold reds, pinks, and cream, with brown touches. "There's an honor bar. Please let us know if you need something you don't see."

As Mary Hannah moved into the room, she spoke to a couple seated in chairs by the fireplace. "Have we decided on lunch?"

The woman was petite with white hair, the gentleman large with a comfortable look about him. His hair was also white, receding on top, but with a full beard and mustache. They both had lovely, welcoming smiles. "We're thinking about trying Five Loaves," said the woman.

"Excellent choice," said Mary Hannah. "Mo and Jim Heedles, please meet Nate and Liz Andrews."

I didn't correct her. I never minded being called Mrs. Andrews. I simply didn't have the patience for all the paperwork involved in making that my legal name at this juncture.

We all shook hands, said hello. "Where are y'all from?" I asked.

"Amherst, New Hampshire," said Mo. "How about you folks?"

"We're local," I said. "We just don't live downtown. So

occasionally we take the opportunity to stay on the peninsula for a few days."

"Makes sense to me," said Jim.

Mary Hannah said, "Let's step across the hall and I'll show you your room and let you folks get settled."

"Maybe we'll see you for wine and cheese," said Mo.

"Oh, I hope so," I said. "Let's plan on it. Y'all have a good lunch."

"Thanks," they said in unison.

"Do you need help with your luggage?" asked Mary Hannah.

"Thank you so much," said Nate. "But I'll grab it later. I think we're going to head out for lunch too."

At least one of us was going to have to go home and pack a bag or else we were going shopping. We had a few things in our cars, but not everything we'd need.

"All right then. Let us know if there's anything you need." Mary Hannah closed the door behind her.

"This is fabulous." The room had a vaulted ceiling with exposed beams, and a large window with rooftop views. Heart of pine floors, white linens on a king-sized bed, and white and teal striped wallpaper made for a soothing vibe. The adjoining bathroom was all glass and marble, with an exposed brick chimney.

"S'nice," said Nate. "What do you think?"

"Either couple could be the witnesses," I said. "But we might still have one or two couples to meet. This room was the only one available for two nights. But that doesn't necessarily mean the remaining two rooms have someone in them right now. But they could. The great thing about a bed and breakfast is that it's normal for everyone to chat. We won't come off like stalkers."

"Yeah, I'm thinking our best bet is to get a few other things out of the way, then come back here at 5:00. There's no guarantee the others will show for happy hour, but typically people who stay at B&Bs like that sort of thing."

"I want to go snoop around Darius's house. See if I can find anything on the son. He worries me. Also on my priority list is Trina Lynn's cameraman, August Lockwood. Her mother claimed he was her best friend. He ought to be able to tell me if there's somewhere else we should be looking."

"Sounds good. You want to pick us up some clothes while you're there?"

"Sure. And I need to talk to Merry about taking care of Rhett for a couple of days. Blake's got his hands full. Maybe she'll want to spend a few days in the guest room, be closer to the beach."

"I think I'm going to head over to Hall's. See if I can find out who Darius and Trina's server was Sunday night, who all might've overheard their argument."

"Good idea," I said. "I'll bring our laptops back. Anything else you can think of?"

"Nah. That should do it. Everything else we'll need is in one of our cars. I'll bring in four listening devices in case it comes to slipping bugs in purses at happy hour."

I drove Nate over to Broad Street, where the Explorer was parked. As he climbed out of my car, he said, "Keep your weapon with you. You never know who else might be snooping around Darius's house. This case will likely bring out the crazies."

NINE

The 12:30 ferry back to Stella Maris was crammed full of reporters. Darius would likely be in jail until Friday morning, and they knew it. But this batch was mostly freelancers. I called Blake.

"How are Nell and Bill doing? Clay?" I asked when he answered.

"They're fine. I talked Grace into renting me the entire B&B at a municipal discount. I'm going to try to get Darius to stay there incognito."

"Fraser's not going to be happy with that plan," I said. "But that'll give you just one place to keep an eye on."

"That, and there's five less rooms for reporters to sleep in on the island."

"There's a ferry full of 'em headed your way."

"S'not the first. Won't be the last. A few of 'em are already camping at the park at Devlin's Point."

"Good grief. This batch isn't heavy with cameras and equipment. I take them for mostly independents looking for a feature article, maybe some background. These are the ones who'll be looking for the Coopers."

"Roger that, thanks."

*   *   *

No cars were parked in front of Darius's house. Did he have personal security people? I hadn't seen any sign of them yesterday. I put my small lock pick set in the back pocket of my capris, then emptied everything from my crossbody bag and transferred my Sig from my larger bag. My summer outfit wouldn't conceal a weapon. If I ran into Darius's security folks, I didn't want to be toting a gun on my hip like Doc Holliday.

I slipped on a pair of nitrile gloves and took a quick stroll around the perimeter. The windows in the garage doors were too high for me to see inside. I tried the walk-thru door, but it was locked.

The infinity pool and landscaping Darius had put in on the ocean side of the house were breathtaking. A fire pit with eight chairs, multiple tables, two dozen lounge chairs around the pool, an outdoor kitchen with two smokers, a charcoal grill and a gas grill, a sand volleyball court...the whole area looked like it belonged at a high-dollar resort. Darius must entertain in lavish scale.

I climbed the stairs to the back deck and tried the screened porch door. Oddly, it had a handle with a keyed lock as opposed to the hook and eye latch on the inside that was more common in our part of the world. It was locked. I cupped my hands over my eyes and looked through a window. No one was in the kitchen. I was certain he had a security system, but had he thought to arm it?

I walked back around to the front, scanned the area, and jogged up the front steps. The lock on the door was impressive. Just for the heck of it, I tried the handle before pulling out my pick set. It was open. Poor Darius had been in such a state when he left that he hadn't locked the front door behind him. And I hadn't even thought to remind him. Good thing Stella Maris was the kind of town where an unlocked front door wouldn't typically be a problem.

No one was around. "Hello?" I called as I pushed the door

open. Somewhere in the house, the alarm panel announced, "Front door." No alarms went off, at least none that were audible. No one answered me. The house felt empty. I wished Colleen were handy to screen it to be sure.

I walked inside and closed the door behind me. A man with his fingers in as many pies as Darius had must have a home office. When the Devlins lived here, the office had been on the front left side of the house. I poked my head into what appeared to now be a living room, or at least a separate conversation area. The doorway had been widened, the door removed.

A quick survey of downstairs revealed that all of the first floor was now entertaining space, from the completely renovated kitchen and dining area to three different living areas, the largest with a projection TV system. The entire floor was done in gleaming hardwoods, white walls, plantation shutters, gauzy white drapes that pooled on the floor, and mixed tan-toned upholstered furniture with an occasional pop of orange or teal.

Time to see what was upstairs. "Anyone home?" I called as I climbed the steps.

No one answered.

A floor to ceiling window at the first landing looked out over the side yard. No one in sight. I continued up the stairs. The only room to the right on the second floor was Darius's office. The decorator had done an excellent job in here as well—dark woods and a nautical theme. Most likely what I was looking for was in here, but I decided to finish my tour before digging in.

Past the top of the stairs, an elevator closet and the laundry room were on my left. Across the hall was a short spur leading to the master bedroom. Massive, with a cathedral ceiling, a fireplace, and a wall of windows overlooking the ocean, it could've come straight out of *Architectural Digest*. The bathroom, done in white marble with industrial accents, featured a shower cave, a steam room, a sauna, and a jetted tub I could have floated in. Still no sign of anyone else in the house.

I stepped back out into the hall and checked out the two guest suites. Neither appeared occupied. Then I went back to Darius's office. I sat down at his desk and surveyed the room. Twin tall file cabinets stood in the corner. But I wanted to see his email first.

I turned on the Mac. What would Darius's password be? I tried his birthday, 123456, 123456789, and the word "password," all combinations a disturbing number of people actually used according to something I'd recently read. Then I heard his voice in my head, "I'm Mr. Main Street USA." Bingo. I was in.

I opened his email and scanned through the most recent subject lines. Then I searched on "Ancestry." A long list of emails filled the screen. Many were actually from the site. I scrolled past those. Halfway down the list was an email with the subject, "Looking for My Birth Family." How had he even gotten Darius's personal email? I opened it and scanned the trail.

His name was Brantley Charles Miller and he'd grown up in Travelers Rest, South Carolina. That was the second time today that quaint town north of Greenville had crossed my radar. I disliked coincidences. It was a long email trail. I scrolled to the beginning.

Brantley had reached out to Darius on the Ancestry site on August 5. The first message had come through their messaging system. Brantley had written:

Hi, I know this sounds crazy, but I think we may be related. I recently had a DNA test done through Family Tree DNA. I uploaded my results to Y-Search. I was tracing my paternal line. It seems we have common ancestors. Would you be interested in discussing our potential common heritage?

Darius had responded in the affirmative, and four messages later he'd given Brantley his personal email address. Because both men had screen names on Ancestry, and living people weren't shown in Darius's tree, it appeared that Brantley had no idea he was speaking to a celebrity until after they'd exchanged a couple of emails. And he had not mentioned that he was looking for his birth family at first.

I focused on the most recent exchange, from Friday. Brantley had written:

I swear to you, I had no idea who you were when I contacted you in the beginning. I was just looking for my birth parents, and I knew we were closely related based on DNA testing.

Darius replied:

I'm sure you can understand how this all seems unbelievable to me. I need a few days to process this information. I'll be in touch soon.

Darius had not revealed Trina Lynn's name, or even that he planned to speak to Brantley's supposed mother. At least he hadn't done that via email. Had they spoken by phone? There was no mention of exchanging numbers.

But had Brantley started investigating Darius when he found out who he was talking to? If he had, the marriage license would have led him to Trina Lynn. Thanks to twenty-four-hour celebrity tracking, everyone who cared to know knew that Darius had just moved home to Stella Maris. And Travelers Rest was only four and a half hours away from Stella Maris—three and a half to Charleston.

I scrolled back to the top of the email trail, then snapped photos of the entire exchange, screen by screen. Then I searched Darius's email, contacts, and calendar for Trina Lynn. There was a contact record with a cell phone number and an address in Mt. Pleasant. It appeared to be her condo. The only other mention was the dinner date from Sunday night. How had he gotten her current phone number?

I opened a browser window and navigated to the WCSC website. Two clicks later I was looking at photos of all the staff and links to their Facebook and Twitter accounts. Trina Lynn's photo had been removed. Had Darius messaged her through Facebook?

Luckily he'd saved his Facebook password, so it was an easy

matter to login as him. Interesting. He had a secret profile under the name DeAndre Baker, with a photo of the donkey from *Shrek* as his profile picture. He had twenty-five friends, one of them his cousin, Clay Cooper. I pulled up Darius's messages.

There it was. He'd messaged Trina Lynn last Wednesday and asked her to dinner to catch up. She'd heard he was back in town. All very civil. No mention of a love child. Had he sprung that question on her at the restaurant? Is that what they'd really argued about?

"Back door." The electronic notification from the alarm panel was faint. There must've been a second control board in the master bedroom, or I would've never heard it. Someone else was in the house.

I closed all the windows and powered down the computer.

Then, I tiptoed to the top of the stairs.

Whoever it was either worked for Darius or they were breaking and entering, like me. Or maybe it was one of the Coopers. Did they have keys? Nell had banged on the door yesterday. If she had a key, she hadn't used it.

I pulled my Sig 9 from my crossbody bag. Holding the gun in both hands, pointed towards the floor, I eased down the steps. Because the staircase switched back at the landing, I could only see the bottom half of the stairs reflected in the window.

When I was two steps above the landing, the reflection of a familiar blonde appeared in the window, stealthily climbing the stairs.

"*Calista?*"

"Liz? Is that you?" she whispered.

I relaxed, slid my weapon back into my bag, and continued down the stairs. "What in the world are you doing here? And why are you whispering?"

"I'm not sure," she said in her signature smoky, breathy voice. Calista was Marilyn Monroe's doppelgänger. A former client, she was one of my best friends. For a while I'd thought she'd be my sister-in-law. So did she.

Calista laughed. "I mean I'm not sure why I whispered, of course. I brought Darius a casserole. See how Southern I've become?"

"How did you get in?"

"Oh. I have a key." She pulled a golden key out of the pocket of her white capris and held it up.

I scrunched my face at her. "Why do you have a key to Darius Baker's house?" Calista had only lived on Stella Maris a few years.

"Well," she said, "we're friends. Sometimes friends exchange keys you know, for emergencies." Her tone might have been the teensiest bit defensive.

"Does that key fit the screen door too?"

"Yes, it does. All the doors are keyed alike."

"How long have you known Darius?"

"We met last Tuesday night at the Pirates' Den."

"Do tell? That was what, his second night in town?"

"I think so. Is that important?" Her eyes were wide with curiosity. Calista was an old soul, world-wise in many ways. But she could also be naive. Or she could be messing with me.

"Only in the sense that in some circles, a key exchange after one week is considered rushing things."

"I see what you mean," she said.

"Why were you going upstairs? I'm assuming your casserole is in the kitchen?"

"Yes. I put it in the refrigerator for when Darius comes home. It's chicken tetrazzini."

"And?"

"Well, I guess he can have a salad with it."

"Calista." I tilted my head and raised an eyebrow at her.

"All right, fine." She rolled her eyes, raised her chin, and looked down her nose at me. "I wanted to leave him a message."

"Upstairs?"

"That's right."

"What kind of message?"

She raised her left hand, which held a creamy envelope with her monogram on the front. "It's personal in nature."

"Calista, exactly how well do you know Darius?"

"Quite well, actually." She lifted her chin another inch.

"Are y'all...involved?"

"I'm not certain why this is your business. And come to think of it, why are you here?"

"And I'd like to know exactly what either one of you are doing here." The voice came from the kitchen doorway.

Calista raised an eyebrow and cast a look in that direction that would have done Scarlett O'Hara proud.

I spun around

The well-maintained black woman could've been a model. Dressed to the nines, she stood with her hands on her hips and a look on her face that said she meant business.

"And you are?" I asked.

"I'm Vivianne Baker."

Vivianne. Darius's second wife. The mean one. "Baker?" I squinted at her.

"That's right. I'm Darius Baker's wife. Who are *you* and what are you doing in his house?"

"I am Liz Talbot. I work for Darius. This is my friend, Calista McQueen. I was given to understand that you and Darius divorced more than two years ago. In fact, he's had another wife and divorced *her* since then." I stared her down.

Vivianne flung both hands in the air, fingers splayed. "That cheap tramp. She was just a fling he made the mistake of marrying. And I don't owe any explanations to the hired help. I think it's time for both of you to leave." She eyed Calista.

"And I don't think that's your call," I said. "Exactly how did you get in here?"

She shrugged, looked innocent. "The back door was unlocked. The door was ajar. For all I knew Darius was being robbed. I still don't know that's not exactly what's going on here. I think we'd better call the police."

"That's an excellent idea," said Calista.

Blake would not be happy to be in the middle of this particular domestic matter. He had his hands full. I slid a business card and my PI license from the side pocket of my bag, offered the card to Vivianne, then held up my license. "As I said, I'm Liz Talbot. I'm a private investigator assisting with Darius's defense. If you'd like, we can call my brother, Blake Talbot, who is the Stella Maris chief of police."

She took my card, eyed it suspiciously, then scrutinized my license. Something shifted in her face.

I continued. "May I see some ID, please?"

She reached into her Louis Vuitton Bandoulière 25, pulled out a wallet, and flipped through an impressive stack of plastic. She handed me her driver's license.

"Says here your last name is Whitley," I said.

She turned her head, looked at something over her left shoulder. "That was a mistake. I was angry at Darius. I should've never changed my name back. I go by Vivianne Baker."

"Is Darius expecting you?" I asked.

"No," she said. She straightened her spine, looked at me directly. "I heard on the news what had happened. I came to be here for him. You said you worked for him."

"That's right."

"Well, he's not here right now. So you work for me."

"Hmmm!" Calista made an indignant noise.

"That's not how this works," I said in my calm, easy tone.

"I'm going to tell *you* how things work," she said. "Darius Baker did not *kill* anybody. Least of all some skank he dated in high school. Now I have hired him a top-notch lawyer. And you can tell whatever backwoods attorney you work for that his services will no longer be needed and he can send a final bill. In the unlikely event that our attorney needs your assistance, I will have him get in touch." She pointed at me with the card I'd given her.

"I'm sorry Ms. Whitley, but you don't get to make those decisions for Darius," I said.

Her eyes got big and her face contorted. "We will see about that. Like I said, it's time for you to leave."

I hesitated. Would Darius want her here, or would he want me to toss her out? I had no idea. They were divorced. She had no legal right to be here. But if she stayed here, I'd know where to find her. I needed to speak to my client.

"Come on, Calista," I said. "Let's go. I need to speak to Darius."

"Oh, you do that," said Vivianne.

Calista said, "I don't understand why we shouldn't get Blake to make her leave."

"Because we don't know yet if Darius wants her to leave."

"*I* know." Calista eyed Vivianne up and down. "Trust me. He does not want her here."

Vivianne's eyes narrowed. "Who were you again?"

"I'm Darius's girlfriend."

Vivianne lunged at Calista.

I grabbed Calista's arm and drug her to the front door.

A primal scream came from deep within Vivianne. She lowered her head and ran towards us. We had the advantage. It was hard to run in Louboutins.

We darted out the front door and bounded down the steps.

Vivianne took off her shoes and charged after us.

We hopped in my car and I pressed the door lock.

Like a woman possessed, Vivianne chased us out of the driveway.

TEN

On the ferry ride back to Isle of Palms I called Blake. "What's all that noise?" I asked when he answered. It sounded like he was in the middle of a riot.

"Reporters. What's up?"

I told him about my encounters at Darius's house.

"You're going to talk to him? See if he wants us to run her off?"

"I'm going to talk to Fraser. I don't know if he wants Nate and me to be seen visiting with Darius. He'll be home Friday. What can it hurt letting her stay there two days?"

"Nothing, I guess," said Blake. "How's Calista?"

"Madder than a feral cat being baptized. I dropped her off at her house. She'd walked down the beach. Did you know she was seeing Darius?"

"How would I know? I'm the chief of police, not head of the social committee." He seemed truly disinterested, which surprised me a bit. He and Calista had been quite the item there for a while. I'd thought she was still on his radar. When he met Poppy Oliver, everything had changed.

"I'm surprised I didn't see a single reporter at Darius's house. Have they found the Coopers?"

"No," said Blake. "They are all congregated at the gazebo."

"In the park? What are they doing there, having a picnic?"

"Darius's most recent ex-wife, Lily, is holding a press conference."

"Hell fire."

"Yep."

"Where's she staying?" I asked.

"I'm about to find out."

"Let me know. I'll need to talk to her."

August Lockwood lived in Cooper River Farms, an apartment complex on Daniel Island, just off Clements Ferry Road. I contacted him the same way Darius had contacted Trina Lynn—through Facebook. He agreed to meet with me at 3:45.

His apartment was on the top floor of a building that backed up to woods, across from the barn-styled club house. As apartment complexes went, this looked like a nice one. He opened the door before I knocked and just stood there looking at me. In his thirties, with dark hair that looked like it was styled to be messy and a body that hadn't missed a workout in a great many years, August Lockwood was a good-looking guy by anyone's measure. I understood immediately why Georgia said she wouldn't have been surprised if Trina Lynn had told her they were dating.

"August Lockwood?" I asked.

"That's right."

"I'm Liz Talbot."

"Right. I was expecting you, of course. I'm a bit unsettled. Please. Come in." He stepped back and opened the door wider. He closed the door behind us and led me down a short hall. The apartment was neat, with brown leather furniture and framed photographs of Lowcountry beaches, marshes, and landmarks. And Trina Lynn.

"Your work?" I asked.

He dug the fingers of his left hand through his hair, distracted.

"Yeah."

"Nice."

"Thanks. Have a seat." He sat on the end of the sofa and gestured to a club chair. "Let me make sure I have this straight. You work for the attorney who represents the man charged with the murder of my best friend."

"That's right."

"Why exactly would I help you, assuming that I could?" His tone was straightforward, but not aggressive.

"Because Darius Baker did not kill Trina Lynn. My job is to discover who did. And you want to help me do that in order to get justice for your friend."

"How do you know, for a fact, that Darius didn't do it?"

I drew a deep breath, released it slowly. "Here's the thing...there's a lot I can't tell you. Client confidentiality and so forth. You'll have to decide if you trust me or not." It would not help my case in the slightest to get into Colleen and her guidance, nor my instincts. Better I allude to facts I didn't technically have in my possession just yet.

He met my gaze and held it, assessing me. His eyes were a warm brown, roiling with a mixture of uncertainty and pain. "Do you think he's being railroaded?"

"I do."

"Because he's black?"

"I don't know why. I know the detectives in charge of his case are good men, not prone to making race-based arrests. I have a sense they're being pressured, but I don't know by whom or what their motives are."

He thought about that for a few moments, nodded. "Okay. How can I help?"

"Trina Lynn was your best friend?"

"That's right. I had been at WCSC for about a year when she started working there right out of college. Trina, she was trying to save the world single-handedly. A bit of a crusader, even when she was just a production assistant. We started hanging out after work. Been friends ever since."

"Were the two of you ever romantically involved?"

"No. I was in a long-term relationship when we met."

"And now?"

"Now I'm not."

"You have a lot of photographs of her." I gestured at the walls. "You and Trina—"

"It wasn't like that. Ever. Two people of the opposite sex can be best friends, you know. I won't say there wasn't chemistry. There was. Just not that kind of chemistry. She was like my sister. Sure, I have pictures of her. We worked together. I was her cameraman. These photos represent our work, stories we covered together."

"Okay. So tell me about who she was romantically involved with."

His eyes widened and he dug both sets of fingers into his hair. "Well, officially, she wasn't dating anyone. She was focused on her career."

"And unofficially?"

"She'd been seeing Grey Hamilton, the news anchor, for about a year. She would've probably been fired if anyone found out."

"She must have loved him very much to take that risk."

He winced. "I think she did..."

"But?"

"Grey was crazy about her. He wanted to marry her. She kept putting him off, said it was because of her career. But I think it went deeper than that. Trina had bad luck with men. I don't think she trusted that he really loved her."

"How did he take this?" I asked.

"He kept hanging in there. Said one day she'd believe him."

"He wasn't angry?"

"No. And Grey Hamilton is the last person on the planet aside from me who would've hurt Trina."

"Any old boyfriends who might've been following her around, caught her with Grey?"

August stared thoughtfully out the window. "No."

"August—"

"Call me Auggie. Everyone does."

"Auggie, can you think of anyone you'd suspect of killing her? Any stalkers? Crazy fans?"

"She got a lot of mail. Emails and the old-fashioned kind. Most people loved her. But there were a few crazies in the mix. One guy— Kevin Looney, hand to God, that's his name—he sent her a letter every week. Seemed to have the idea they had a relationship. I thought it was creepy. Trina felt sorry for him. He's a sad case, I guess."

"Is he local?"

"Lives on Johns Island. Runs one of those pet washing vans. I've seen him, many times, watching Trina when we were taping spots or broadcasting live."

"Do you think he'd hurt her?"

"Who knows what anyone's capable of?" he said.

"What about the stories she's been working on? I understand she was meeting a source in Philadelphia Alley the night she was killed."

"Yeah, she said a woman called her. Said she had information about the missing petty officer case Trina Lynn had been investigating. This was Trina's most recent passion project. She had it in her bones that the petty officer was somehow tied to the attempted abduction of a sixteen-year-old girl the night he disappeared."

"You disagreed with that?"

"Not so much that. It's just that she'd been chasing it for months, and there were no new leads."

"What's the petty officer's name?"

"Fielding Davidson. Last seen February 2, at 9:15 p.m. leaving his girlfriend's apartment in Goose Creek."

"And what did Trina think that had to do with the sixteen-year-old girl?"

"Mia Moretti. Someone tried to snatch her that same night, along the route Davidson would've taken home—between his girlfriend's apartment and his. She was grabbed from behind in the parking lot at a pizza place on Red Bank Road."

"How'd she get away?"

"Good Samaritan intervened. Started whaling away on the guy who tried to grab her. She ran inside and called 911. When the officers arrived, both the attacker and the Good Samaritan were gone. Fielding Davidson hasn't been seen since. Trina believed he was the Good Samaritan, and it got him killed."

"Wow. What did the police think of her theory?"

"Zero evidence. Mia couldn't describe either her attacker or the guy who saved her."

"And the person Trina Lynn was supposed to meet Sunday night had information connecting the two incidents?"

"That's what she told Trina."

"Did she say why she needed to meet in Philadelphia Alley? Seems a bit out of the way. Why not a coffee shop?"

"No idea."

"Was Trina worried at all about that?"

"She would've met her in a barnyard. All she could think about was getting whatever information the woman had."

"Did it worry you? Did you think about going with her?"

"Of course I did. Trina was adamant that she had to go alone."

"Have you or anyone else heard from this source since Trina's death?" I asked.

He shook his head. "No. I figure she's freaked out. Whatever she knows, she'll be too afraid to share it now. Probably thinking the information got Trina killed and she doesn't want to be next."

"But why would someone kill Trina and not the woman holding the incriminating information?"

Auggie shrugged. "I have no idea. I didn't say it made sense. I just don't expect to hear from that source again."

"When you heard that Trina Lynn had been killed, what's the first thing that popped into your head? Who did you think had done it?"

"Honestly, I thought it was a robbery. Trina was in the wrong place at the wrong time. I cursed myself for not going with her."

"And now?"

"It was either a robbery or someone connected to Fielding Davidson's disappearance."

"Just so I have it for my records, where were you Sunday night between 10:00 and 11:00?"

He gave me a look that said I was trying his patience. "I was at the community fire pit drinking beer with half a dozen neighbors."

"Could I get those names, please?" I asked.

He muttered something, stood and crossed the room to a desk. He grabbed a pad and pen and dashed something on a note pad, then tapped and scrolled on his phone, alternately adding to his missive. After a few moments, he spun and delivered the piece of paper without a word, exasperation all over his face.

"Thank you so much." I stood. "And thank you so much for seeing me. I know this is a difficult time." I took a step towards the door.

"Anything I can do to help."

"Hey, just one more question while I have you."

"Okay." His tone held a note of warning.

"Did Trina Lynn ever tell you that she had a child?"

"She did. She thought about her son a lot. But she thought she did the right thing by him."

"Did she talk about Darius?"

Auggie shrugged, shook his head. "Not really. I mean yeah, she told me he was the father. But he was part of her past. She never mentioned him."

"Were you surprised that she agreed to have dinner with him Sunday night?"

"I guess I didn't give it much thought," he said. "He was back in town and wanted to see her. They had history."

"Did you know that Darius did not know about the child?"

"Yeah. I think Trina really loved Darius. When they were in high school, I mean. She knew he had big dreams. Giving up the baby was heart-wrenching for her. She didn't see any reason to put Darius through the pain. It wouldn't have changed her mind. He wasn't in a position to raise a child any more than she was."

"One thing that I just can't wrap my head around is how in the world she kept that pregnancy a secret in a small town like Stella Maris."

"She told everyone she was going to take a year off and backpack through Europe. Then she went to stay with family friends in Travelers Rest. Came home after the baby was born and enrolled in Trident Tech. It was the mid-nineties. Facebook wasn't invented yet. No one was expecting daily updates from Europe."

"She really did tell you everything, didn't she?"

"I told you. We were best friends."

"I can see that. If you think of anything else, here's my card." I offered him a small smile laced with something he could interpret as regret for having troubled him, if that suited him, and headed towards the door.

When I opened the door, a petite redhead with bright blue eyes stood on the other side. She drew back, surprised.

"I'm sorry," I said. "I didn't mean to startle you."

"It's fine," she said in a soft voice. Her hands twisted each other nervously. "I just came to check on Auggie."

"Hey, Camille." His voice rang a bit tired to my ear, like maybe this wasn't the first time she'd been by.

"Bye now." I waved to them both and headed to the elevator.

When the doors opened, a brunette got off. She looked over her shoulder at me as she walked towards Auggie's door. I'd be willing to bet there was a hoard of young women seeing after his well-being.

ELEVEN

They didn't skimp on happy hour at 86 Cannon. Nate poured us each a glass of Veuve Clicquot while I put together a small plate of cheeses, sliced baguette, nuts, and fruits from the cheese board. Then we went out to the second-floor piazza. It was decorated similarly to the one below, but with more seating, and white grommet drapes around the perimeter, pulled back and tied at each column with a length of rope.

To the right, Tanna and Eric Mullinax occupied two chairs against the rail with a small table between them. Across from them on a sofa was a couple we hadn't met. Mo and Jim Heedles were seated on one side of an outdoor sectional sofa on the end of the porch to our left. On the other side of the sofa, two women were taking turns telling a story. We were late to the party. We smiled and waved in both directions. The wicker chairs directly in front of the door were available, but not what we needed at that particular moment. They were isolated from everyone else.

"Let's head over here," I murmured to Nate and gestured right with my head. I wanted to speak to the folks from Travelers Rest. "Hey, y'all."

"Hey," said Tanna.

Eric stood. "Here, have a seat."

"Oh no, thank you." I waved away the notion of taking his

chair. "I've been sitting in the car. I need to stand for a while."

"I insist." He smiled, held onto the chair as if holding it for me.

"You are a true Southern Gentleman," I said. "Thank you so much." I sat and placed my glass on the small table to my left. I glanced to the couple I pegged at mid-fifties across the porch. They were sipping something red. From the hue, I gathered it was the pinot noir. "I don't think we've met. I'm Liz, and this is my husband, Nate."

"Wynonna and Sam Williams." She slurred the last name slightly. How many glasses of the pinot noir had the plump, sandy-haired woman had? "We're from Dayton, Ohio."

"How long y'all in town for?" asked Nate.

"We just got here yesterday afternoon," said Wynonna. "We're here 'til Wednesday, then we're headed to Savannah." One down. They hadn't been here Sunday night.

Sam rattled the ice in his rocks glass. Apparently he'd been to the honor bar in the library for a stouter libation. "Hot out here. Think I'll grab another." He stood and headed towards the doorway.

"Tanna—it's Tanna, right?" I took a sip of my champagne. "Such a lovely name."

"Thank you." Her smile was warm and genuine.

"You said y'all are from Travelers Rest, right?"

"Uh-huh." She nodded.

"We met someone from Travelers Rest not too long ago. I'm trying to recall where. You remember, sweetheart?"

Nate furrowed his brow. "Young guy?"

"Yes. I believe his name was Brantley..." I looked up, like maybe I was searching for the name on the porch ceiling. "Brantley Miller. Now where did we meet him? Do y'all know the Miller family?"

Tanna paled, looked at Eric.

Eric cleared his throat. "I wouldn't say we *know* them. We

know of them."

I gave Tanna an inquiring smile and took a bite of cheese.

Her hand went to her chest. "It's a sad story, I'm afraid. Most of the Miller family passed away in a fire about six months ago. Mr. and Mrs. Miller. Their two teenagers. Brantley was the only one who survived."

"Oh dear Heaven," I said. "I had no idea. I'm so sorry to bring up sad memories."

"Well," said Eric, "it's not like we knew them well."

"It was just sad, is all," said Tanna. "I understand they were very nice folks. The story on the news was filmed outside the Methodist Church during the funeral. It was overflowing with people."

"I wonder how on earth Brantley was able to survive," I said.

"The newspaper said he wasn't home at the time of the fire," said Tanna. "He's in college now. Clemson, I think."

"Do the authorities know what caused the fire?" asked Nate.

"A clogged dryer vent, of all things," said Tanna.

I was hoping hard that was exactly what happened. But I couldn't help but wonder if Darius's son was a seriously disturbed young man. Imagining the worst was an occupational hazard for me.

"I'm terribly sorry to have brought it up," I said. "Please, let's talk of more pleasant things. What did y'all do this afternoon?"

"We had lunch at Cru Cafe over on Pinckney and then took a carriage tour," said Tanna. "How about y'all?"

"Oh, I adore Cru! Their catering side did our wedding reception, didn't they, sweetheart?" What we'd done that afternoon wasn't very touristy.

"Well, you and your mamma put an awful lot of work into that menu, if I recall. But it was outstanding," said Nate.

"Where all else have y'all eaten?" I asked.

"Saturday night we ate at Hank's. Eric had to have fried

seafood or he was gonna bust something. It was delicious. Then Sunday we spent the day on the beach over at Isle of Palms and grabbed a burger at Poe's on Sullivan before we headed back. Monday was Poogan's Porch and Tuesday was BBQ at Smoke. It sounds like all we've done is eat."

"It all sounds delicious," I said. "I'd love to have a day just to hang out on the beach and relax. That sounds heavenly to me. But being in the sun all day purely exhausts me."

"Oh, me too," said Tanna. "We came back here and fell into bed. I don't think I even turned over 'til 8:00 the next morning."

Two down.

Nate said, "Darlin', I'm just going to step over here and speak to Jim."

"Oh, wait," I stood. "Y'all excuse us, please. We do need to go say hello."

"Of course," said Tanna.

Nate and I made our way to the other end of the porch. The two ladies were still talking in animated fashion, over the top of each other, while Mo and Jim smiled and nodded. We stood at the end of the sofa smiling.

The two women were maybe in their early forties, one blonde, one brunette. The story involved a sunrise kayak tour they'd taken from the marina at Isle of Palms, dolphins, and an alligator.

"It sounds fabulous," said Mo when the blonde paused for breath. She looked at Nate and me. "Have you guys met Faith and Paige?"

We all said hey and exchanged pleasantries.

"We actually live on Stella Maris. We take the ferry ride from that same marina every time we come into town. Where are y'all from?" I asked.

"Atlanta," said Faith, the blonde. "We came for a long weekend but decided to extend our stay."

Why had they done that?

"You are so lucky," said Paige.

"We are indeed," said Nate. He looked at Mo and Jim. "Did y'all have a nice afternoon?"

"We did," said Mo. "We had lunch at Five Loaves, then went on a walking tour. We just love all the historic homes."

"Ah—Rainbow Row, the Battery. I especially love the houses along East Bay," said Faith.

"Have y'all done any of the Plantation tours?" I asked.

"We have," said Paige. "We left early Sunday and started at Middleton Place—the gardens are breathtaking. Then we went to Magnolia Plantation. I loved the gardens there too. I can't decide which I liked better. Anyway, we had reservations at The Peninsula Grill, but we were so tired when we got back, we ordered takeout and crashed."

If she were telling the truth, and I had no reason to suspect otherwise, Jim and Mo were our witnesses.

"Where's everyone headed for dinner?" asked Nate.

Faith looked at her watch. "We need to change. We changed our reservation for Peninsula Grill to tonight."

"Y'all enjoy," I said. "If you like scallops, theirs are fabulous."

They stood, said their goodbyes and left.

"What about y'all?" Nate and I slid into Faith and Paige's recently vacated spots on the sofa.

"We thought about trying to get into McCrady's," said Jim.

"Restaurant or Tavern?" asked Nate. "The Tavern closed back at the end of July."

"No, we were thinking about the restaurant," said Mo. "The tasting menu sounds out of this world."

"We've actually never been." I looked at Nate. This was true. Charleston hosted a great many superb restaurants. We had our favorites and a long list of those we'd like to try. McCrady's was on the list. But their single long U-shaped table was not the ideal setup for conversation amongst a party of four.

Nate lifted a shoulder, gave me a skeptical look. "Middle of the week in September. It's possible, I guess. How would y'all feel about some company?"

"We'd love company," said Mo. "Please come. If we can get in." She sounded eager.

Nate pulled out his phone. "I'll just step inside and give them a call."

"We'd be happy to have you join us," said Jim. "If they don't have a table, maybe you could recommend a restaurant. You guys probably know all the best places to eat."

"I think you'd be hard pressed to pick a bad restaurant in Charleston." I mulled the best place for conversation. "Have y'all ever been to Charleston Grill? They have a tasting menu. But they'd likely be just as hard to get into on short notice."

"Sounds great," said Mo. "Really we're fine with anything. I'm sure you're right. We couldn't go wrong. It'll be nice to have company."

Mixed emotions wrestled on Jim's face. What was he thinking?

Nate stepped back to the porch, holding his phone to his chest. "McCrady's has a spot for two. Shall I reserve it for y'all?"

Mo said, "Would you see if Charleston Grill has room for the four of us?"

"Certainly." Nate stepped back into the kitchen.

"Oh, I hope they can work us in. Shall we walk?" I asked. "It's a little more than a mile, but it's straight down Cannon to King, then a nice stroll down King Street to the Shops at Charleston Place. Charleston Grill's inside."

Mo and Jim exchanged a glance. "I guess that'd be fine," said Mo.

"Or we could drive," I said, "or take a couple Scoops?"

"Scoops?" Mo squinted at me.

"It's an electric car service on the peninsula. It's free. You just tip your driver."

"How do they do that?" asked Jim.

"Businesses advertise on tablets on the back of the headrests," I said.

Nate walked back onto the porch. "All set. I hope 7:00 works for everyone."

"Sure," said Mo. "It's fine."

"We need to change," I said. "If we want to walk, we'll need to leave here by 6:30."

"Let's just take the electric cars," said Mo.

"All right," I said. "I'll call and arrange for two of them to pick us up at 6:45."

Behind the closed door of room number five, I said, "It has to be them, right?"

"By process of elimination, has to be."

"What was up with you offering them a table for two at McCrady's?"

"I was testing to see if they really wanted company this evening. If they'd have gone for it, the table would've been snatched right out from under them by a pair of scallywags while we were talking."

"I can't believe Charleston Grill had a table available at 7:00. I was prepared to have to eat late this evening."

"There's a story there, but I can't tell it. Wouldn't be in my best interests. Best to let you think I pulled a rabbit out of a hat."

"Well done," I said.

"All in a day's work."

"Listen, you know Jenkins told them not to talk to anyone about what they saw. In particular, he probably said, don't talk to any other investigators who approach you."

Nate winced. "I know. They seem like such nice folks. I really hate to play them, but I think we're gonna have to."

"I can't see any way around it either. The second we tell them who we are, they're not going to talk to us at all anymore."

Nate reached up, held my chin, and smoothed his thumb across my lip. "Stop biting that gorgeous lip of yours. This can't be helped. Darius's life may depend on it. We have to do our jobs."

His blue eyes went smoky. He kissed me once, slowly, then propped his forehead against mine. "You'd best get in the shower if you're going. I'm happy to help if you need me."

"If you help me, we'll miss dinner." I grinned, pulled away.

"There is that."

I grabbed a quick shower, redid my makeup, then slid into my navy and white dot poplin shirtdress and navy sandals. A simple silver starfish necklace and a pair of medium hoops completed my ensemble. I ran a brush through my hair and fluffed it a bit with my fingers.

"I'm ready whenever you are." I moved away from the bathroom mirror and walked into the bedroom.

Nate waited by the door in his traditional khakis and a soft blue button down with the sleeves rolled up. "You look gorgeous," he said.

How had I gotten so lucky? I walked over and placed a hand on his chest. "So do you."

TWELVE

The Scoops dropped us off just before the corner of King and Market. Mo, Jim, Nate, and I made our way across King and underneath the green awning into The Shops at Charleston Place. Nate held the door, then followed us in. Charleston Grill was just past the Louis Vuitton store on the left. Tall planters with greenery flanked the dark wood French doors, which both stood open in welcome.

The hostess greeted us warmly and led us to a corner table by the glass wall overlooking the courtyard. With rich paneling, white tablecloths, pear green upholstered chairs, and carefully set tables, the restaurant exuded elegance. A quartet in the bar area played atmospheric jazz that wafted through the restaurant but wasn't so loud as to make conversation a challenge. I smiled at Nate. He had done well.

"This is lovely," said Mo. "Thank you for suggesting it."

The waiter introduced himself as Adam and asked about our water preferences. Nate and I asked for bottled flat. Jim looked a bit uncomfortable, like maybe he could see how this meal was going to cost more than his first car. He wasn't wrong.

Mo asked for bottled water as well and gave Jim a look I'm sure Nate recognized. He and I exchanged a quick glance. We needed Mo and Jim relaxed, having a good time, and not shy of ordering the alcoholic beverages of their choice.

"Listen." Nate spoke in a conspiratorial tone. "Now I know this is going to sound highly inappropriate, and the last thing I'd ever want to do is offend guests in our fair city, but Liz and I have just had a run of luck. We're celebrating this evening. That's actually why we're staying downtown. We'd be honored if you'd be our guests for dinner."

"Oh, we couldn't possibly." Mo looked slightly horrified. "That's not necessary."

When my husband set his mind to charm someone, they would be charmed. He leaned in. "Mo." He met her eyes with his deep blue ones and deepened his drawl. "This is important to us. It's a very special evening, you understand? Liz and I, we're probably gonna go slap crazy, hog wild, off our rockers and order enough food for ten people. We're gonna get downright sinful. We're approaching this meal with wild abandon. We need you and Jim to come along for the ride without hesitation. We need this, Mo." He turned to Jim. "Jim. Would you oblige me, please?"

Jim looked at Mo. "My dear, I think this may well turn out to be the most unusual trip we've ever taken." He turned back to Nate. "Very well. If you insist."

Nate smiled broadly. "That's what I'm talking about. Thank you so much. This is going to be fun. Where's Adam?" He looked around and motioned Adam over. "Adam, this is a special occasion. We'd like to start with a bottle of champagne." Nate flipped through the wine list, ran his finger down the page, then tapped it when he saw what he wanted. "Bin number 498, please."

Adam nodded. "Yes, sir." Then he verified. "The 1985 Krug, sir?"

"That's the one."

Adam nodded again. "Right away, sir."

I was reasonably certain Nate had just ordered a wine ten times more expensive than any either of us had ever had in our entire lives. He was setting the stage. To keep his momentum going, I said, "I think we all know we want the tasting menu, right?"

"Sounds good." Mo wore an expression that said she thought we might both be crazy but seemed harmless enough.

"Let's go for the eight courses and add the caviar," I said.

"Perfect," said Nate, "and we'll get the wine pairings to go along. Y'all do like wine, don't you?"

"Indeed we do," said Jim.

"They do nice combinations here," said Nate. "But if y'all would prefer, we can choose the wines ourselves."

"No, the pairings sound fine to me," said Jim.

"I assume the Scoop cars will come back for us?" said Mo.

"Absolutely," said Nate.

"That's good," said Mo. "Because I don't think we'll be able to walk back to the bed and breakfast."

"That's the spirit," said Nate.

"What are we celebrating?" asked Jim.

"Jim, my lovely wife has just been promoted. She works for a defense contractor. Now, I can't say which one, and I can't tell you what she does exactly. Hell, I don't even know for sure myself. But she just got a damn impressive promotion, and I'm just so proud of her I can't contain myself."

"Congratulations." Jim and Mo both smiled warmly.

"Thank you ever so much," I said. "I'm pretty excited about it myself."

"As well you should be," said Mo.

A gentleman who introduced himself as Steve showed up with our champagne, and another server slipped champagne glasses into place and then disappeared so quickly it was like the glasses had just appeared on their own recognizance.

Steve went through the ritual of presenting the bottle for approval, opening it, pouring Nate a taste, and waiting for his go ahead before filling the rest of our glasses. Then Steve placed the bottle in an ice bucket on a stand near the table and slipped away.

Nate raised a glass. "To my beautiful, brilliant wife. Congratulations, sweetheart."

Mo and Jim raised their glasses. "Congratulations."

"Thank you all so much, truly." I sipped my champagne. It was ridiculously good. I was going to have to be very careful. I dearly loved champagne. But I needed to keep my wits about me.

Adam returned to the table and Nate ordered the eight-course tasting menu with the caviar supplement for all of us. Adam went through a series of questions about food allergies and preferences so the chef could be certain not to send us something we wouldn't enjoy. We were all eager for whatever she decided to send.

"We'll have our champagne with the caviar," said Nate, "and then the wine pairings after that, the top tier."

"Yes, sir. Good choice. We'll get the caviar right out."

I savored another taste of champagne. "So tell us, what all have y'all done since you've been here? You got in...when did y'all get into town again?"

"We drove down from New Hampshire," said Mo. "Took the scenic route. We spent a night in New York and another in Virginia Beach. Got here on Friday."

"That your green BMW convertible in the parking lot at the B&B?" asked Nate.

"It is," said Mo. "That's my toy car. It's a 1997 Z3. I've racked up 160,000 miles on it in the eighteen years I've had it. I love it."

"Convertibles are so much fun," I said.

"I wouldn't take anything for mine," said Mo.

"Is this your first time in Charleston?" Nate asked.

"It is," said Jim. "We've traveled a good bit, but this is our first time here. Beautiful city." Jim took a long drink of champagne. I was thinking he liked it as much as I did.

A server approached the table with a tray and served us each a standing silver spoon with an amuse-bouche—perhaps two bites of watermelon salad with feta and mint. "From chef." His accent was perhaps Russian.

We all picked up our spoons with interest.

"It's certainly pretty," said Mo.

It tasted bright and refreshing. We all murmured appreciatively. With impeccable timing, shortly after we'd all finished, Adam delivered the caviar. The inky black beads were mounded in a small oval crystal dish, with matching dishes of crème fraîche, chopped onion, and shaved egg whites on a crystal platter. Toast points and circles were artfully arranged around the dishes.

"Bon appétit, y'all," said Nate.

I'd never had caviar in my life, and I wasn't sure I'd like it. I sipped my champagne. To my surprise, my husband dug right in, seemed a bit nonchalant. But that was part of the role he was playing. I would play my part as well.

I smiled, took a toast point and scooped on some of the caviar, then dressed it with a bit of onion and some crème fraîche. With far more nonchalance than I felt, I took a bite. The Hallelujah Chorus started playing in my head. Good grief that stuff was good. No wonder it cost so much. I washed it down with a generous swallow of champagne.

"So y'all arrived Friday," I said. "What's your favorite thing you've done so far?"

Mo said, "I just love walking around the city. It's like walking back in time. Well, if you ignore all the cars, anyway."

"I know what you mean," I said. "The old houses are truly lovely."

We all paid attention to our caviar and champagne for a few moments, oohing and aahing. Why had I been convinced I wouldn't care for caviar? Steve came by and refilled our glasses, and we toasted everything from the band to Scoop cars.

Like they were performing a perfectly rehearsed dance, the

waitstaff delivered plates of a mixed vegetable salad with an olive-caper vinaigrette, fresh glasses, and a bottle of Pinot Grigio, which Adam left on the table in case we wanted more after he filled our glasses. Next came a South Indian fish in a curry sauce with a Riesling, followed by the best crab cake I'd ever put in my mouth and a bottle of a friendly, fruity Spanish white wine, the name of which I couldn't pronounce. We were into the fifth course—halibut with brown butter and a Russian River Valley Chardonnay—and had asked so many questions about Mo and Jim's activities since Friday that I was beginning to fear they felt like they were being interviewed.

Despite my efforts to pace myself, the wine made me perhaps a bit bold. "Did y'all hear about that reporter who was killed Sunday night in Philadelphia alley?"

Mo and Jim studied their plates, played with their halibut. Finally, Mo said, "Yes. That was tragic. Did you know her?"

"No," said Nate. "I never met her. Had you, darlin'?"

"No," I said. "But she did go to school with some friends of mine. She was a few years ahead of me."

"How about them arresting Darius Baker?" asked Nate. "Hard to believe he'd be a killer. Seems like such a nice guy on TV."

Mo looked at her glass, swirled the wine. "It is awfully hard to believe."

Jim looked at her, drained his glass, and set it on the table. "Mo saw him."

"*Jim.*" She turned towards him, gave him a look that said, *What are you thinking?*

"It will do you good to talk about it," he said. "I know you're preoccupied by the whole ordeal."

"We're not supposed to talk about it," said Mo.

"We're not supposed to talk to the press," said Jim. "And that one detective certainly did his dead-level best to discourage us from talking to investigators for the defense. But I keep telling you, that's not illegal in the slightest. Witnesses do it all the time. Defense attorneys could hardly do their jobs otherwise. In any case, I hardly think discussing what happened to us with friends is what the detective meant."

"Perhaps you're right," said Mo.

"You saw the murder?" Of course I knew she hadn't.

"No." Mo took a deep breath. "We went to dinner at East Bay Meeting House. After dinner we felt like a walk. So we went down Vendue Range past the fountains and walked out and sat on the swings for a while."

"We don't have to tell them every step we took," said Jim.

"I'm telling this," said Mo. "Then we took the path along the waterfront. We walked past the pineapple fountain and just walked along the waterfront. At some point, I don't recall exactly what street we were at, we cut back over to East Bay and just walked on down to The Battery. We'd gotten all the way down to Oyster Point—there at White Point Garden—and were just looking out at the harbor. We walked back a little ways up East Battery, not far. And we stopped to look at a boat out in the harbor. Then I turned around and was just looking at the park, and the statue and the cannons across the street when all of a sudden, there he was."

"Darius Baker?" I asked to confirm.

"That's right," said Mo. "He came walking down the sidewalk across the street. I just love his show. I don't watch much television. A few crime shows. But I do watch *Main Street USA*. We both do."

"That's right," said Jim.

Mo continued. "He had on a baseball cap, but I knew it was him. I climbed down the steps off The Battery and ran across the street. He was carrying a white bag. I called out to him, 'Excuse me, Mr. Baker.' He looked around, smiling, like he was happy to be recognized. But he stopped and threw that bag away in the trash can there at the park—the one in front of the last cannon. Then I was standing right in front of him and telling him how much I loved his show. Jim finally caught up to me—"

"I thought she'd lost her mind."

"You were happy to meet him too."

"I was."

"I asked him for his autograph," said Mo. "He signed a receipt from dinner I had in my fanny pack. The police took it."

"I don't understand," I said. "What did you actually see him do?"

"I just told you," said Mo.

"What was in the white bag?" asked Nate.

"How would I know?" asked Mo.

"The police claim there was a gun in it," said Jim. "A Glock."

"Why would they have looked to see what was in it?" I felt my face scrunch into one of those expressions Mamma is forever fussing at me about.

"Well, that's the crazy part," said Mo. "We talked to him for a few minutes, then walked back across the street to The Battery, walked the rest of the way around—down Murray Boulevard—then cut up Rutledge and back to the B&B. Of course, we heard sirens. Noticed something was going on way down Queen Street when we walked by. But we never dreamed it had anything to do with Darius Baker."

Nate and I were both riveted by her story. The waitstaff came and cleared away the halibut and brought pasta and pinot noir. They seemed ruffled that we showed little interest. When they stepped away, Mo continued. "The next morning, the police detectives came to the B&B and asked to see us. Mary Hannah came to get us. She was disconcerted, to be sure. Anyway, we went down to the parlor, and these two detectives are asking us about seeing Darius Baker at White Point Garden the night before. They said *we'd* called them. We told them that was crazy, and that we hadn't done any such thing. Then they asked us if we saw Darius Baker put anything in the trash can, and of course I had to say, yes I did. I saw him throw away a white bag. They had me come in and make an official statement. Sign it and everything."

"We just don't understand how they located us," said Jim. "It was all very odd."

"Sounds like," I said.

"They claim we reported it," said Jim. "Seem to think we're confused senior citizens, or maybe we don't want to admit that we called. Like we had second thoughts and didn't want to get involved. But that's not what happened."

"No," said Mo. "We did see on the news that the reporter had been killed, and we put together that's what the commotion on Queen was about. But we did not call the police and say, 'Darius Baker threw away a suspicious package at White Point Garden.' Nothing like that. Why would we? There was nothing vaguely suspicious about it."

"Indeed," I said. "Why would you? Was there anyone else around when you were talking with Darius?"

"Lots of people," said Mo. "I mean, it wasn't crowded. It was after 10:00 at night, but there were people out walking."

"And the young lady," said Jim.

"That's right," said Mo. "I asked a young woman to take our picture with Darius. She took one with my phone, so I didn't get her name or anything. It's not like she needed to send us the photo."

"Did you see where Darius went?" asked Nate.

"He was standing on The Battery the last we saw of him," said Mo.

I took a bite of pasta and chewed thoughtfully. It was a mushroom and asparagus cavatelli, the flavors so good they were a distraction.

"That's some story," said Nate. "What do y'all make of all that?"

Mo said, "Well, we read a lot of crime fiction. And I have to tell you, it seems to me that someone is framing Darius. But I did see him put that bag in the trash can. I can't say I didn't."

"No," I said. "I can certainly understand that. I wonder if the gun was registered to Darius."

"They didn't tell us that one way or the other." Jim washed down the last of his pasta with the rest of his pinot noir.

"What are you going to do?" I asked.

"We've given a statement," said Jim. "If there's a trial—"

Jim paused as servers cleared the pasta and brought venison tenderloin with huckleberry-port reduction and a nice Côtes du Rhône. Having been raised by a mother whose primary expression of love was feeding us all silly, I was accustomed to large meals. But all of the servings were more generous than I'd anticipated. I tried to pace myself on the food. The Côtes du Rhône was so delicious I had to speak sternly to myself.

When the waitstaff had moved away from the table, Jim continued. "If there's a trial, I guess we'll have to come back to testify. Nothing else we can do."

"But..." Mo shook her head. "I can't get over the feeling we're helping someone frame Darius. I wish I knew what to do."

"Nah," said Nate. "Jim's right. You told the police what you saw. Now you just have to leave it up to the investigators to get to the bottom of it."

"But it's maddening," said Mo. "According to that detective, we can't talk to the very people who will be looking for some other explanation than Darius killed that girl and put the gun in a trash can. Those police detectives have made up their minds, that's for sure. And that prosecutor. She's a piece of work."

"You spoke to the solicitor?" I asked.

"Scarlett Wilson," said Mo. "Yes. She was there when we went in to give our statement."

"I wouldn't worry about it, Mo," said Nate. "The thing is, the investigators for the defense? They're working hard right now to get to the bottom of things. Trust them to do their jobs."

Mo prepared a bite of venison, stopped with the fork halfway to her mouth. "I just detest feeling like we've been used."

The venison dish was delicious. It was followed by lamb chops with lamb au jus and mint chimichurri, puréed potatoes and a vegetable medley, paired with another lovely French red wine with a complicated label. By the time we got to the sorbet to refresh our palates, mine was exhausted. But we all rallied when dessert arrived—fried waffle and cherry-vanilla ice cream sandwiches with cream cheese mousse, orange-cherry coulis, and white chocolate crumbs. A lighter, sweeter, French red wine was served with it. My wine horizons were definitely broadened over the course of the meal.

Just when we thought we were finished, Adam brought another plate of small-bite confections, which none of us could manage. We chatted briefly about the highlights of the meal, then I excused myself and headed towards the ladies' room.

"I'll come with you," said Mo.

We made our way through the dining room and through an arched doorway, then went left down the hall to the restrooms. The ladies' room was empty except for the two of us. When we'd washed up, I reapplied my lipstick and a light coat of gloss.

Mo watched me in the mirror. "What would you do if you were me?"

I put my lip gloss away in my purse. "I'd enjoy the rest of my vacation and try not to worry about what's happened. It's an anomaly. Charleston is safe. And like Nate said, there are investigators for the defense hard at work getting to bottom of all this."

"I know it's not my job. But I'd love to be a part of that, help them." She had a gleam in her eye.

"I bet you'd make a great detective. You know, I always wanted to be Nancy Drew myself."

THIRTEEN

It was 10:30 before we got back to 86 Cannon. We talked while we changed into soft clothes—pajama shorts and a tank for me and pajama pants and a T-shirt for Nate.

"I don't even want to know how much that dinner cost," I said. "I'm just happy Darius is paying for it."

Nate gave me a quizzical look. "Now don't act like we've never had a nice meal in a restaurant before."

"Of course we have," I said. "But that was so far over the top it's ridiculous. We could've paid half our property tax bill with that much money."

Nate studied me for a minute. "Do you worry about paying the taxes on our house?"

"Taxes, insurance, a new roof, painting, new HVAC systems in a year or so. I worry about all that. Don't you?"

He looked perplexed, like this was a trick question. Then he rubbed his eyes and said, "You know what, it's done. We'll bill Darius. No sense getting all worked up about it."

"I'm not worked up. I'm just sayin'..."

He raised his eyebrows at me. "You're a little worked up."

I threw a pillow at him with a quelling look.

"Oh, you wanna have a pillow fight?" He flashed me a devilish grin.

I tilted my head at him. "We've got work to do."

"Have it your way."

"I make a point of it."

"Damn if that's not the truth."

Was he still joking around? The tease in his voice told me he was.

We piled up pillows at the padded headboard and leaned against them, each with our laptop.

"Until we can talk to Darius, I think we have to assume the gun was planted," I said. "If he *did* put a gun in the trash can a few blocks from where Trina was killed, immediately following the crime, and it *was* the murder weapon, well, given that Colleen assures us he's innocent, that's got to be one hell of a story."

"I've never met the guy, but I think he has to be innocent. You don't think he's that stupid, do you?"

"Of course not," I said. "If he were guilty, with his resources, he'd have chartered the first plane out of here, not waited at home to be arrested. And I guarantee you that's exactly why Sonny has a problem with this case. That, and the whole gun in the trash can with witnesses who say they didn't report it...Sonny knows that smells wrong."

"Do you know anyone else at Charleston PD well enough to ask a few questions?" Nate asked.

"Unfortunately, I don't. But I'd surely like to know who pressured them to make an arrest, and what their motives are. Blake knows a few people. Let's see if he'll nose around."

"That most likely went straight down the chain of command." Nate typed something into his laptop. "I'm just looking at the CPD website. Looks like there's several divisions under the Investigations Bureau. Homicide...that'd fall under Crimes Against Persons, and Violent Crimes under that. So Sonny and Jenkins report to a team leader, could be a sergeant. But that's probably more logistical than anything else. They all report to a lieutenant,

I'm guessing, who reports to the captain over investigations. That person likely reports to a deputy chief. I can come up with a pretext to get those names."

"That makes me feel queasy, but okay." My experience with the Charleston Police Department had been mostly positive. We needed to keep things that way, protect our professional reputation. Questioning the integrity of someone in the command staff could prove a career-limiting move for us.

"All I'm looking for right now is names. See if there's a connection we're missing. I'll be cautious. Next, we need a detailed outline of Darius's movements after he left the restaurant," said Nate.

"We won't likely get that until Friday. What did you find out at Hall's? You haven't had a chance to tell me."

"I got the name of the downstairs hostess from Sunday night, tracked her down. She was able to tell me who the lead server was for Darius and Trina Lynn's table. Guy named Glenn O'Brien. He remembered hearing an argument, but I had to pull that much out of him by making it sound like he was single-handedly responsible if an innocent person went to jail. Professional waiters are trained to be discreet, no doubt. Swears he has no idea what the argument was about. Says they stopped talking and glared at each other when the waitstaff came to the table. Glenn's convinced other diners could not overhear anything they said. He added that if that had been the case, someone from management would've quickly gotten involved. They're alert to any whiff of unpleasantness."

"Sounds right," I said. "But the net of all that is, there's no witness at Hall's who's bolstering the prosecution's case."

"Not as far as I've been able to find out," said Nate. "I think their whole case is the gun."

"That's a pretty damning piece of evidence," I said. "Sonny would've remembered Darius and Trina Lynn dating. He knew there was history there. So they get this call, retrieve the gun, test it, it's the murder weapon. Then they go talk to the people they think led them to it, only Mo and Jim don't know what they're talking about. Sonny and Jenkins go talk to Darius, who is so sure he's innocent that he talks to them without a lawyer present. He tells them he and Trina had dinner together that evening."

"Okay, so their theory of the crime is obvious," said Nate. "What are our alternatives?"

"Hang on. I want to get all this down." I opened a spreadsheet to serve as a temporary case board and created a tab for "Facts" and one for "Questions." I named a third tab "Narratives," and created columns labeled "Suspect" and "Motive."

"While you're getting set up," said Nate, "the other thing I did today was spend some time in Philadelphia Alley."

I looked up from my laptop. "Find anything?"

"There are cameras on the back of the Footlight Players Theatre building."

"Surely Sonny and Jenkins asked for the footage."

"They did," said Nate. "I spoke to the folks at the theatre. Unfortunately, for some unknown reason, the cameras weren't working that evening. They're motion activated. But they didn't come on at all between 9:30 and 10:30."

"Are they Wi-Fi?"

"They are," said Nate. "Someone who knows how tampered with them."

"Whatever happened was premeditated, and carefully planned to happen exactly where it did. Not a crime of passion arising from an argument over dinner that night."

"Exactly. I also looked at all the possible exits from the alley. It's not like you can only get in or out at Queen Street or Cumberland. There's a parking lot off State you can cut through and come through an iron gate. That's open, but it's pretty close to the Cumberland end. There's another gate on the other side leading to the church property. There are multiple doors leading into the

Footlight Players' building, but they stay locked. No indication any of them were disturbed. And there's one gate leading to a courtyard, one to a private residence, and one to a church building."

"Whoever killed Trina had multiple escape routes," I said.

Nate made a face like maybe he wasn't ready to commit to that assessment. "Potentially. But with a couple of exceptions, he or she would've needed an accomplice inside the Footlight Players or the home on the corner of Queen and Philadelphia Alley."

I chewed on all that for a minute, then filled him in on what Auggie had told me about Trina Lynn, the missing petty officer case, and the woman with so-called information. "I'm thinking the most likely scenario is that whoever called Trina Lynn and set up that meeting lured her to her death. Killing her was about the story Trina was working on involving the petty officer, covering all that up. Whoever called her wanted to shut her up, not help her. It was a trap. And it's highly unlikely another party to that situation would've killed Trina and let someone with the information she wanted live." I listed "unknown fake informant" as our first suspect, and "coverup a crime/keep a secret" as the motive.

"I'll do some digging tomorrow into the missing petty officer," said Nate. "See what I can find out about who all else was connected to that case. But at least as likely, based on statistics alone, would be that her boyfriend—the news anchor—killed her," said Nate.

I added "Lover/Grey Hamilton" and "Crime of Passion" to my list. "Continuing with the crime of passion theme, we need to find out if Grey Hamilton had any spurned lovers who might've wanted Trina Lynn out of the way." I talked as I typed.

"Which brings us to family," said Nate.

"I think we have to consider her child, Brantley Miller, a suspect. That fire story made the hairs on my neck stand up."

"Yeah, mine too," said Nate. "We need to track him down

yesterday. What about the Causbys?"

"We can't rule them out yet, but my sense is they're unlikely suspects." The vast majority of homicide victims were men. But when women were victims, they were statistically far more likely to be killed by a lover or family member. I added Billy Ray or Georgia Causby, Sawyer Causby, and Laura Beth Causby Coleman to my suspect list, with unknown motives.

"What about Darius's ex-wives?" asked Nate.

"Well, I thought they were long shots until they started turning up." I filled him in on my encounter with Vivianne Whitley, and then told him about Lily McAdams's press conference. "I'm just wondering when his first ex-wife is going to turn up. But now that I'm thinking about it, I don't recall Darius ever mentioning divorcing Trina Lynn. I didn't see a record of that, either. If that marriage was legal and they didn't divorce, none of his subsequent marriages are legal."

"That could have a serious impact on their claims to his money," said Nate.

"Maybe," I said. "But surely a family court would take into account these women *thought* they were married to him."

"Probably varies state by state. But the first question is, did any of them even know Darius was married to Trina Lynn?"

"Adding that to my questions list," I said. "Auggie, Trina's cameraman and best friend, told me about a stalker. She may have had more than one. The station would have all the letters and emails. But apparently Kevin Looney showed up regularly to wherever they were taping or broadcasting." I added "Wannabe Lover/Kevin Looney" to my list with jealousy as a motive.

"What about the best friend?" asked Nate.

"I ruffled his feathers when I asked for an alibi, but he gave me a list of six people he claims he was with. Says he was drinking beer at the community fire pit. He lives at Cooper River Farms on Daniel Island."

"That'd be what, thirty minutes or so away?"

"About that."

"Shall I speak with his friends?" Nate asked.

"Sure, thanks. We need to cross him off our list."

"What about someone connected to another story Trina Lynn was working?"

"That's a real possibility," I said. "Her job carried a certain amount of risk. And then we have the hardest culprit to find: the random unknown robber."

"I'm exhausted," said Nate. "You ready to call it a night?"

"Yeah, I think we have plenty to keep us busy tomorrow. Hang on…I just need to see what the funeral arrangements are." I pulled up Trina Lynn's online obituary. "The funeral is at St. Andrews in Mt. Pleasant tomorrow afternoon at 2:30. The family is receiving friends in Sam's Hall on the church campus from 1:00 p.m. until the service starts. Private, family only interment following the service at Christ Church cemetery."

"You planning on attending?" He closed his laptop and set it on the bedside table.

"I'd like to go, but if I did, it'd have to be incognito. I truly don't want to intrude on the family's grief. It won't comfort them in the least to see me there. If I were some anonymous face, that'd be different. But we have history."

"They don't know me," said Nate. "I'll go."

"You've already got a lot on your plate tomorrow," I said. "The petty officer's case, Sonny's chain of command, Auggie's alibi…"

"Two of those things won't take ten minutes. The petty officer…that may take a while. But I can still get to the funeral. You're planning on going to Trina Lynn's condo, aren't you?"

"You know me so well." I grinned, put my laptop away, and crawled under the covers.

"Hey, we got what we needed here. Do you want to stay here tomorrow night or head home?"

"Let's play it by ear," I said. "As nice as this place is, I'd rather be home when we're working. And I hate leaving Rhett so much."

"There's no place like home." He smiled, leaned over to kiss me goodnight.

"Does it really feel like home to you now? Stella Maris?" For a while that had been a real issue with us. While I'd grown up on Stella Maris and had deep roots and family there, Nate grew up in Greenville.

"Slugger, I'm at home wherever you are."

FOURTEEN

When most people thought about Shem Creek, they imagined the stretch where it flowed into Charleston Harbor, not far from where the shrimp boats tied up and you could buy shrimp so fresh it was just caught that morning. They saw the bridge on Coleman Boulevard, and all the waterfront restaurants—Red's Icehouse, Vickery's, Shem Creek Bar and Grill—and the boat landing. But Shem Creek continued deep into Mt. Pleasant, and though it narrowed substantially before it reached Bowman Road, several communities between there and the business district had lovely views. Tucked into a shaded neighborhood off Anna Knapp Boulevard, Trina Lynn Causby's condo sat on the banks of Shem Creek.

It gave me pause, breaking and entering on the day of her funeral. But I was on the side of the angels, wanting nothing more than to find the truth about what had happened to her and to bring her killer to justice. I parked the Explorer—Nate and I had switched cars for the day because I needed gas and he was a gentleman—in front of an adjacent building, grabbed a tote with a crossbody strap filled with the things I was most likely to need, and strolled down to the creek bank. Trina's condo was a first-floor end unit in a building with eight homes, four down, four up.

Through the screened porch on the back, I noticed the security system sticker on the window. The company used a Wi-Fi signal and door and window sensors. I'd have to disable it. I continued around to the front of the building. Thankfully, the front door was recessed and hidden from view of the random neighbor who might walk by. I pulled out a Wi-Fi jammer, activated it, and slid it back into my tote. Then I slipped on a pair of nitrile gloves and used my pick set to let myself in.

As I eased the door open, I listened intently for the beeping of an alarm, just in case I'd miscalculated. All was quiet. I carried my bag inside and relocked and bolted the door behind me. Should family show up, or Sonny and Jenkins, I'd need time to get out.

It wasn't a large condo, maybe 1,100 square feet, with two bedrooms and two baths. But it looked cozy for one or two people. With light-colored hardwood floors, it was decorated in soft neutrals—sand, cream, and white—with blue and green accents. It was clean and uncluttered. Trina had clearly been a neat freak, or perhaps she'd just cleaned.

The floor plan was simple, with two bedrooms and a laundry closet off the foyer, and a living room with sliding doors to the screened porch. To the left of the living room was a dining area open to a galley kitchen. The window shades were the variety that virtually disappeared when open, and the curtains on the sliding doors were pulled back letting in lots of natural light. Mature oaks shaded the back of the condo. A variety of shrubs and grasses lined the bank of the creek beyond. It was a lovely view. Had Trina been happy here?

I started with the front bedroom, which Trina had used as an office. The wooden file cabinet had been emptied. There was a single framed photo on her writing desk. Taken a few years back, it was of Georgia and Billy Ray Causby and all four of their children. They were all smiling, happy. Troy had an arm around Trina Lynn. That picture took my breath away. How many similar photos had we taken—Mamma, Daddy, Blake, Merry, and me? It was hard to fathom the hole in the Causby family.

The only other items on Trina's desktop were a box of tissues and a ceramic jar of pens. On the floor underneath was the power supply to the laptop the police had no doubt taken. I sat at her desk and opened the single drawer. Nothing but office supplies there. I rotated in her chair, taking in the room. Where would I put personal mementos?

Across from the desk was a comfortable reading chair in front of a wall of bookcases. On one side of the chair was a small table with a coaster. On the other side was a stack of five artsy leather-covered boxes. Was that a non-functional accent piece? I sat in the chair and opened the smallest box—the one on top. Empty. I opened the bottom box to find it also empty. Perhaps because I'm a bit OCD, I continued opening all five boxes until I found something in the box in the middle of the stack. I pulled it onto my lap.

Inside were maybe two dozen cards, the kind that come with flowers when they're delivered. All came from the same florist in Mt. Pleasant, Sweetgrass Flowers. All were signed the same way: "Always, W."

Who was "W"? Not Grey Hamilton, unless it was a nickname of some sort.

Nothing else was in the box. I examined the inside more closely. The leather on the bottom was loose at the corner. I peeled it back. Underneath it was a single photo of Trina Lynn with a man who looked familiar, but who I couldn't immediately place. The photo appeared to have been taken at a formal occasion of some sort, perhaps a charity ball. Trina and the man were smiling and posing for the camera. Who was that? It came to me after a moment. His photo was on several billboards in the area and countless other ads. It was Walker Nance, one of the area's most prominent real estate agents. When had this been taken? Why was it hidden? The two were in a room full of people.

I looked at the photo closer. It appeared to be a recent photo of

Trina Lynn, within the last year would be my guess. Clearly, Walker and Trina were involved, but the body language in the photo wasn't intimate. I snapped a photo of the picture and the florist cards. Had Trina been seeing Walker before she started dating Grey Hamilton? Perhaps she'd forgotten she even had these mementos.

Taking great care to put everything back like I found it, I restacked the boxes. I scanned the office one last time, then moved on to the bathroom adjacent to Trina's bedroom. The toilet tank was empty except for the customary mechanism and water—no envelope of money in a ziplock bag. Her medicine cabinet had the usual over-the-counter cold remedies, ibuprofen, and the like. Trina's beauty products—shampoo, conditioner, body wash, toothpaste, makeup, et cetera—were drugstore brands.

I moved to the bedroom, sat on the edge of the bed, and opened her top bedside table drawer. Prescription nasal spray, a flashlight, a bookmark, pen and paper—nothing remarkable there. I checked the remaining two drawers and found one with scarves and other accessories and one with miscellaneous electronic cords. Nothing of interest here either.

Trina's closet was well-organized. I spent close to an hour going through hatboxes and checking the pockets of coats, suits, and dresses, but came up empty. After searching each drawer in her dresser, running my hands through the clothes and along the inside frames, I found nothing else related to Walker Nance. I let my eyes slide around the bedroom. There were two pretty watercolor paintings on the walls, and one collage of Trina with Auggie and a few other WCSC on-air reporters. Grey Hamilton wasn't in any of them. I walked through each room of the apartment. There wasn't a single photo of Grey Hamilton anywhere. Trina had taken discretion seriously where their relationship was concerned.

I went back to the office and took a closer look at the bookcases. No photo albums were nestled among the collection of literary novels, biographies, and other non-fiction titles. Did Trina simply use electronic photos? Or had the police taken all the photos from her apartment except the one family photo and the work-related collage? I'd need to ask Auggie.

Had she had any girlfriends? Or was Auggie her sole confidant? Perhaps she had been close to her sister, Laura Beth, and that had fulfilled her feminine companionship needs.

It didn't take me long to go through Trina's kitchen. She had very little in the way of groceries, and some leftover takeout from P.F. Chang's. Her kitchen had the customary items in the way of gadgets, dishes, and flatware, but nothing of interest was hidden amongst any of it.

I unlocked the door, let myself out, and turned off the signal jammer. For a moment I looked at the door, fighting the urge to go back in and look some more. I knew there was nothing else to find. But I had a lingering feeling that I had an incomplete image of Trina Lynn.

It was barely 10:00 in the morning. We'd stayed up late and had a lot of wine the night before. I could use another shot of caffeine. I zipped over to Brown Fox Coffee Company on Simmons Street, parked in the small gravel lot beside the grey painted brick building and stepped up to the window. I ordered my favorite, the Mexican Fox, a dark mocha latte with a kick of cayenne. Given the heat, today I ordered it iced. I'd brought my laptop with me and wanted to dig a little, so I set up shop at the back spot in a row of wooden picnic tables with bright orange umbrellas on the far side of the building.

I activated the hot spot on my phone and plugged it into my laptop. I could access the hot spot via Wi-Fi, but the cord made it more secure. From Trina Lynn's profile, I created a branch for Walker Nance. Immediately, my query returned the information that he'd been married to the former Julia Kensington for fourteen years. They had three children, two boys and a girl. What had Trina's relationship to him been? How long had it lasted? Did Grey

Hamilton know about it?

Would Walker Nance show up at her funeral?

I texted Nate his photo. *Be on the lookout for Walker Nance at the funeral.*

Then I dug deeper. Neither Walker nor Julia had a criminal record, nor any civil claims. The Walker family home was on oceanfront on Sullivan's Island. They owned it through a family trust, and I couldn't find record of a mortgage. I'd known Walker did well in real estate. But this was an oceanfront compound, probably worth close to eight million dollars. Did either of them have family money?

A few clicks later I had my answer. Walker Nance came from a middle-class background, had grown up in Mt. Pleasant. Julia's father owned a technology company that specialized in banking software. Julia had grown up a few doors down from where she currently lived. Whether or not she'd been given part of the family fortune, I couldn't tell. But she surely came from money.

I pulled up Julia's Facebook profile. She was a lovely woman with blue eyes and warm brown hair she wore in a classic bob. She didn't post often to Facebook, and when she did, it was some sort of funny meme or video. But people tagged her often in photos they posted.

One of her friends, Bunny Porter, had just tagged her and two other friends an hour before. She was looking forward to their regular "Seashell Sisterhood" Thursday lunch at The Obstinate Daughter. I clicked Bunny's profile. Both women had an air of the well-maintained about them. Both were in their late thirties and had grown up on Sullivan's Island. I was mightily curious about the "Seashell Sisterhood."

The Obstinate Daughter sounded good. Remarkably, I was feeling peckish myself.

FIFTEEN

In the spring and summer, you typically needed a reservation to get a table at The Obstinate Daughter on Sullivan's Island, even for lunch. In September, I could probably walk in and be seated. If push came to shove I could eat at the bar.

The restaurant was on Middle Street, diagonally across from Sullivan's Island Town Hall. I parked on the street in front of a small park with a clear view of the restaurant's parking lot and waited. It wasn't quite 11:30, so I was betting I had beat them there. The Facebook post had tagged two other friends. Apparently it was a party of four.

At quarter 'til twelve, a Lexus SUV pulled into the gravel parking lot, and Bunny, a petite woman with shoulder length blonde hair and large sunglasses, hopped out on the drivers' side. A few seconds later, Julia came around the car and they meandered towards the outdoor stairs to the second-floor restaurant, continuing a conversation that involved the dramatic clutching of each other's arms. I zoomed into the parking lot and hopped out of the car, looking around, rushing to meet imaginary friends. I followed Bunny and Julia up the steps.

"I need to run to the little girls' room," said Bunny.

"I'll come with you," Julia said as they passed through the door. "Libba and CeeCee aren't here yet."

I loved the vibe in The Obstinate Daughter. With light wooden floors, grey, weathered wood walls, rope-accented ceiling fixtures, and soft seafoam green chairs, it felt like a restaurant at the beach. The pendant lamps with various shapes of orange shades were a nice accent.

"Hey, darlin'." Bunny smiled as they strolled straight past the hostess. "Could we please have our usual booth?" Both ladies headed straight for the restrooms, certain their wish would be granted.

"Of course." The hostess glanced at me, perhaps wondering, as I did, about the type of women who traveled in pairs to a restroom with accommodations for only one. "I'll be right with you."

Perfect. I slid a hand into my crossbody bag and palmed a small, flat, disc-shaped listening device. "I'd love to eat at the bar if that's okay."

"Sure. Grab any open spot." The hostess crossed to the corner booth by the window overlooking the parking lot and laid four menus on the table. She turned around and walked towards the open kitchen.

With her back to me, I took the scenic route, passing by Bunny and Julia's regular booth. I faked a dropped earring just in case anyone was watching and bent down to look for it.

"Where on earth did that earring go? There it is." As I rose, I stuck the magnetic bug to the metal support plate underneath the wooden tabletop and continued to the bar, smiling at anyone who cared to look.

The bar—really the white solid surface more resembled a lunch counter—was L-shaped, beginning where the tiled half wall to the open kitchen ended. Had I sat in that section, my back would have been to the booth. I proceeded to the first counter stool on the corner, which gave me a direct view of the front booth by casually turning my head only slightly.

The waitress slid me a menu. "Do you know what you'd like to drink?"

"I'd like a glass of unsweetened iced tea, please."

"Did you see today's specials?"

"I'm afraid I didn't."

She rattled off a list of delectable sounding choices, but I was already thinking about a couple of my favorites on the menu. "I'll be right back with your tea."

I opened the menu and quickly decided on the roasted beets and the Geechie fries, though it was a mystery how I could eat after last night. I pulled out my phone and opened the app to listen and record what my device picked up. I popped in my earbuds.

When the waitress came back with my tea, I placed my order, and gestured towards my earbuds. "Audio book." I smiled.

"I understand," she said. "I love to listen to them in the car. I just finished one by James Patterson. Do you like him?"

"Yes." I smiled and nodded, hoping she didn't have time to chat further because Libba and CeeCee had just come through the door and were hugging Bunny and Julia, fresh back from freshening up. One was a redhead, the other a dark brunette. All four women were dressed in well-accessorized shorts outfits and sandals.

Bunny and Julia sat with their backs to the wall, Libba and CeeCee across from them.

"Jason?" Bunny summoned their server. "Darlin', we're going to need four stout Lady Sullivans. You know how we like them."

"Right away." Though his back was to me, I could hear the indulgent smile in Jason's voice.

I'd be willing to bet they tipped him well every Thursday. I'd never tried a Lady Sullivan, but according to the menu, it was made with Tequila, strawberry, key lime, and basil. That sounded like a fancy margarita to me, and I had a particular fondness for margaritas.

The four women discussed food briefly, each seeming to have

already decided what she wanted. Jason delivered the cocktails, which they tasted and declared divine. He took their food order and slipped back to the kitchen.

Bunny raised her glass. "I call this meeting of the Seashell Sisterhood to order."

"Forever faithful," the four women said in unison.

"Is it just me, or do these drinks need more tequila?" asked Julia.

"Mine's fine." There was a bit of reproach in the redhead's tone.

"Seriously, Libba?" said Julia. Libba was the redhead, then, CeeCee the brunette.

The others murmured non-committal "Hmmms."

They waxed poetic about how glad they were to be through Labor Day weekend and have the kids back in school for a while now. I glanced up occasionally, and noticed Julia seemed subdued. Bunny noticed too.

"Sweetie, are you okay?" Bunny asked Julia.

The other two women stopped chatting and leaned in. CeeCee reached across the table to take Julia's hand. "How *are* you?"

"I'm fine, truly." Julia smiled brightly.

"How are you holding up, really?" asked Libba.

"Well, my stars in heaven, y'all, it's not like she was a friend of mine. Far from it," said Julia.

"We know *that*," said Bunny. "But all this is bound to stir up talk."

"It probably has," said Julia. "But it's not the sort of thing people will mention to my face, now is it?"

"At least you know for sure now it's over," said Libba.

"*Libba.*" Julia gasped. "You make it sound like I wished the woman dead."

"Well, pardon my saying so," said Libba, "but didn't you?"

Julia raised a hand to her mouth, but didn't say anything.

Bunny said, "Now Libba, you know Julia didn't *mean* what she said. She was angry, is all."

"Have the police been by?" asked Libba.

"The po-*lice*?" Julia drew back, looked at her friend in utter disbelief. "Surely you don't think they'll want to talk to me?"

No one said anything. Bunny looked down at the table.

"All of you are thinking that, aren't you?" asked Julia. "You think the police will think I murdered that husband hijacker because of a moment of—of—" She blinked, raise both hands to her mouth.

"You dropped your basket is all, sweetheart," said Bunny. "It happens to the best of us."

Libba said, "Julia, you know I'm your friend and I love you. It's because I love you that I think you should talk to an attorney. Just in case...so you have someone to call."

The waitress put my plate in front of me. I unrolled my flatware from my napkin, chose a Geechie fry and bit the top of it off. Yum. Geechie fries are basically French-fried grit sticks and I had a particular fondness for them. I was not typically a fan of the beet. But they performed magic on the beets at The Obstinate Daughter, I was certain of it. There was something about the combination of pomegranate molasses, ricotta cheese, and pistachios that made the beets not only palatable, but delicious. I picked up my fork and put together a bite.

CeeCee piped in. "The thing is, you made rather a scene. In front of several hundred people. Someone will recall that and make mention of it."

What on earth had happened? I bit off another bite of Geechie fry and studied the foursome across the restaurant.

"When one pushes over an eight-foot ice sculpture at a black-tie cancer benefit, well, it's bound to cause talk," said Libba.

"It's a miracle you were able to keep it out of the papers," said CeeCee.

Bunny put her arm around Julia. "That woman—not to speak ill of the dead—had no business being there. She should have known better. It's bad enough, running around with a married man. But to show up at his wife's signature charity event—that's just beyond the pale."

Was that the very event where the photo I'd found of Trina Lynn and Walker Nance had been taken?

"Well of course she had no class," said CeeCee. "But that's not the point, is it? The point is, she's dead, and poor Julia here had one hell of a motive to kill her."

"But I didn't kill her." Julia practically wailed. "I wouldn't have any idea how to shoot someone. I certainly don't own a gun. Why, I've never fired one in my life. I couldn't hit the broad side of a barn."

Bunny looked around the restaurant. She almost caught me looking. "Shhh. Of course you didn't shoot anyone. Do you have an alibi? I mean, you know I don't think you did it, but an alibi would come in handy."

Julia was quiet for a minute. "I was at my parents' house Sunday night."

"How late?" asked Bunny.

"'Til about midnight."

"Well, there you go," said Bunny.

"Who else was there?" asked Libba.

"Why does it matter?" asked Bunny.

"You know very well why it matters, Bunny Porter," said Libba. "If it's an alibi you need, it's better to have people who aren't your blood relatives providing it."

"Besides Mamma and Daddy and the kids, Carlene and Isaac were there most of the evening."

"I'm afraid paid help isn't much better than family," said CeeCee. "You'd best talk to an attorney."

"It just makes me so angry," said Julia. "First, Walker

humiliates me, strutting around with that cheap piece of TV trash. Then, he has the nerve to bring her to my benefit—"

"Well now, in fairness, sweetie, he didn't bring her," said Libba.

Julia glared at her friend. "Whose side are you on?"

"Yours, of course," said Libba. "But I think it's best to deal in facts. Especially if you're recounting this to police officers. They're especially keen on facts."

"Fine," said Bunny. "The horse's ass did not technically bring the cheap piece of Christmas trash to the cancer benefit that our lifelong friend spent a year planning. But the tramp was there. So was he. And he was caught red-handed in the coat closet with her in a position for which there simply is no polite explanation."

"If anyone *besides* Catherine Calhoun had caught them, it would've been a different story," said CeeCee. "Ever since her husband got caught in that bawdy house scandal last Christmas, why, she simply cannot resist spreading bad news involving anyone else's husband."

"I think she told everyone she ran into," said Libba. "She surely told me. And she was quite gleeful about it."

"No one had to tell me anything," said Julia. "There was this moment...I'll never forget it as long as I live. They'd just given me a thank-you toast. And they wanted me to say a few words. I walked up on that stage, and I looked out into the crowd, and every person I looked at was talking behind their hand, or just looking at me like they felt so, so sorry for me. Sorry for *me*...Julia Kensington. Why, no one's ever felt sorry for me my entire life. I couldn't abide it, the pity. Y'all understand, don't you?"

They all murmured, "Of course we do."

"And I have to say," said CeeCee, "it was quite satisfying to watch you nearly take her out with that ice sculpture."

"But we need to circle the wagons," said Libba.

"Exactly," said Bunny. "As I recall, I was at the Kensington's home Sunday evening as well. Until midnight. Didn't I see both of y'all there too?"

"No," said Julia. "No, thank you, dear Bunny. But I couldn't possibly let you do that. I'll speak to an attorney, just in case. But I really and truly was at Mamma and Daddy's house. They'll just have to believe me. It's the truth. My children were there. I wouldn't have my children lie for me in a million years."

"Darlin'?" said Bunny. "Where was Walker?"

"Why, I haven't the faintest idea," said Julia.

Apparently well-trained to their routine, Jason delivered fresh drinks and took the empty glasses. "Your food will be right out."

"You don't think that Walker—" CeeCee asked.

"Don't even think such a thing," said Julia. "Whatever else he is, and I have a very long list of names, he's still the father of my children. He's not a murderer."

"Perhaps she was pressuring him," said Libba.

"But so what?" said Bunny. "She had no leverage. The secret was out. Everyone knew Walker was having an affair with the trashy blonde on TV. And everyone knew for certain that Julia knew. The bimbo had nothing to pressure Walker with. I mean, she could have said, 'Oh please leave her and marry me or I'll never see you again.' But that would have gone one of two ways. If God gave him half a brain, he'd have said, 'Okay, fine. This was the worst mistake of my life,' and that would've been the end of it. But if he'd thought he was really in love with her—forgive me, Julia—but if he was that stupid, well then, he wouldn't have killed her, would he?"

"It could've been a crime of passion," said Libba.

"Libba, that is just not a helpful thing to say," said CeeCee.

"I'm just trying to prepare her for what the police are probably thinking," said Libba.

They all went quiet as Jason delivered their food. When he stepped away, Bunny said, "We're all here for you, Julia. You let us know what you need. We'll get through this together."

"Are you going to divorce him?" asked CeeCee. "Honestly, I'm surprised you haven't already filed papers and thrown him out."

"I haven't decided," said Julia. "We're in counseling."

"When did you start that?" asked Bunny, surprised.

"A month or so ago," said Julia. "I didn't say anything because I know what you all think. You all think I'm weak, and I should've kicked him out the night of the benefit. But it's not that easy. The children adore Walker. And I—I'm just so hurt."

"We've all said way too much about Walker and what we would and wouldn't do, many times," said Bunny. "This is your decision, and yours alone. Now come on, y'all, let's have another drink and enjoy our lunch. We're going to have to get in the carpool line before you know it."

"Hear, hear," said CeeCee.

They all lifted their glasses and clinked them together in the center of the table. Bunny signaled Jason for another round, and they all tucked into their plates. Until 2:00, they chatted about their kids and the fall sports they were playing. Then they paid their bill and left.

After the table had been bussed, I discreetly retrieved my bug and headed to the car. I weighed my options, then headed back into Mt. Pleasant. I wouldn't attend Trina Lynn's funeral, for all the reasons I'd told Nate I shouldn't. But I could watch to see who all came out of that church and observe how deeply they appeared to be grieving.

SIXTEEN

Julia Nance and her friends understandably held a low opinion of Trina Lynn Causby. But based on the traffic gridlock in the Old Village of Mt. Pleasant, she was well-loved. The Causby family had been in Mt. Pleasant for generations, so naturally everyone knew them. Then there was Trina Lynn's WCSC family and all the people her stories had touched over the years.

St. Andrews Church occupied the corner of Whilden and Venning, three blocks from Charleston Harbor. The historic church, which dated back to 1857 and was now used primarily as a chapel, fronted Whilden Street. The large, contemporary-style ministry center, where Trina Lynn's service was no doubt being held, faced Venning. Live oaks along both streets wept Spanish moss, adding to the somber mood of the afternoon.

When I arrived in the neighborhood at 2:15, police officers stood watch outside the church, relieved from the duty of directing traffic by virtue of the fact that everyone who'd come for the funeral was already inside. The parking lot was packed to overflowing, and every available spot on the surrounding streets was taken. So many cars were illegally parked, the police would've been hard pressed to tow them all. This was a blessing for me. I'd blend in just fine.

Across Venning Street was the church parking lot, and behind it ran a private drive that provided access to a newer row of homes tucked in behind the homes on Morrison Street. I drove around the block once, then rolled down Morrison Street and parked in front of a small painted brick building that was once probably a store of some sort, but was now, according to the sign, New Ebenezer Baptist Church. I banked on the church's goodwill in light of the large funeral going on a block away.

I opened the lift gate, grabbed my good camera out of the back, and put it in a small, lightweight backpack. Then I slid into a lightweight utility jacket. Flipping through a box of identification, I selected a fake press ID that claimed affiliation with no news outlet in particular, but looked official enough for casual observers. I pulled together a few other items I might need—my pick set, Wi-Fi jammer, and gloves—added them to the backpack, then secured it snugly to my back.

If I walked around the block and down the private drive, I risked being spotted by someone who knew I didn't belong, or perhaps one of the police officers on guard at the front of the church. I scanned the homes across Morrison, looking for one with no cars out front and a deserted feel, then walked confidently down the driveway of the cream-colored house directly across the street.

As soon as the six-foot privacy fence in back registered, I started running. I charged it, jumped, put my hands on the top, and hoisted myself up. My right foot found purchase and I pushed myself the rest of the way over, landing in a low crouch. I stayed low, prayed no one was home at the two-story house I was looking up at. For a couple minutes, I watched. There were no signs of life. What I was about to do was all kinds of risky.

According to the sticker on the window, the security system on this house was the same as Trina Lynn's. I reached for my signal jammer, then stopped. This house was elevated, like many this close to the harbor. How high was the front porch?

I walked around the side of the house, scanned the area, and climbed the steps. This would work well. From here, I could see across the parking lot. I couldn't make out much, but my camera lens would take me much closer. The line of trees between the parking lot screened me from view. I raised my camera, looked for the door of the church and zoomed in. Perfect.

I settled into a rocking chair and waited. The service would just now be starting. Just in case, I popped in my earbuds, and slipped my phone into a utility pocket. I mulled Julia Nance and her Seashell Sisterhood. Sonny and Jenkins likely had no idea there were two people with motives just as strong as Darius's. The problem was, once they'd made an arrest they stopped looking at alternate theories. They'd probably stopped looking the minute ballistics came back on that gun. It was hard to blame them. At 3:00, I heard the church doors open. Using the camera as a monocular, I scanned the faces coming out of the church and started snapping.

First came pallbearers with the casket, followed by the family. Billy Ray Causby was holding Georgia upright. Without his strong arms, she no doubt would have crumbled into a heap. Sawyer and his wife and sons came next. Sawyer was stoic, with a rigid look about him. Laura Beth and her husband and children followed. Tears streamed down her face as her husband tried to comfort her. I had no right to be here observing their raw grief.

Into my frame came three-year-old Marci, my cousin. No, of course that was Sara Catherine. But the resemblance took my breath away like a gut punch.

Staff from J. Henry Stuhr's funeral home helped the family into limousines and they pulled away from the curb. Then the ushers stepped back and the remaining mourners streamed out of the church.

The first face I recognized was Walker Nance. He must've been sitting near the back. He looked serious, but not particularly affected. If he was grieving, his was a private grief. Someone spoke to him and he smiled his million-dollar smile. I kept on snapping.

There were many faces I didn't recognize, but I recorded as many as I could. After a few minutes, Grey Hamilton came out with some of the other WCSC team members. His eyes were red and he had a pallor. I'd bet plenty of people there didn't recognize their nightly news anchor.

Not far behind Grey came a wild-eyed man clutching his hair and openly crying. He appeared somewhere in the neighborhood of forty, and was dressed simply in a plaid shirt and jeans. I snapped several photos of him, wishing I could get license plates from here. But there was no possible perch from which I could get faces and tags.

A long stream of people came out before Auggie's face came into the frame. He was with the brunette I'd seen getting off the elevator at his apartment. I widened the shot a bit. There was the redhead. Camille, he'd called her. And two blondes. Auggie had what looked like a harem. They all seemed to be jockeying for position to hold onto him, comfort him. Auggie. Why hadn't he told me about Trina Lynn and Walker Nance? He knew all of Trina Lynn's other secrets. Surely he knew about her affair with the realtor.

And then there was Nate in my frame. Nate and one of the most gorgeous women I'd ever seen in my life. She was nearly as tall as him, runway thin, with platinum hair styled in a messy look that probably took a stylist to achieve. Her tailored black suit contrasted perfectly with her pale skin and red lipstick I bet her mamma never had to remind her to put on.

If I hadn't already profiled her and knew exactly who this woman was, I'd have been fit to be tied at the way she clung to my husband—the way he allowed it. But that was Arianna English, a model and brand ambassador, wealthy in her own right. She was Darius Baker's first ex-wife.

My phone rang, startled me. "Call from Mamma," Siri announced.

I pressed the button on my earbuds to answer. "Hey, Mamma." I was distracted, still busy watching a super model with her hands on Nate. Mamma can read me well.

"What's the matter?"

"Nothing, Mamma. Is everything all right? How's Daddy?"

"Your father is fine. I'm losing my ever-loving mind. He was entertained by being waited on hand and foot for about two days. Now he's bored with being stuck in the house. He says he's feeling up to company. We didn't have family dinner last night. It's the first Wednesday we've missed in a while. Can you and Nate come this evening?"

"Sure. Six o'clock?"

"Earlier if you can make it. I—".

Arianna ran her hand up Nate's arm. "Mamma, I have to go." I ended the call.

"Call Nate," I ordered Siri.

I watched him extricate himself from her grasp to answer the phone.

"Please tell that high-dollar floozie that if she'd like to keep her hands, she'd best keep them off you."

"Liz."

I watched his eyes search the tree line, trying to find where I was. He scanned past me, then backed up, looked straight at me, though he couldn't possibly have seen me. "I'm just leaving the funeral now. Ms. English needs a ride back to the Belmond. I'm going to drop her off, then I'll meet you at the office."

"Best not take too long," I said brightly. "We're having dinner at Mamma and Daddy's at 6:00."

"I'll look forward to it." I could hear the grin in his voice. He was enjoying how I had noticed Arianna pawing him.

I'd remind him of that later.

SEVENTEEN

I called Auggie Lockwood from the car and told him I needed to see him immediately. Of course he was still in the car as well, and from the sounds of it, several of his entourage were with him.

"Sure," he said. "Come on over. I'll be home in fifteen minutes."

When he pulled off the Mark Clark Expressway at exit twenty-three, I was right behind him. I didn't bother hanging back, but followed his Subaru Outback until he parked, pulling the Explorer into a spot right beside him.

I climbed out of the car, waited for him. He took his sweet time. The brunette and one of the blondes eyed me through the windows. The redhead got out of the car first, a challenge in her eyes. What was up with these women?

Finally, Auggie got out of the car. "You want to talk upstairs? I need to change."

"Fine." My voice might've held the teensiest bit of irritation.

I followed him to the elevator, not sparing a glance for his companions.

We rode up silently. I studied him. This was Trina Lynn's best friend in the world. I knew people worked through grief differently, but he seemed quite composed for someone who'd just witnessed his best friend's casket being wheeled out of a church.

As soon as we were inside his apartment, he removed his jacket. "Have a seat," he said. "I'll just be a minute."

By the time he got to his bedroom door, he had his tie off and his shirt unbuttoned. I stopped in front of the club chair I'd sat in the day before.

He turned back towards me. "If you'd like anything, help yourself." He wasn't wearing a t-shirt, but stood bare chested in front of me, showing me his six-pack abs.

I blinked. Was this guy coming on to me?

"I'm good, thanks." I kept my eyes on his, letting him know how I was completely disinterested in anything he might be offering.

He left the door open. I walked over to the patio doors that opened to the balcony and looked outside. His bevy of beauties were still by the car chatting. The brunette cast a hateful look towards the apartment. I was certain it wasn't directed at Auggie.

He walked back into the room wearing utility shorts and a T-shirt. He sat on the sofa and gestured towards the chair. "What's up?"

I stayed where I was, but turned to face him. "I think we established that Trina Lynn told you all of her secrets."

He shrugged. "I guess so. I mean, I think she did, yeah."

"Why didn't you tell me about Walker Nance?"

He winced. "I honestly didn't think it was important."

"Seriously? Was she still seeing him?"

"No," he said. "That was over a few months ago. It was...she was embarrassed by it. I thought it was history and couldn't be related. I didn't want to make her look bad, you know what I mean?"

"You need to let me decide what's important. How serious was it? Did she love him?" Women who saved the cards that came with flowers were in love.

He tilted his head back and forth. "It was complicated."

"But she was so in love with Grey Hamilton that she risked her career to date him. She must've been seeing both men at the same time."

He shrugged. "She was."

"Explain that to me, please."

"I can't. She couldn't explain it to me. She said she loved both of them. I just figured, you know...monogamy isn't for everyone."

"Clearly not. But can't you see how this makes Walker Nance and his wife both serious suspects in Trina Lynn's murder?"

"I told you, I thought it was over."

"Because of Julia Nance's meltdown at a cancer benefit?"

"Who told you about that?"

"You should have. How do you not see Julia Nance as a suspect?"

"Women like that don't kill people."

"You can't sincerely believe that, can you?"

"I can and I do. She has far too much to lose. So does Walker."

"Which is what makes them excellent suspects," I said.

"I'm sorry, I just don't see it that way. Which is why I didn't mention it to begin with."

"When exactly did they stop seeing each other?"

"Right after that benefit. That was in June. Trina Lynn was afraid they'd use their influence to have her fired. Her career was the most important thing in her life."

"And yet she risked it by dating Grey Hamilton."

"Which is why I think she really loved him. Walker...that was just a distraction."

"From what?"

"The fact that she couldn't have a traditional, out in the open, dates in restaurants kind of relationship with Grey."

"But she couldn't go out in public with Walker either."

"Which made him safe."

"I understand this all makes sense to you, but I have to tell you, I find it batty and quite sad."

He drew a deep breath. "I'll give you that much. It was sad. I wish she'd married Grey and let the career chips fall where they may. But like I told you, she didn't trust that he loved her. Didn't trust that he would still love her if she stopped being Trina Lynn Causby, investigative reporter."

"Back to Walker...how did he take it when Trina stopped seeing him?"

"It was mutual, I think. She was afraid of losing her job. He was afraid of losing all his wife's money. They just simply never saw each other again after that blue-blood brawl."

"You're certain of that?"

"Yes. I'm certain. Trina would've told me."

"But Julia had no way to trust that was the case, even if Walker swore it up and down. Why would she believe anything he said after he cheated on her?"

"She might not've believed him. I have no way to know one way or the other. But I can't see her shooting Trina Lynn in a Charleston alley three months later."

"And that's exactly why she'd get away with it if she did."

EIGHTEEN

I caught the 5:30 ferry, and just barely made it to Mamma and Daddy's house by 6:00. Nate and I met there, arriving at the same time. He'd likely arranged it that way. We used a tracking app on our phones and smart watches to mind each other. It was a necessary precaution in our line of work. But it also came in handy on a day-to-day basis.

"Well, I'm happy to see you were able to extricate yourself from Arianna's clutches." I raised an eyebrow at him as we climbed out of each other's cars.

"Now darlin', you know very well that woman is nothing more than a client's ex-wife to me. A source of information."

We stopped for a kiss where the driveway met the front walk. How easy it was for him to smooth my ruffled feathers. Perhaps too easy. I pulled away, looked up at him. "I've had a front row seat to marital misconduct today. I may be a bit sensitive on the subject."

From inside the house came Chumley's—my daddy's basset hound—earnest, mournful howl, punctuated with the occasional bark.

"Sounds like trouble," said Nate.

"He's probably just tired of being cooped up, with Daddy sick and all," I said.

We continued up the path. Nate said, "You don't seriously

think I give other women a second look, now do you?"

I smiled up at him. "No. Because you know precisely how good a shot I am."

He laughed. "I did find it interesting, her showing up at the funeral."

"Did she say exactly why she did that?" We climbed the steps to the front porch. Chumley continued to howl.

"She did," said Nate. "She came to town to help Darius prove his innocence. She was looking for clues at the funeral, because that's what they do on TV."

"Oh dear heaven. They're all three here. At least she's staying in Charleston."

"She was," said Nate.

"Where is she now?"

"She came over on the 4:30 ferry with me. Her luggage was waiting downstairs at the hotel."

"She rode home with you?"

"It was an opportunity to talk to her. She was going to get a car service to bring her, but I figured it'd be better for her to come with me. Gave me an hour of uninterrupted interview time. She was a captive audience. Or rather I was her captive audience. And she does enjoy an audience."

I was reaching for the door when it swung open. Nothing in my life prepared me for the sight on the other side.

"Mamma?" I gasped.

She was covered, head to toe, in pluff mud.

"Mamma, what happened?"

"Carolyn, are you all right?" asked Nate.

Chumley came running through the foyer, dragging a leash behind him. He was likewise completely coated with pluff mud. They both stank to high heaven. Chumley sat by Mamma and howled at me.

Mamma said, "Does it look like I'm all right?"

"Where's Daddy?"

As if on cue, he called from somewhere inside the house, "Carolyn, I've got the hose hooked up. Come back outside and I'll rinse you off."

A tiny crab ran down Mamma's arm. She jumped, shook her arm frantically. "Get if off me. *Get it off me.*"

"Mamma." I gentled my tone. "Let's go out back and get you rinsed off."

"I need a very hot shower," she said.

"Of course you do," I said. "But let's get the worst of it off outside, don't you think?"

I soothed her back down the foyer, through the kitchen, out the back door, through the screen porch, and onto the pool deck. Daddy waited with a hose pipe with a large spray nozzle on the end.

"What in the world were you doing in the house?" asked Daddy.

"I went for help," said Mamma.

"Help?" said Daddy. "Come over here and let me squirt you off."

"You're just loving this, aren't you?" Mamma asked.

Daddy grinned. "What makes you say such a thing?"

"Oh please," I said. "Mamma, you want me to hose you off?"

"I've got it." Daddy pressed the handle on the nozzle and a fast, hard stream of water came out. He directed it at Mamma.

"Ow! Frank, that's too hard."

Chumley barked at Daddy.

"Hush up, hound dog. I'll get to you in a minute."

"Here, let me fix it." Daddy twisted the end of the nozzle, and the spray widened into a soft shower. He sprayed Mamma's legs. "Is that better?"

Mamma didn't answer, but she didn't object.

Daddy sprayed and sprayed her legs, but the pluff mud barely noticed.

"I don't think this is going to work, Carolyn. I'm going to have to spray harder."

"Why don't you let me squirt you with the hose?" she said.

"I'm sick," he said. "And I'm not covered in pluff mud."

"Frank, maybe you should go inside," said Nate. "You being sick and all. We can get Carolyn and Chumley cleaned up."

"That's an excellent idea," said Mamma.

"No," said Daddy. "I've got this." He turned up the sprayer and squirted Mamma's legs, adjusting until he found a pressure that was effective but didn't cause her to scream.

"Dad?" Blake and Poppy came through the screened porch into the backyard, followed by Merry and Joe.

Daddy squirted Mamma in the face.

"Frank! Stop that!" she sputtered.

"We've got to get that mess off you," said Daddy.

"What on earth happened?" asked Merry. "Mamma, are you okay?"

"No, Esmerelda," said Mamma. "I am not one teeny bit okay."

Talking distracted her from being squirted. "Mamma, tell us what happened," I said.

"What happened," she said through gritted teeth, "is that your father would not shut up about how his poor little hound needed to go for a walk. After being shut up in this house for ten days with him and that dog, *I* needed to get out of the house. So I put the dog on the leash, and we went for a nice walk. It was so nice, in fact, I walked him all the way over to Marsh View Drive."

"That's a long walk for Chumley," said Blake. Chumley was plump, and not accustomed to walking much farther than a few blocks.

"We were both enjoying the fresh air," said Mamma. "But he got tired and sat down in the middle of the road."

"That's too far for the hound," said Daddy.

"He needs to be walking at least that far every day," said

Mamma. "So do you."

"How did you get him out of the street?" asked Poppy.

Mamma stared at Poppy. "Oh dear goodness. What you must think of this family. Nearly every time you've been here for dinner there's been some sort of disaster."

"That's not true at all," said Poppy. "Tell us how you got Chumley to move. I've seen him get stubborn."

"He does," said Mamma. "He gets just as stubborn as an old mule." She looked at Daddy.

"So what did you do?" asked Merry.

"I coaxed him over into the grass. It was softer. I thought maybe he'd walk there," said Mamma.

"That was a great idea," said Poppy.

Daddy continued to rinse while we all distracted Mamma, getting her to tell us what had happened.

"Well," said Mamma, "it was a great idea for about five minutes. Until he saw the fiddler crab."

"Oh no." Blake smothered a grin.

"A fiddler crab?" said Joe. "Basset hounds chase fiddler crabs?"

"This. One. Does." Mamma gestured at Chumley.

Chumley commenced howling again.

"Hush up," Daddy, Mamma, Blake, Merry, and I all said at once.

Mamma turned around so Daddy could hose her back. "The strip of grass isn't wide along that section of Marsh View Drive. It starts getting muddy quick, then there's patches of spartina grass, and mud flats, and, well, the marsh. The tide was out, so there was a wide swath of mud. Chumley started barking at the crab right along the edge. The crab skittered right out across the mud, and Chumley found his second wind, just like that."

"Oh, no." I could see this playing out vividly in my imagination. It was not a pretty sight.

"Lightnin' here was on one of those retractable leashes," said Mamma. "I had it set to give him a lot of slack. He took it. He chased that crab about ten feet into the pluff mud before he started sinking."

"We're lucky we didn't lose the hound dog," said Daddy. "His short little legs, portly physique..."

"You're lucky you didn't lose *me*." Mamma turned around, leaned into her roar.

Daddy stopped spraying her.

"That muck is like quicksand," she said. "Chumley sank into it up to his stomach. He couldn't move."

"Poor Chumley," said Poppy.

Blake's eyes got big. He, Merry, and I all gave Poppy warning glances. She had a soft heart for animals. But right then, we all knew the smart play was to show Mamma sympathy, and Chumley had drug her through the mud. Literally. Sympathy for Chumley just then was downright dangerous.

Mamma looked at Poppy, raised an eyebrow. "I went into the mud after him. I sank into it up to my knees."

"Oh, Mamma," I said. "That just sounds like a nightmare to me." And it did. Pluff mud was full of the bacteria that ate the decaying spartina grass, plus decaying material from fish, shrimp, and all manner of things I didn't care to think about.

"It was a nightmare," said Mamma. "I wrapped my arms around Chumley and pulled and pulled. Finally he came free, but I fell backward, him on top of me. We were both wrestling around in that revolting mud for what seemed like hours. I thought we would both be sucked under and never be seen or heard from again."

"Mamma, that's horrible," Merry said.

We both moved closer to her, wanting to comfort her, but neither of us wanting to touch her.

Mamma said, "I think that's good enough I can go indoors, Frank. Let me see the hose for just a second to get a bit of it out of my hair."

"I can squirt your head." Daddy demonstrated.

"Frank." I just knew Mamma was giving him the look, but you couldn't really tell it because she still had mud on her face. She held out her hand.

Daddy handed her the hose, grinning.

She turned it on him full force.

"What are you doing?" Daddy sputtered. "You know I've practically got pneumonia."

"This mud has bacteria in it," said Mamma. "You may have gotten some on yourself." She squirted him gleefully.

"Stop that, now," said Daddy.

"No." Mamma got closer, squirted him in the face.

Daddy ran. "Look here now, I'm gonna end up in the hospital."

"You have no idea exactly how true that is," said Mamma.

She chased him around the pool deck 'til he was good and wet. Then she handed Blake the hose.

"I'm going inside to shower," she said. "I've already made the tomato pie, field peas, and potato salad. The chicken is soaking in buttermilk in the refrigerator. Liz, you'll have to fry it, and make the gravy. The biscuits are ready to bake."

"Okay, Mamma," I said.

"Merry, set the table, and help your sister warm things up."

"What can I do to help?" asked Poppy.

Mamma's shoulders raised and lowered in a long sigh. "Try to forget what you've seen here today."

"Blake, after I've gone inside, give your father the hose. Frank, get Chumley cleaned up. Somebody please get the mud off the pool deck and where it's tracked in the house. I can't believe I did that. I took temporary leave of my senses."

Thank heaven, it seemed as if she'd returned.

"I'll wash up out here after we get the mud off the dog," said Blake.

"I'll help," said Joe.

Nate said, "I'll mop up inside."

"I'll help out in the kitchen," said Poppy.

"Thank you all." Mamma walked inside, head high, her posture impeccable.

We all watched her go. Once she was inside, Merry started to giggle. That got me started. Poppy chuckled. Blake snorted. Then we were all laughing so hard we were holding onto each other.

An hour later, Merry, Poppy, and I were in the kitchen. The dining room table was set, Nate had opened two bottles of pinot noir and put them on the table, with two in reserve on the sideboard. I took the last of the chicken out of Mamma's two large cast iron frying pans and started the gravy.

Nate popped into the kitchen. "Anything I can do to help in here?"

"I think we've got it. Thank you, sweetheart."

"I uhh...I mopped the foyer. But when your daddy took Chumley upstairs, well, the floor got all messy again. I'm going to remove that right quick before your mamma comes down."

"Wait...Daddy took Chumley upstairs?" I turned away from the gravy to look at him.

"He got most of the mud off him, but some of it was deep into his fur. And he still stank pretty bad. Your daddy put him in the bathtub. Blake's up there with them."

"This isn't good," I said.

"Does Mamma know?" Merry asked.

"I don't think so," said Nate. "She hasn't come out yet."

"Mamma doesn't allow Chumley in the bathtubs in the house," I said. "He takes a bath outside. In the wintertime, he gets a bath at the vet."

"Desperate times," said Nate.

Merry grabbed a bottle of bleach from the pantry and handed it to Nate. "Take this up to Blake."

"Tell him he'd better clean that bathroom up like it's a crime scene," I said.

"Roger that." Nate took the bleach and left the kitchen.

"I'll go help." Poppy took off after Nate.

It was 8:00 before we all sat down to dinner. Merry had cut fresh hydrangeas and arranged them in a low crystal vase. I lit the candles before I took my place to Mamma's right.

Everyone was quiet all of a sudden. I looked at Blake for assurance all was well upstairs. He nodded. Hopefully Mamma would never know Chumley had taken a bubble bath in the guest room.

Mamma drew a deep breath. She looked her usual regal self, if a bit tired. "How is Chumley?"

"The hound dog is clean as a whistle," said Daddy. "He's in there in his bed by my chair, taking a nap."

"The house looks so clean. Thank you, whoever got all that mud up off the floor."

"That was Nate," I said.

"Of course it was," said Mamma. "Thank you, darlin'." She smiled warmly at Nate.

"Nothing to it," he said.

"Dinner looks delicious," said Mamma. "Thank you, girls."

"Well, Mamma, you did all the hard parts," I said. "All we did was heat things up."

Mamma pressed her lips together, looked at me from under her eyebrows. "Nonsense. See there, you can fry a chicken when you set your mind to it." She held out her hands to Merry and me. "Let's say grace."

Mamma prayed, "Father in Heaven, thank you for this food. Bless it to our use, and us to thy service. Thank you, Father, for delivering me from the depths of that horrible, vile, sucking, mud.

Thank you for my family, who set things to rights. And please, Father, be with Darius. He had a hard start in this life, Father. He's been gone a long time, and has no doubt been led into temptation while in Hollywood. But he's one of us, Father, part of our Stella Maris family, and he's returned home to us. Protect him and help those who are working to clear his good name. In Jesus' name we pray."

We all said amen and commenced to passing serving dishes and platters.

"Mamma, you have outdone yourself once again," I said. "This all looks amazing."

"It's nothing fancy," said Mamma.

"It looks pretty fancy to me." Poppy's eyes were large.

Daddy poured gravy on a biscuit, looked at Blake. "You get things settled down downtown?"

Mamma glanced my way. "Your brother's been tied up with these protesters."

"Protesters?" I scrunched my face at her. "Who's protesting what?"

Blake said, "People are all worked up because Darius is in jail."

"You didn't arrest him," I said. "He's not in jail here."

"Yeah, I know," said Blake. "Everyone just wants to show support. Reverend Wilson from over at First Baptist has a prayer vigil going. The group marched through town with signs saying, 'Free Darius,' and all such as that. No one showed up to argue with them, so it all worked out. Everybody's heart's in the right place. Except the press. They're looking for dirt, anywhere they can find it."

"Well, there isn't any here," said Mamma.

"Are you sure about that?" I asked.

"What do you mean?" asked Mamma.

"Just asking." I was thinking about secret marriages and babies, wondering how long it would be before someone dug all that up. "I'm worried for Nell and Bill. Are they still at the B&B?"

"Yeah," said Blake. "So far no one's found them."

I turned to Nate. "Where is Arianna staying?"

"Who's Arianna?" asked Blake.

"Darius's first ex-wife," I said.

"How many does he have?" Blake gave me an incredulous look. "When did she get here?"

"Three," I said, thinking about Trina Lynn, and how the number varied based on whether that marriage was legal or not. "And this afternoon. Nate brought her over." I raised an eyebrow at my husband.

Blake looked at Nate, then at me. "What am I missing?"

Nate said, "Not a thing. She needed a ride. I gave her one. Dropped her off at Calista McQueen's house."

"I'm sorry, what?" I looked at him.

"*E-liz-a-beth,*" Mamma said. "Wrinkles. Untwist your face this instant."

"She asked to be dropped at Calista's house. Said she was expecting her," said Nate.

"Well, at least she has a place to sleep," I said. "I'd love to know the story there."

"Would you now?" Nate grinned.

I tilted my head at him. "Did she tell you how she came to know Calista?"

"They've never met," said Nate. "Calista called her right after her altercation with ex-wife number two."

"How did she get her number?" I asked.

Nate said, "Now that, I don't know. But Arianna hopped on her private jet and came running. She wants to help clear Darius's name."

Blake closed his eyes. "When are they going to release Darius?"

"Hopefully in the morning," I said.

Blake raised his glass. "Let's hope everything goes well at the bond hearing. Things'll settle down once he's home. What did Fraser say about the ex-wife at Darius's house?"

"Oh shit. I forgot to ask him. Things have been happening fast."

"Elizabeth. Language." Mamma gave me the look.

"Sorry, Mamma."

Blake said, "Well, I guess Darius can handle his ex-wives when he gets home."

"Have there been any more press conferences?" I asked.

"Yeah, the third ex-wife had herself another one this afternoon. The folks from First Baptist came out for it. The thing is, everyone here likes Darius. Not a soul believes he killed Trina Lynn. If the TV people would just stop agitating everyone, putting microphones in peoples' faces, asking ridiculous questions that have nothing to do with Trina Lynn's murder, things would be fine."

"Eat your dinner, son," said Mamma. "All this is too upsettin' to be discussing at the dinner table. Did you girls see there's banana pudding in the refrigerator in the pantry?"

"Banana pudding?" Joe's eyes got big.

"Yummy," said Merry.

"Better save room," said Mamma.

"I found my horn while you were out on your walk," said Daddy. "It was hidden in the attic. I can't imagine how it got up there, can you?"

Mamma laid down her fork. "I'm going to have a long talk with Warren Harper. The man has obviously been reading trashy new age magazines."

"What kind of horn?" asked Poppy.

Blake said, "Dad, please." If I were him, I'd've been worried too. Poppy had already seen too much crazy.

Merry said, "I think it makes perfect sense. Daddy has bronchitis. Playing a didgeridoo has been proven to be good for your lungs. How did it get in the attic?"

Merry had given Daddy the didgeridoo for Christmas a few years ago. I'd thought it was a joke—we all did. Daddy was infamous for asking for odd things to send us all on scavenger hunts at Christmas time and around his birthday. But he'd hauled it out a few months back and commenced playing it. Mamma was sorely vexed with Dr. Harper for encouraging Daddy's musical pursuits on the grounds it might be good for his overall lung health, an idea Mamma set no store by whatsoever.

"I haven't the faintest notion." Mamma picked up her fork and took a bite of tomato pie.

"Maybe after supper I can play it for you," Daddy said to Poppy.

"My nerves can't take that this evening," I said. Daddy made a godawful racket with that didgeridoo, perhaps similar to the moans of a wounded wooly mammoth.

"Your nerves?" Mamma looked at me like I'd lost my mind. "I've been shut up here with him for ten days."

"Dad," said Blake, "are you just bored with being sick?"

"You know what, I forgot," said Daddy. "I've got to go out after dinner."

"Go out?" Mamma stared at him. "Out where?"

"Over to the Pirates' Den."

"Have you lost your mind?" asked Mamma.

"The mayor, John, Robert, and I need to talk," said Daddy.

John Glendawn and Robert Pearson were two members of our town council. Daddy was one as well. My godmother, Grace Sullivan, and I made up the rest of the current council. What was Daddy up to?

"Talk about what?" asked Mamma.

"We have business to discuss, Carolyn." Daddy picked up a chicken leg.

"What kind of business can't wait until you're well?" I asked.

"I can tell you exactly what they're up to," said Mamma. "The mayor wants to have an informal meeting with your father and a few other members of the town council to discuss who will fill Michael Devlin's recently vacated seat."

"No one mentioned it to me." I was on the town council.

"Liz, darlin'." Mamma's tone notified me how I was being obtuse. "You know very well how this works. Before they can officially discuss anything, these old coots have to drink over it and decide what they think, what they're all going to say, officially."

Daddy said, "There's not a thing wrong with old friends getting together to talk these things over before somebody's there writing every word we say down for God and everybody to pick over, analyze, and twist all around if they feel like it."

"You're sick, remember?" asked Mamma. "So sick I risked my life this afternoon to walk your dog."

"I told you I could walk the dog."

"And Warren Harper told you to rest."

"So now he's a genius and we should listen to him," said Daddy. "But when he tells me to blow my horn, he's a quack."

"You have been outside too much today already," said Mamma. "And you got wet, for heaven's sake."

Daddy looked at her slack-jawed. "Well whose fault is that, I'd like to know?"

Mamma inhaled slowly, smiled at Poppy, whose head was rotating back and forth between the two of them like she was watching a tennis match. "You're not going anywhere until the doctor tells you it's all right to be out and about."

Blake said, "Dad." There was a plea in his voice.

Daddy smiled at Poppy, pushed some peas onto his fork with a biscuit, and delivered the bite to his mouth. The rest of the meal passed in relative peace. We chatted about harmless things: the hydrangeas, how chicken always tastes better fried in cast iron, and Mamma's remarkable banana pudding. Then Merry, Poppy, and I cleared the table.

We wandered into the den, where Mamma and Daddy had reconvened the discussion of Daddy going to The Pirates' Den. "Blake, take his keys," Mamma directed.

"I took them an hour ago," said Blake.

"Where are my keys?" Daddy leveled a serious look at Blake.

"I'll tell you later," said Blake. "Poppy and I need to be heading out. Dad, try to be a more cooperative patient, would you?"

"I need my keys," said Daddy.

"They're someplace safe, I promise," said Blake.

"FT, how about we make us a hot toddy?" said Joe. "That'd probably be good for what ails us, wouldn't it?"

"A hot toddy?" Daddy wavered.

"That's a sensible idea," said Mamma. "Perhaps I'll have one as well. I probably have mud in my lungs."

Blake and Poppy headed towards the door. They were so close.

"I need to get over to The Pirates' Den." Daddy stood and headed to the kitchen, which had a pass-thru to the garage.

"If you go out that door, I'm calling J. Henry Stuhr's to come pick you up," said Mamma. J. Henry Stuhr's was the local funeral home, with five locations in the Charleston area.

"Call 'em." Daddy grabbed his didgeridoo from where it was propped in the corner and stalked across the room, through the foyer and the kitchen, and out the door to the garage.

"You reckon he's planning on walking over there?" asked Nate.

"Mamma, is the key to the golf cart on the same ring as his truck and house keys?"

"The golf cart," said Mamma. "No. I keep the key on a hook by the door."

We all ran out the front door.

Daddy waved as he pulled out of the driveway.

"What do you think he's going to do with that didgeridoo?" asked Poppy.

"Maybe he thinks John will let him play onstage at The Pirates' Den," said Nate.

NINETEEN

I considered going to The Pirates' Den, but I was pretty sure Colleen had someone in mind for Michael Devlin's council seat, and I had a pretty good idea who that was. Daddy and that bunch would be hard pressed to thwart whatever Colleen had planned.

Nate and I headed home and settled into the office with a bottle of pinot noir. Nate poured while I powered up my laptop and opened the spreadsheet I'd started at 86 Cannon.

"I want to get this on the case board," I said. "That helps me process things."

"You want me to do it?" asked Nate.

"I've got it." I sat my laptop on a small table near the whiteboards, grabbed a black dry erase marker, and started transferring our possible theories of the crime.

Nate sat in the corner of the sectional, propped his feet up, and watched. A few minutes later, I stepped back and looked at all the possibilities.

Suspect	Motives
Unknown Informant	Cover up a crime/Keep a secret
- Petty Officer Case	
- Some other story	

Lover	Crime of Passion
- Grey Hamilton	
- Walker Nance	
Wannabe Lover	Jealousy
- Kevin Looney	
Unknown Wannabe Lover	Jealousy
Spouse of Lover / Wannabe	Jealousy
- Julia Nance	
Family	
- Brantley Miller	Rage
- Billy Ray	Unknown
- Georgia Causby	Unknown
- Sawyer Causby	Unknown
- Laura Beth Causby	Unknown
- Brother or Sister-in-law	Unknown
Darius's Ex-Wives	Jealousy/Financial
- Arianna English	
- Vivianne Whitley	
- Lily McAdams	
August Lockwood	Unknown
Unknown Subject	Robbery
	Random

"I saw Kevin Looney at the funeral," said Nate. "Guy was all kind of tore up. Still could be him."

"Was he the one in a plaid shirt and jeans?"

"Yeah. I thought one of the guys from J. Henry Stuhr's was gonna escort him out of there. He was very emotional. It was awkward because no one seemed to know who he was. I chatted him up a bit. He definitely had an unrequited—unnatural, even—attachment to Trina Lynn, given that she didn't know him."

"All right, so he's a priority."

"I see you found something at Trina's condo," said Nate. "She had a second lover?"

I filled him in on Walker and Julia Nance. "I believed Julia when she told her friends she was at her parents' house. She was convincing. But that leaves Walker Nance as a serious contender without a known alibi."

"Well done." Nate took a sip of wine, studied the board. "I think we can eliminate August Lockwood. I checked his alibi first thing this morning. Unless he convinced six friends to lie for him, he was at the fire pit at the apartment complex."

"I hardly glanced at that list. Just out of curiosity, how many of those friends were women?"

"All of them." Nate set down his glass on the tray on the ottoman, tapped at his phone. Both of us kept temporary case notes in lists. "Bailey Hart, Camille Shaw, Finn Weathers, Jaelyn White, Saige Martin, and Yeats Collins. All but Saige and Bailey were with him at the funeral today."

"They all live at that same apartment complex?"

"Yep."

"There's something odd about that guy," I said. "He gives me the creeps."

"He's a narcissist, if you ask me. Set up court in a corner at the visitation. According to him, Trina Lynn being shot is something that happened to him. Turned my stomach. Her family didn't have much to do with him. Can't blame them."

"Any reason to think his groupies would lie for him?"

Nate rolled his lips in and out. "It's a possibility, sure enough.

But what motive would he have to kill Trina? By all accounts, including his, they were best friends...a successful team. She was the on-air talent. He'll be reassigned, no doubt. But I'd say her death was not a good thing for his career."

"Let's kick the tires a bit more before we erase him from the board," I said.

"As you wish."

"Did you get a chance to look into the petty officer's case?"

"I did. I met with Antonia Flores, the girlfriend whose apartment Fielding Davidson left the night he disappeared. She was almost certainly the last person to see him before he disappeared into thin air, other than the person or persons responsible for his departure, of course. She was cleared in his disappearance, by the way. The couple across from her had a problem with their washing machine. She let them use hers, and they were in and out of her apartment until past midnight. She never left."

"Does she have a theory about what happened to him?" I asked.

"Indeed she does, and she was eager to share it. Seems none of the investigating officers took her input seriously, in her view, anyway. You know how that goes. They had good reason, I think, to believe her scenario wasn't likely."

"What did she think happened?"

Nate said, "Miss Flores believes her ex-boyfriend, one Mark Wentworth, killed the petty officer in a fit of jealousy. Seems Mark is a bit of a stalker and a bully."

"Did the police look at him? That sounds like a credible lead to me."

"They did," said Nate. "But...there was jurisdictional ambiguity with that case. You had the Goose Creek PD, Charleston County Sheriff's Office, and then you had NCIS involved. The Navy folks wouldn't talk to me, but a helpful sheriff's deputy told me that the one thing they all agreed on was that Trina Lynn's theory was correct. They think a local human trafficking ring was behind the attempted kidnapping of the girl, Mia Moretti. There was some evidence the petty officer was at the scene. The deputy wasn't helpful enough to tell me what that was, but he said it was solid. Witnesses saw a van they've connected to the trafficking ring in the area around that time. Apparently, there's an ongoing task force investigation into that organization. The petty officer is almost certainly dead, and no one thinks they'll ever find his body."

My stomach roiled. "So if Trina Lynn was stirring that particular pot, and she was, the gang wouldn't have hesitated to come after her."

"That's true enough," said Nate. "But framing Darius...that's definitely not their MO."

I mulled that. "That's an excellent point. We have a number of possibilities here. Normally we'd eliminate the least likely first, but that would mean asking family for alibis, something I'd like to avoid if we can. How about we look at this through the lens of who had the motive, means, and opportunity to plant the gun in the bag Darius reportedly threw in the trash can at White Point Garden."

"That makes the most sense to me," said Nate.

"The motive could be as simple as 'make anyone look guilty but me.' They maybe weren't necessarily out to frame Darius in particular. Maybe he was just handy."

Nate said, "But whoever it was had to know Darius had a connection to Trina Lynn. That wasn't common knowledge. No one would get that lucky—to implicate someone who happened to be handy and have him turn out to have a connection to the victim they didn't even know about."

"Agreed." On another section of the case board, I started a list of facts about the killer. "We're looking for someone who knew Trina Lynn had a history with Darius. He or she also knew Trina Lynn was investigating the petty officer's case, because they used it to lure Trina Lynn to Philadelphia Alley. They owned or had access to a handgun and knew how to use it."

"He or she was in Charleston Sunday night," said Nate.

I stood back and looked at the case board. "So we've established it wasn't the gang responsible for the petty officer's probable death. Who else can we eliminate?"

"It damn sure wasn't random," said Nate.

I erased "Unknown Informant/Petty Officer Case" and "Unknown Subject/Robbery." "We need to talk to the ladies who found Trina Lynn. See if they saw anyone leaving Philadelphia Alley. Maybe that will help us narrow things down."

"That's a good idea. Can you talk to them tomorrow morning?"

"Sure." I took my wine and joined him on the sofa. "Right now, Brantley Miller looks like our best suspect to me, followed by either of Trina Lynn's lovers and her stalker."

"Why don't I make a quick trip to Travelers Rest?"

"Assuming he's still in school at Clemson, he'd be there," I said.

"Less than an hour between the two."

"I'll feel better after we look him in the eyes, talk to him. Maybe we should both go."

Nate said, "Nah, we've got too many bases to cover. Besides, if he's a stone-cold sociopath who could burn down a house with his family in it, looking into his eyes likely won't tell us a thing. I'll just make a day trip of it. Leave early. I'll be home by bedtime."

I studied his face. "You're trying to keep me away from Brantley, aren't you?"

"What makes you say that? We always divvy things up, cover more territory faster."

"Then I'll go to Travelers Rest and Clemson."

Nate shrugged. "If you'd rather do that, fine with me."

"Really?"

"Really." He took a long sip of wine. "Of course, the ladies from Texas would probably be more comfortable talking to you."

"You think so?" He was absolutely trying to keep me away from Brantley Miller.

"Don't you?" he asked, all innocent.

"I'm on to you."

"Are you now?"

"You're trying to protect me again."

"Look me in the eye and tell me you never worry about me." Nate had been shot earlier that year. I worried about him often and he knew it.

"Worrying's one thing," I said. "But not letting me do my job is another thing altogether."

"Slugger, there is plenty of work to be done here. It's going to take both of us. I'm not trying to keep you from doing your job. Now, would I rather you stayed here while I went to get a look at Brantley Miller? Yes, okay. I admit it. You got me. Especially given that Colleen is tied up twenty-four seven protecting Darius as long as he's in jail. I'd appreciate you not telling her this, but I really do miss having her around."

"*Oooh!* I knew it. I am perfectly capable—"

"But on the other hand, if I go check out Brantley Miller, that means you're going to stay here and track down three other men who could just as easily have killed Trina Lynn, right?"

"But your gut tells you it's Brantley, just like mine does."

"Based on what we know right now, yes," he said.

"Let's flip a coin."

Nate's phone rang. He glanced at the screen. "Fraser."

He slid the button to the right, put the phone on speaker. "Nate Andrews."

"Mr. Andrews, I will be in bond court first thing in the morning. Mr. Baker will appear remotely via video from the Charleston County Jail. I anticipate his release. However, I will not be available to escort him home due to a commitment regarding another case. There will undoubtably be a plethora of media at the jail. You and Ms. Talbot will need to escort him directly to his home. See to it that he does not speak to the press."

"I think the plan is for him to stay at a local bed and breakfast with his family," said Nate.

"Whoever's plan that was, it is not *my* plan. Take him home, Mr. Andrews."

"What time do we need to be at the jail?"

"I will call you. It will likely be early afternoon," said Fraser.

"We'll take care of it." Nate ended the call.

"I guess that settles that," he said. "Neither of us is going to the Upstate tomorrow. It'll definitely take both of us to keep the reporters at bay."

"Damnation. Let's get as much out of the way as we can in the morning. Then maybe we can both go Saturday."

"Sounds like a plan," said Nate. "We should divvy the rest of those folks up first thing in the morning."

"Right after breakfast at The Cracked Pot," I said.

"You seriously want Moon Unit's country fried breakfast with gravy after the meals we've had the last two nights?"

"It's not in our best interests, for sure," I said. "But I'm wondering if Moon Unit has any more information to pass along. Hey, what did you find out about Sonny's chain of command?"

He tapped at his phone. "Not much of use, at least at this point. I know the names. Their lieutenant is Randall Johnson. The captain over the Investigations Division is Olympia Price. Deputy Chief is Tyrone Latimer. All three are highly decorated and respected. So far nothing's popped as a connection between any of them and any name we've run across on this case."

"You never did tell me about Arianna English." I sipped my wine.

"I told you everything there was to tell." His voice was even, not defensive.

"She sure seemed taken with you. Couldn't keep her hands off you."

"I wouldn't say that. She's just one of those physically demonstrative people."

"Do tell?" I leaned closer, spoke softly. "I'm going upstairs to slip into something involving garters and heels. If you'd care to join me, I'll show you how physically demonstrative your wife is."

He kissed me long and hard. Then he put his hand under my chin and lifted my face so that I was looking into those deep pools of blue. "I can't even begin to conjure a more enthralling image than you in garters and heels. But the thing is, it's clear to me that I'm the one who has something to demonstrate right now. Because you seem to be confused as to who the only woman in the world whose hands I want on me is. And I need to clear that right up."

Then he scooped me up, carried me up the stairs, and laid me gently on the bed.

I never had the chance to change.

TWENTY

There was a line outside on both sides of the door at The Cracked Pot the next morning.

"No tellin' how long we'd have to wait for a place to sit. Let me out and I'll run in and try to catch Moon Unit," I said.

"I'll swing back by the house and grab coffee. Some yogurt and some fruit. That sound okay?" asked Nate.

"Perfect, thanks." I leaned over and kissed him, smiled, and climbed out of the car.

I couldn't even hear the bells when I went through the door. Every seat at the counter, every table, every spot at a booth was taken. People were crowded inside the door waiting for a seat. I didn't see a soul I knew. The noise level was overwhelming. Everyone was talking louder to be heard over the crowd, so the volume seemed to be cranking up by the moment.

I scanned the dining room and behind the counter for Moon. There. She had a tray balanced on her hand as she delivered platters of eggs, grits, biscuits, bacon, ham, and sausage to a table near the back. I zigzagged through the restaurant, sliding between chairs, and made my way to Moon.

She lowered the tray and turned towards me. "I don't have any idea how long it'll be. Blake took his breakfast to go. First time that's ever happened."

"Are these all reporters?"

"Most of them. There's also some folks from out of town here to support Darius. And people who work for his first ex-wife. Have you met her? She's at Calista's. But her people showed up today. She's renting a house—"

"Moon, real quick. Is there anything else you think Sonny might want me to know?"

She raised an eyebrow at me. "Now that you mention it, he said something very odd. I don't know what to make of it." She looked at the ceiling. Wiggled her finger back and forth a few times. "It was something like, 'I wish Liz knew the true price of this case.' I thought it sounded real philosophical. But it didn't make any sense to me. Does it to you?"

Indeed, it did. Price. Sonny was telling me Captain Olympia Price was pressuring him. "Not a lick. I think Sonny's working too hard."

"I've tried to tell him that, but you know men don't listen."

"I've gotta run. Good luck with all this."

"Hey, business is business. These are paying customers. I'm happy to see 'em."

I stepped out under the pink awning and scanned Main Street for the Explorer. It would likely be a few more minutes. The crowd outside The Cracked Pot had gotten larger. A woman I recognized as Lily McAdams, Darius's most recent ex-wife, stood against the side of the building talking on her phone and checking her nails. She reminded me a bit of Trina Lynn. She had that same blue-eyed, fresh-faced, wholesome look. Except for Vivianne, Darius seemed to favor blondes. How were Calista and Arianna getting along?

I started to call Calista, but then I caught part of what Lily was saying. "...just trying to get his money. Darius would have told me if he'd had a son. We're soul mates. We didn't keep that kind of thing secret from each other."

I eased closer, not looking at her.

"No, he just came up to me after the press conference," she said.

Brantley Miller was here. I needed to talk to Lily, fast.

I leaned against the building with one hand, held my chest with the other, and faked a pained grimace. Lily looked at me. "You okay?"

I winced. "I think so."

"Hey, I'll call you back," she said into the phone. "You need to sit down?"

"No, thank you. You're sweet to ask. It's nothing, really. Hey, aren't you Darius's wife?"

She held out her hand. "Lily McAdams. Technically, Darius and I are divorced. But that was such a huge mistake. I guess I needed to grow up a little bit. As soon as we get this mess behind us, I'm sure we'll patch things up."

"I'm Liz Talbot." I handed her a card. "I work for Darius. Well, not exclusively, but I'm on retainer. My husband and I are private investigators."

"Oh, wow. It's great to meet you," she said. "So you two are helping Darius with these ridiculous charges?"

I chose my words carefully. "We are, yes. I'm so sorry, I wasn't trying to eavesdrop, but did you meet the young man who's claiming to be his son?"

"As a matter of fact, he walked right up to me and introduced himself yesterday afternoon. The whole thing's bizarre. Darius does not have any children."

"That's my understanding. Did this young man tell you where he was staying? I'd like to talk to him."

"Somebody needs to. Somebody needs to tell him to stop spreading these lies about Darius. That is not helpful, to say the least."

"So, do you know? Where he's staying?"

"Oh. No, he didn't mention it. I didn't ask. I just wanted to get away from him."

"Why is that?" I asked.

"Well he's obviously trying to scam Darius. Who knows what else he's capable of?"

Nate pulled to the curb.

"You have my card in case you need to reach me," I said to Lily. "Where are you staying?"

"The Stella Maris Hotel."

"You were lucky to get a room," I said.

"Tell me about it," she said. "This island could use a nice resort or two."

Oh sweet reason, please don't let anyone else get that bright idea. It was always a risk when this many new people came to town. "With the ferry, and no bridge, it's just not practical to have big hotels and all like that."

She smiled. "You never know. I'd be willing to bet you good money Darius is planning to put a resort here with its own private ferry. This place is gorgeous. So relaxing—well, aside from the legal difficulties. I'm going to talk to him about it as soon as we're through this nightmare. You'll see."

Why had it not occurred to me until that moment that Darius might be interested in developing Devlin's Point, most of which he now owned? After everything we'd been through to prevent Devlin's Point from being turned into a high-rise resort. That had been Colleen's first assignment. Was it possible she'd been at the jail for days protecting a man who planned to work against everything she'd been sent to us to accomplish? I wasn't accustomed to sharing Colleen, and I didn't care much for her being tied up with Darius all week.

"Bye now." I waved to Lily and climbed in the car.

"Who was that?" Nate asked.

I grabbed my stainless steel coffee mug from its typical holder and gulped. "Lily McAdams. Ex-wife number one. But that's not even in the top three headlines."

"Oh?"

"Captain Olympia Price is the one who pressured Sonny and Jenkins to arrest Darius. Brantley Miller is here. And Lily thinks Darius plans a resort for Devlin's Point."

TWENTY-ONE

Two Meeting Street occupied the corner of Meeting and South Battery, across from White Point Garden. The lovely white Queen Anne style house reminded me of a wedding cake, with its turrets and wide wrap-around double porches with arches between the columns. Built in 1892 by Warren Carrington and his wife, the former Martha Williams, with money her father gave them as a wedding gift, the house was arguably the most iconic inn in Charleston, which was somewhat ironic given that it was built twenty-seven years after the Civil War ended.

Nevertheless, it was quite lovely. Margie Sue Frentress and her twin sister, Mary-Lou Willis agreed to meet us on the porch. The twins had blonde hair, blue eyes, and sweet smiles. One of them had a touch of strawberry in her hair. I pegged them at mid-fifties, but well-maintained. We all said our hellos, and we showed them identification and gave them each a business card. Then we settled into a round wrought iron table with four chairs on one of the rounded porch corners under a turret. The lush landscaping in the garden beyond and the canopy of live oaks shaded the porch and lent it a quiet, private atmosphere.

"I'm sorry to ask you to meet out here," said Margie Sue. "It's just..." She looked at her sister.

"We understand," I said. "I can imagine this has all been very upsetting."

Mary-Lou added, "And, well, to be honest, how did we know y'all were who you said you were? You could be anyone, really. Nearly witnessing a murder has made us a bit paranoid."

"Are you satisfied with our credentials?" Nate asked.

"Yes, thank you," said Margie Sue. "We appreciate you offering your identification and all. Of course, we're not supposed to talk to y'all."

"The police told you not to?" I asked.

"Well, they told us not to talk to the press," said Margie Sue. "And they certainly discouraged us from talking to investigators for the defense. The one detective kept reassuring us we didn't have to talk to you. But the other one, he kept adding unless we wanted to. We looked it up on the internet. It's not against the law for us to talk to you."

"No, it certainly isn't," I said.

"We've planned this trip for months," said Mary-Lou. "Our getaway—just the two of us. I can't believe we're involved in a murder. Everyone wants us to come home, but we've decided to stay through tomorrow. That's when our airline tickets are for."

"Could you walk us through Sunday evening?" I asked. "Just take your time and start with dinner."

"Well," said Margie Sue, "we had late reservations at The Peninsula Grill. We really wanted to go there, but the only time they could take us was 8:30. We don't usually eat that late. I know I should've made the reservations weeks ago."

"Margie, stop that," said Mary-Lou. "We had a fabulous dinner. We can stay up late on vacation if we want to."

"What time did you leave the restaurant?" I asked.

They exchanged a glance.

"About 9:45. It might have been later. We can't be a hundred percent sure," said Margie Sue.

"Did you walk back to the inn?" I asked.

"Yes," said Margie Sue. "We had a big dinner, and we wanted to let it settle. It's less than a mile straight down Meeting Street, but we decided to take our own walking tour."

"Tell us about that," I said. Nate and I had agreed that I should ask most of the questions.

"We walked down North Market towards the Cooper River," said Margie Sue. "Then we went right on Church Street, but we backtracked up Cumberland to see the Powder Magazine. Did you know that's the oldest surviving public building in the Carolinas? It was built in 1713. They stored their gunpowder in there before the revolution—the walls are thirty-two inches thick. But they had to move the powder during the siege to hide it. It's all so fascinating."

I smiled. "It is, isn't it? Where did you go next?"

"We went back over to Church Street and walked partway down to St. Philips, but then I remembered that Dueler's Alley ran behind the church. The story of the Whistling Doctor just breaks my heart. I wanted to see if we could hear his ghost whistle."

"I wasn't nearly as enthusiastic about chasing ghosts down a back alley, but I'd had wine with my dinner, so I agreed," said Mary-Lou.

"We walked back up to Cumberland and went right on Dueler's Alley," said Margie Sue.

"Don't call it that," said Mary-Lou. "It sounds so Wild Wild West. Philadelphia Alley."

"Y'all sure seem to know your way around the city," I said.

"We studied the tourist maps they give you at the Visitors Center like we were studying for exams," said Mary-Lou. "We wanted to make sure we saw everything we could."

"Anyway," said Margie Sue. "We'd just taken a few steps in. That's when we heard arguing. Two women. We couldn't make out what they were saying. They were yelling, but they were talking over the top of each other. We stopped and just looked at each other, like, what should we do? That's when we heard the gunshot."

"We didn't even talk about it, we just ran down the alley," said Margie Sue. "I confess I considered if maybe we were hearing the ghosts of duelers, but I didn't think those were women. It was confusing."

"And I thought at first it was a ghost tour of some sort," said Mary-Lou. "You know, a dramatization."

"But I guess in the backs of our minds, we both thought maybe someone needed help," said Margie Sue.

"You ran towards the gunshot?" I asked.

"It was stupid, I know," said Mary-Lou.

"What did you see?" I asked.

"This beautiful young blonde woman was lying there. We found out later of course she was a local reporter. I called 911 on my cell phone," said Margie Sue.

"Did you pass anyone before you got to the victim?" I asked.

"No." They both shook their heads.

"Did you ever see the other woman?" I asked.

Margie squinted. "Not really. It was dark. There are some lights along the alley. But we were a good ways away when we heard the gunshot. I caught a glimpse from behind, but all I saw was black clothes. She had a hood up or something. I couldn't tell the color of her hair."

"Was she tall, short, thin, fat?" I asked.

Margie pressed her lips together, shook her head. "She wasn't overly anything that I noticed. But really, I just caught a glimpse."

"I didn't see her at all," said Mary-Lou.

"Did you see anyone else in the alley that night? Someone going in a door or through a gate?" I asked.

"No, just the poor reporter and the other woman walking away down the alley in the other direction, towards Queen Street. Well, she walked a little ways. Then she started running."

"And you're positive it was a woman you saw?" I asked.

"Well..." said Margie. "Honestly, no. We thought we *heard* two women. But I can't swear the other person wasn't a man with a higher-pitched voice. And I had the impression it was a woman, from behind. But I wouldn't swear to it. Things have gotten awfully muddled in that department."

"What happened next?" I asked.

"We waited for the police," said Margie Sue. "Neither of us knew if she was alive or dead, or if we could help. We were afraid of doing more harm than good."

"Oh," said Mary-Lou. "And we met Vicki."

"Who's Vicki?" I asked.

Margie Sue reached for her purse, rustled around in there, and came out with a slip of paper. "Vicki Turpitt. She and her husband are staying at a campground over at James Island County Park. She came down the alley from the other direction while we were waiting on the police."

"Did she see the other woman?" I asked.

"She did say she saw a woman dressed in black leaving the alley," said Margie Sue. "But she didn't wait for the police to come. Said her husband was waiting for her at the waterfront swings. I think she was really shook up."

"Did you give her name to the police?" I asked.

"We did," said Mary-Lou. "But we have no idea if they spoke with her."

"How long before the police arrived?" I asked.

"Not long," said Margie Sue. "Minutes. Vicki just missed them. EMS came about the same time, but that poor woman was already gone."

"How long were you there, talking with the police?" I asked.

The sisters exchanged a glance. "Not that long. Maybe fifteen minutes. But then they came by the next morning to follow up. Asked us to come in and make sworn statements. We did that."

"Did they drive you back to the inn?" I asked. "Sunday night."

"Why no," said Mary-Lou. "We walked on back."

"Tell us about that," I said. They were staying at Two Meeting Street. Had they happened upon Mo and Jim with Darius? It would have been on the way if they'd walked along the waterfront. But the timing was probably off.

Margie shrugged. "We walked out the other end of the alley. Came out at Queen Street. We went left, walked over to East Bay. And we took that all the way back to South Battery, then turned right and here we were."

"Did you see anything peculiar, anything that caught your eye?" I asked.

They squinted at me with identical expressions of confusion. "Like what?"

"Just go back over the walk in your minds and tell us anything you think of," I said.

They both tilted their heads, looked off into space.

After a moment, Margie said. "We were in shock. Chattering about what had happened. I didn't notice anything at all until right before we turned on South Battery. And that was just some poor soul rummaging through the trash. It's sad, really, in a city this beautiful, you still have people that desperate."

"I'd forgotten about that," said Mary-Lou. "It is sad."

"Tell me about who you saw," I said.

Margie Sue looked surprised. "I guess it was a homeless person."

"Man or woman?" I asked.

"Woman," they both said.

"Old or young?" I asked.

"It's hard to say for sure," said Margie. "She had on a baseball cap. Her hair was up underneath it. She had on way too many clothes for the heat—a big flowy skirt and a paisley jacket. And she had a big shopping bag."

"White, black, Hispanic, Asian...?"

"White, don't you think, Mary-Lou?"

"Definitely white."

"And her build?" I asked.

"It was hard to tell," said Margie Sue. "She had on so many clothes. She wasn't dressed for the weather at all."

"Where was the trash can she was going through?" I asked.

"Right at the side entrance to White Point Garden," said Margie Sue.

"Did you see anything specific that she took out or put in the trash can?" I asked.

"No, I didn't," said Margie Sue. "Did you?" She turned to her sister.

"She had a white bag in her hands when I saw her. But I couldn't tell you whether she took it out or put it in."

"Did you tell the police detectives about this?" I asked.

"Well, no," said Margie Sue. "They never asked us anything about after we left the alley."

TWENTY-TWO

James Island County Park sits along the Stono River, a tidal channel that separates James Island from Johns Island. The park is lovely, with mature trees and lots of natural areas. The Turpitts' Catalina Legacy travel trailer was parked at site one twenty-five, tucked into the shade. The white Chevrolet 4x4 had Arkansas plates.

The couple sat under the awning in outdoor zero gravity recliners having coffee when we pulled up. They smiled and waved like they knew us. The black and tan dachshund stretched out between the chairs stood and commenced barking.

"Missy, shh," said the man. He was bald with a sturdy look about him.

"Hey, y'all," I said as Nate and I climbed out of the Explorer.

"Good morning." They looked to be active sixty-somethings. They both lowered their chairs, stood, and walked towards us.

Nate and I showed them our identification. As with the twins, I did the talking.

"I'm Liz Talbot. This is my husband, Nate."

"Jim and Vicki Turpitt." He held out a hand.

We all shook hands, said hello again.

"We're private investigators looking into what happened downtown Sunday evening," I said. "We were wondering if we could have a few moments of your time."

"Sure," they both said.

"But I'm afraid I can't tell you a thing," said Jim. "I was waiting for Vicki on the swings."

"Vicki, would you tell us what you remember?" I asked.

She was a strawberry blonde who wore her hair styled short and straight, but with a little lift and a scatter of bangs. It suited her. She regarded me with intelligent eyes. "We had dinner at Hank's around 8:00. It was maybe 9:30 when we left. We went for a walk. Headed down Church to Market, then over to Concord. We walked down to the north entrance of Waterfront Park—where the fountain is. We sat on a bench nearby, in the terraced area under the trees. Then we walked out to the swings. I wanted to walk some more, but Jim wanted to enjoy the swing."

"I knew it was a mistake, letting her take off by herself," he said.

"I walked down Vendue Range, crossed East Bay," said Vicki. "I was a little more than a block down Queen Street when I heard what sounded like a gunshot. Then I saw a woman come running out of Philadelphia Alley. She was dressed in black from head to toe. Had on a hoodie drawn tight around her face, and large sunglasses."

"You're positive it was a woman?" I asked.

"She had a woman's shape, curves. And she moved like a woman, if you know what I mean," said Vicki.

"Could you make out anything else about her appearance? Race? Height? Her build?"

"She was white, I'm almost positive. But I couldn't see much of her face. It's possible she was Asian, or a light-skinned Hispanic. She was average height, I guess. Trim."

"Which way did she go?" I asked.

"She crossed the street and ran down Queen, back towards East Bay," said Vicki.

"Did you see if she had a gun?" I asked.

"No. She could have. The hoodie was the kind with a big pocket in front," said Vicki.

"Then what happened?" I asked.

"I had to decide whether I should follow her or see if someone needed help. I thought that was more important. And then I saw that poor woman, just lying there in the alley. There were two other ladies there. They had already called the police. I knew Jim would be worried, especially with the sirens, which I could already hear. I gave the women my name and went back to the swings."

"Did the police come and talk to you?" I asked.

"No," said Vicki. "I really thought they would. But then we saw in the news they'd arrested Darius Baker. We just love *Main Street USA*. We couldn't believe it. After that, I figured the woman I saw was another witness. But you asked me if she had a gun. Are you thinking maybe she's the one who shot that reporter?"

Just then I was busy thinking how Sonny had to be under the threat of being fired or worse. He was too good a detective to have not followed through and at least spoken to Vicki.

"We don't know yet," I said. "We're just gathering information. Did you see anyone else come out of Philadelphia Alley, either before or after the woman?"

"No," said Vicki. "Just her."

"Did you see anything else out of the ordinary?"

"No," said Vicki. "I just feel awful I didn't get a better description of her or something."

"You did the right thing," I said. "And you've been very helpful."

Nate's phone rang. "Excuse me." He stepped away.

"Please call us if you think of anything else," I said.

We both waved and climbed into the Explorer.

Nate ended the call and pressed the button to start the car. As we drove back towards the gate, the Explorer hesitated.

An irritated look crossed Nate's face. "Dammit. I'm going to have to take a look at that. We've got a cylinder misfiring. It's either a plug wire or the coil connection."

"Should we take it in for service?"

"It's probably something simple I can take care of. But I can't do it now. We need to be at the jail by 1:00."

TWENTY-THREE

The Sheriff Al Cannon Detention Center was situated on Leeds Avenue in North Charleston. The original structure was comprised of two four-story square, grey concrete buildings connected by a smaller grey rectangle. There were few windows, and it wouldn't have been hard to figure out what the place was without the sign. That's where Darius had been held since his arrest.

Nate parked the Explorer in the parking lot and we walked towards the lobby. Three news vans were already broadcasting or taping a spot—I couldn't tell which—with the jail as a backdrop, bringing any viewers who hadn't heard why Darius was here up to date. Fortunately for us, they had no idea we were there for Darius.

We passed underneath the metal awning and into the utilitarian lobby. We spoke to the deputy serving as hostess and she directed us to the row of connected metal chairs to wait. We stood in the general vicinity.

Shortly after one, Darius came out through a grey door under a sign that said, "Secure Area." His head jerked left to right. He saw us and walked towards us. Colleen walked just behind him, in ghost mode.

"Darius," I said, "this is my husband, Nate. He's also my partner."

"Nice to meet you." Darius shook Nate's hand. "What's y'all's plan for getting me past the vultures outside?"

"I'll create a diversion," said Colleen.

"We're going to walk right past them," Nate said. "Me on one side, Liz on the other. We'll be fine." He looked at Colleen like he was thinking *Get to diverting*.

"So we gonna run for it. Okay. All right then. Let's go." Darius headed for the door.

I moved to his left. Nate pushed the door open and we all walked through.

A small crowd of reporters waited, microphones in hand.

They erupted in shouted questions. Darius couldn't have answered any of them if he'd wanted to. It was impossible to understand who was asking what. We walked fast towards the Explorer. They followed. We just kept walking, eyes down.

"Holy shit, get that on video," one of them yelled.

They all turned to look. I glanced over my shoulder to see what appeared to be a waterspout in Brickyard Creek, the stream that ran behind the detention center. As waterways in the Lowcountry go, this one rarely made the news. Perhaps other sections of it were lovely, but this stretch was narrow and completely obscured by a thick stand of trees. It was easy to miss. Lots of folks probably didn't even know it was there.

"What in the *hell* is that?" asked Darius.

"I have no earthly idea," I said. "Quick, get in the car."

We each ran for a door. The doors unlocked as Nate touched the drivers' side handle. We hopped in, Darius behind me. Nate locked the doors and pressed start. The engine coughed, then clicked.

"Aw, hell," said Darius. "I know you didn't come to pick me up from the jailhouse in no broke down car."

"Dammit." Nate pushed the button again and the car started.

I stared out the window at Colleen's diversion, which was admittedly a doozy.

"Whew," said Darius. "I don't know what's going on over there with that mud cyclone, but let's get the hell out of here."

Every one of the reporters had abandoned Darius to check out the towering funnel of muddy water. As soon as we'd cleared the parking lot and turned right off Leeds onto the on ramp to the Mark Clark Expressway, the mud spout collapsed, splattering every reporter in the jail parking lot. Colleen appeared in the backseat beside Darius.

"That was fun," said Colleen. "I haven't played in the mud in a long time. But I'm exhausted."

Spectacular special effects typically left Colleen drained.

"We'll have to watch that on the news tonight," said Darius. "Maybe the weatherman can explain it."

"Oh, that won't be on the news," said Colleen. "None of their cameras worked. They'll all talk about this for a while."

Of course, Darius couldn't hear her. Nate shook his head. I met her eyes in the rearview. *Thank you.*

"You're welcome." Colleen curled up on the seat, leaned against the door.

"Darius, are you okay?" I asked.

"Yeah, I'm fine," he said. "Y'all wouldn't believe what all has happened the last three days if I told you. I saw some wondrous things in that jail. Make that mud mess look downright ordinary. I tell you, God looked after me in there. I'm sure of it."

Colleen sighed. "These past three days have worn me out. Troy Causby's friends weren't the only ones trying to get to Darius."

"A lot of folks were sending up prayers," I said, thinking of Mamma.

"Listen," said Darius. "I owe you one, for sure. If you hadn't a come by my house the other morning, I wouldn't a known who to call. That lawyer you hooked me up with seems to be a good one. He's damn snooty, I'll tell you that much right now. But I don't care about that if he can fix this mess."

"Fraser's the best," I said. "Listen, we need to ask you some questions."

"Let's hear 'em," said Darius.

"First, about your son..." I said.

"Oh, hell, here we go," said Darius.

"We need to know," I said. "Did you tell him Trina Lynn was his mother?"

"Naw," he said.

"Is he what you and Trina Lynn were arguing about at Hall's?" I asked.

"Yeah. I asked Trina Lynn about him. And she told me what she did. She covered the whole thing up and went out of town to have that baby, then put him up for adoption without even telling me I had a son."

"I know that made you mad," I said. "Did the police ask you about that at all?"

"Not at first," said Darius. "But I think someone told them, because Jenkins came around asking about it after I was in jail."

"The only people who knew were Trina's family and Brantley himself," said Nate.

"Brantley ain't got nothing to do with any of this," said Darius.

"How can you be sure of that?" I asked.

Darius was quiet for a minute. "I guess I can't be. But he seems like a nice kid. Think about it...kids that age into they ancestry...those are the nerds. He ain't getting into trouble. He's in college. Gonna make somethin' of hisself."

"You may be right," I said. "But we have to check out every possible angle."

"Yeah, I get that." He sounded depressed at the thought.

Nate changed lanes to pass a truck as we crossed the Cooper River. "Walk us through your movements after you left Hall's Chophouse Sunday night."

"Trina said she had to meet somebody. She called a Scoop. I

waited with her 'til it came. I went back to my car. It was parked on John Street. I started to head home. Damn sure wish I'd done that. But it was a nice night. I got me a baseball cap outta the car. Cover up my bald head and most people won't recognize me right off.

"Then I just wandered around. Hadn't been home in a long time. Things sure have changed. I walked down King Street, looking at all the shops and restaurants. Cut over on Society. Went right on Meeting. Left on North Market, then over to East Bay. I stopped at a bakery on the corner of East Bay and Cumberland. Carmella's. Bought two cannoli, thinking I'd eat 'em the next day. I love me some cannoli. Walked on down East Bay towards The Battery. Them cannoli was talking to me. Time I got to Rainbow Row, I started munching on one of 'em. By the time I got to the The Battery, they was both gone. Then—"

"What did you do with the bag?" I asked.

He screwed up his face at me. "I threw it in the trash can."

"Which one?" I asked.

"There at White Point Garden. Why are you asking me about litter?"

"I take it you and Fraser haven't discussed the evidence the police have against you?" Nate asked.

"Naw. I just talked to him the one time he came to the jail. Right after I was arrested." Darius looked out the window at the Wando River. "What evidence? They can't have evidence I did something I damn sure didn't do."

Nate said, "They found the murder weapon in a white bag in the trash can at White Point Garden. They have a witness who saw you put a white bag in that particular trash can."

Darius got loud. "And I just told you I put a white bag in that trash can. Do you think I'm stupid on top of being a cold-blooded baby-mamma killer? I was right there at The Battery. The Cooper River and the Ashley River were pooling together right there in front of me. Why would anybody throw a gun they had just used to kill somebody into a trash can when there's a perfectly good harbor right in front of them?"

"That's a very good question." Nate's voice was calm, even.

"All right," I said. "Calm down and back up. You put the paper bag in the trash can. Then what happened?"

"Some nice lady recognized me. Came running across the street wanting my autograph. She didn't have nothing for me to sign except a receipt from dinner. But I signed it. Somebody took our picture."

"Who was that? Who took your picture?" I asked.

"Just some random lady. We didn't ask her name. She used the nice lady's phone and took our picture."

"Then what did you do?"

"Then I realized what time it was, and I needed to get myself back to the ferry dock or I wasn't gonna be sleeping in my bed. I flagged down one of those li'l bicycle rickshaw taxis to take me back to my car. Had a damn parking ticket on top of everything. Still almost missed the ferry."

"Did you save the receipt?" I asked.

"I didn't ask for no receipt for a taxi." He gave me a look that inquired after my sanity.

"I meant from Carmella's," I said.

"Naw. The girl at the counter tried to hand me a receipt," he said. "I waved it off."

"That's too bad," I said. "The time stamp could've cleared you. Did you pay with a credit card?"

"Cash."

"Still. If we need it, I'll talk to the folks at the restaurant. You're a celebrity. Surely whoever you bought the cannoli from remembers you," I said.

"Young girl," said Darius. "Not my primary demographic."

"She might still remember you," I said. "The next thing we need to talk about is your marriage to Trina Lynn. How did y'all pull that off? You were both underage."

"I got my mamma to sign an affidavit. We uh, we forged Trina's mamma's signature."

"But that has to be notarized," I said.

"And we talked somebody into notarizing it. We were teenagers in love, and it was Valentine's Day. That poor lady's retired now, maybe dead. We don't need to drag her into this."

"So you got married because it was Valentine's Day?" I asked.

"I told you. We were in love," he said.

Nate looked in the rearview mirror. "And she was reluctant?"

Darius's face was quite expressive. Just then it was saying, *You got that right.* "Trina Lynn was a good girl. She wasn't giving away no free milk. So, I bought the cow."

"Oh my stars," I said. "You got married so you could have sex?"

Darius started shaking with a chuckle. "You think that's unique? Let me tell you something, most men get married so they can have sex."

Nate turned to me. "Ah, he doesn't speak for the group." He looked back into the mirror. "When you married her illegally at age seventeen, Trina Lynn was not pregnant?"

"That's right. We were secretly married in February. I never knew she got pregnant at all. Last time I saw her, she surely didn't look like she was expecting a baby. But when I asked her at the restaurant Sunday night, she told me she thought it was a prom night baby."

"And if you had known she was pregnant?" I asked.

"I honestly don't know. I'd like to think I woulda stayed here, talked her into keeping the child. But that woulda been a hard sell. Her parents didn't really approve of me, and she was real close to her family."

"But she married you," I said.

"Yeah, she did, didn't she?" He stared out the window again.

Nate got off of 526 on Hungry Neck Boulevard. "Did you ever get divorced?"

"We did. I'm not sure which was more legal, the wedding or the divorce. Before I married Arianna, I got in touch with Trina and she agreed to a quickie divorce. My attorney said it was legal. He went to Mexico and took care of everything. Mexican divorces were a thing back then. Do people still do that? Anyway, Trina nor I either one even had to show up."

"When's the last time you spoke to any of your ex-wives?" I asked.

Darius thought for a minute. "I told all of 'em when I decided to move here. It's been a couple months."

"What's your relationship with them like?" I asked.

"Why? Ain't none of them killed Trina Lynn, if that's what you're thinking."

"Darius." I gave him a quelling look in the rearview.

"Arianna and I are friends. If I'd a married her when I was more mature, I might a just had the one wife. Vivianne...whoo law. Vivianne and I are like gasoline and matches. We stay clear of each other. Lily...that was me being stupid again. That girl's way too young for me. We don't even know any of the same music. But I guess we get along okay. Now why are you asking me about them?"

"Because they're all three in Stella Maris right now." I watched his reaction in the mirror.

He drew back, eyes large. "What?"

"Vivianne is at your house—"

"How did she get in?"

"I'm afraid Calista let her in, but it was by accident," I said.

Darius put a hand over his face. "Oh Lord. You can't take me home then."

"I'm afraid we have to," I said. "Fraser is insistent that we allow the press to video in front of your house and generally make your life miserable, at least for a few days. It builds sympathy in a potential jury pool, apparently."

"Listen. You don't understand. If you leave me there with Vivianne, bad things will happen," said Darius. "If I have to go home, you have got to get her outta my house. And that won't be an easy thing, I'm just telling you that up front."

I looked at Colleen. *Can you handle that?*

"Please." She yawned. "I'll take care of that right now. She'll be gone before y'all get there." Colleen faded out.

"We'll handle Vivianne," said Nate.

"God bless you," said Darius. "Where are the other two?"

"Arianna is at Calista's house—"

"*What?* How? How in the hell did that happen?" He got loud again.

"Long story," said Nate. "I dropped her off."

"I thought you were on my side," said Darius. "You better be on my side. I'm the one paying your bill. If you took her over there, you can go get her out of there."

"I think she's leaving under her own steam," I said. "I heard at The Cracked Pot this morning she'd rented a house. No idea whose."

"Rented a *house*? How long is she planning on staying?" asked Darius.

"Indefinitely, is what she told me," said Nate.

"Why would she do that?" asked Darius.

"Said she's here to help you prove your innocence," said Nate.

Darius heaved a heavy sigh. "Well, I guess it's more than I deserve that she cares whether they lock me up or not."

"Which brings us to Lily," I said. "She's been holding daily press conferences at the gazebo at the park."

"Oh lord, lord." Darius shook his head.

"She seems to think the two of you are on the verge of patching things up," I said.

"Unh-uh. No. No way," said Darius. "I strongly suspect that

sweet young thing married me for my money to begin with. And I'm already giving her plenty of it."

"And that reminds me," I said. "What are your plans for Devlin's Point?"

He squinted, blinked at me. "I'm gonna live there. What do you mean? Are you asking me if I'm planning to throw big parties or something? 'Cause I'm not really a party kind a guy, in case you worried about that."

"I'm asking if you have plans to develop it—put up a hotel, a resort, anything of that nature," I said.

"*Hell* no. Why in this world would I do something like that? One reason I came home was to get away from crowds."

"Something Lily said." I felt a bit of the tension in my shoulders ease.

"That girl has always got big plans for something." Darius shook his head. "I've got to get my house in order, I can see that. But none of those women have anything to do with Trina Lynn."

Nate followed Palm Boulevard as it turned left, then stayed straight onto Forty-first Street. We were nearly to the marina. "We're going to have to wait for the 2:30 ferry. Darius, you hungry? Liz and I didn't have a chance to have lunch."

"Yeah, I'm starving. I haven't hardly eaten a damn thing since Tuesday morning," said Darius.

"I don't see any signs of the media," I said. "The reporters must've all stayed behind to compare notes on the creek spout. We're clear for the moment."

Nate pulled down to the parking lot in front of Morgan Creek Grill and we got out and climbed the steps to the Upper Deck. It was still plenty hot, in the high eighties, but the breeze was nice, and there was a roof over the deck to keep the worst of the sun at bay. We didn't need to be told Darius wanted to be outside.

We grabbed a table by the rail. Our server put down menus and asked for our drink order. Nate and I ordered unsweetened tea.

Darius glanced at the menu. "Bring me a Corona and one of every appetizer on this menu. And a Creek Burger, medium, add mayonnaise." He looked at us. "I'm gonna need help eating them appetizers. What ch'all want?"

Nate ordered a burger, and I went with the mahi mahi tacos. I knew we weren't going to eat all that food, but went with the spirit of the occasion. When the food arrived, we had to slide another table over just to hold it all. Darius ordered another beer and told the waitress to bring the check. He paid the bill and we munched until we saw the ferry approaching. We all grabbed one more bite as we stood, then rushed down the steps and piled into the car.

Nate pushed the button, and the car misfired again. He muttered a couple curses and tried again. It started on the third try.

"How old's this car?" asked Darius.

"Less than a year," said Nate.

"They sure don't make cars like they used to," said Darius. "If I was you, I'd be having a serious conversation with a car dealer."

"It's something simple. I'll pop the hood and check things out myself as soon as we get home." Nate drove around to the Stella Maris ferry dock and pulled the car onto the ferry.

It wasn't rare for mid-afternoon ferries to be mostly empty. We were relieved and grateful to be the only car that trip. We all got out and climbed to the upper deck to enjoy the fresh air. As the ferry glided across the water, we all turned to our own thoughts. I puzzled over everything we'd learned that day. There was no way around the fact that Trina Lynn's killer was a woman. That made things easier in some respects. We could eliminate a few possibilities. But just because Brantley Miller was innocent in the matter of her death didn't mean he wasn't dangerous. Then again, he could be exactly who Darius thought he was, a slightly nerdy college kid.

When we were closing in on the ferry dock, but still a ways out in Pearson's Inlet, we all went back downstairs and climbed into the car. Colleen reappeared in the backseat. "I'm still working on Vivianne. She's stubborn. And apparently not given to fear of spirits and such. I went full on poltergeist on her. She's fixin' to do a sage cleanse on the whole house. But I'll get her out of there."

I've met her. She's a piece of work.

Nate pushed the button, and the car misfired again.

Before he could push it a second time, Colleen yelled, "Freeze."

Nate and I looked at her.

"Out of the car, *now*." She disappeared, then reappeared on the deck.

We scrambled to follow her.

"Out. Out. *Out*." Nate yelled.

We both flung open our doors and dove out of the car.

Darius opened his and hopped out. "What's the matter with y'all?"

Colleen said, "*Get off the ferry*."

"You mean jump in the water?" Nate forgot and spoke out loud.

"*Now!*" Colleen reared back and touched her temples. *Jump in the water, now!*

She was broadcasting, throwing the thought to the crew.

"Jump," hollered Nate. "Everyone, into the water."

"You crazy," said Darius. "I ain't jumping in no damn water."

Nate and I grabbed his arms and ran towards the rail. We hopped over and pulled him with us.

"Let go a me—" Darius yelled. "Ahhhh!"

We hit the water and went under.

I kicked towards the surface and breached it just in time to see Colleen blowing the ferry captain and his single crew member off the ferry with a gust of wind she conjured with a wave of her arm. She spun around. Everyone was in the water. She shot upwards in a golden column of light and disappeared.

The Explorer exploded in a fiery ball. Seconds later, the ferry went with it.

We all treaded water staring at the flames.

"Sonavabitch." My mind raced through everyone we'd interviewed that week. Who had done this?

"Day-um," said Darius. "That's a recall gonna set Ford back. How did y'all know it was gonna explode like that? Has it been in the news? Exploding Explorers?"

Nate and I exchanged a glance.

"No," I said. "We just have finely tuned instincts."

"I'll never question that again," said Darius.

TWENTY-FOUR

By the time we swam to shore, Blake, his number two Clay Cooper—Darius's cousin—a fire truck with four Stella Maris volunteer firemen, and the EMTs were in the parking lot. A crowd of curious Stella Maris residents had begun to form. Blake had the area roped off with crime scene tape. Because they went off the other side, the ferry crew reached land before we did, and were being examined.

I'd lost my sandals in the water—the second pair of Kate Spade shoes the inlet had claimed. The rocks along the waterfront near the dock dug into my bare feet. Nate had ahold of my arm, helping me navigate.

Blake offered me a hand. I grabbed it, and Nate handed me over.

"You all right?" The look in Blake's eyes told me exactly how shook up he was.

"I'm fine." I stepped into the grass alongside the parking lot and stayed there. The asphalt was rough and no doubt scorching hot.

"Nate?" Blake turned back towards him.

"I'm good, thanks." Nate cleared the rocks and came to stand beside me. "Darius, you got it?"

Darius picked his way through the rocks, muttering curses.

"Oh yeah. I'ma tell you what, though. This has been the most stressful week of my entire life. And I've been on TV for years. I don't remember things being this exciting on this lil' island. I came home for peace and quiet. Seems like you all outta that here." He looked at Blake like maybe he was responsible.

"And from where I sit, it looks like you brought all the crazy with you," said Blake.

Darius muttered something, continued picking his way slowly across the rocks.

Blake turned to me and Nate. "What the hell happened?"

Nate said, "The Explorer started giving me trouble this morning. Lurching, misfiring. I was gonna take a look at it as soon as we got home. Didn't had a chance. We rode up top on the ferry. When we got back in the car, I went to start it to run the air conditioning as we approached the dock. It missed again. And then something didn't smell right." Nate ran a hand through his hair, looked around, shook his head. I knew he was struggling to explain why we all jumped in the water. We couldn't say, *because our guardian spirit told us to.*

Colleen appeared beside him. "I remembered reading this article where some guy's car was acting just like that and someone had rigged it to explode. As soon as I recalled that, something just told me we should get out of the car and off the ferry. I just knew."

Nate repeated what she'd said verbatim.

Blake blinked at him. "You think somebody bombed your car?"

Nate hesitated.

Colleen said, "It's not a bomb. In the article I read, someone ran a wire from a spark plug to the gas tank. Just a piece of wire. And it caused the car to explode, after it misfired for a day or two."

Nate parroted Colleen.

Darius's face was contorted in disbelief. "Was somebody trying to kill *you*, or me?"

"That's a fair question," said Nate. "I don't know. Of course it will probably take weeks for forensics to analyze whatever they're able to pull out of the water. I could be wrong. It's just a guess."

"No," said Colleen. "That's exactly what happened."

Who did that? I threw the thought at her.

"No idea," she said. "That's all I've been given."

One of the EMTs approached our group. "Everyone okay over here?"

We all assured him we were fine. None of us wanted to be examined.

Blake said, "Charleston Sheriff's Office is sending an underwater recovery team. I've got an emergency call in to the mayor. We've got to replace the Amelia Ruth as quickly as possible. I'm hoping for a loaner from the North Carolina Ferry System. Otherwise, we could be down a while. Plenty of folks have private boats for pleasure, but most everyone on the island depends on the ferry."

"We're going to need to charter something to get some of the visitors back to Isle of Palms, aren't we?" I asked. "I mean, there are a lot of folks here with no place to sleep."

"I'm already on it," said Blake. "Their cars will be stuck here temporarily. But I've rounded up volunteers who can take anyone back who needs to go. The Robinsons are going to coordinate it all through the marina."

"I've got a boat," said Darius. "Chris Craft. It's docked over at the marina."

"That's excellent news," I said. "We're going to need to borrow it."

"Borrow it? I'll take you wherever you need to go..." said Darius. "Aww, hell. I can't leave the island anyway. I got this damn ankle monitor. And that's a brand new boat. I ain't even driven it but once myself."

Blake said, "Darius, I thought you might want to stay at the bed and breakfast. It'll be quieter there, and that's where Nell and

Bill are. Coop too, when he's off duty."

"Thank ya," said Darius. "But I understand my lawyer wants me at home. But I could use your help getting my second ex-wife out my house."

Blake lifted his cap, dug his fingers through his hair, then resettled the cap. "I'll send Clay with you. He can run her off and keep an eye on things. Hey, Coop." He motioned for Clay to join us.

"Drop Liz and Nate off, then take Darius home. Clear out any trespassers. I need you to stay there with him tonight instead of going back to the B&B. Maybe a few nights. You okay with that?"

"Sure." Clay grinned. "It'll be just like old times."

Darius smiled. "Sounds good. Thank ya, cuz."

Clay said, "Blake, you ready for me to take them on now?"

"Yeah," said Blake. "I know where they are if I need them. Hey—nobody go running off on that boat tonight. Let's let some of the dust settle. See if we can figure out what we've got here. For now, you're all safer here."

I was thinking how we were all virtually trapped on the island with at least four potential murderers.

TWENTY-FIVE

The first thing Nate did when we got out of Clay's squad car at our house was check my car over with a fine-tooth comb.

"No extra wires under the hood or around the gas tank." He slammed the hood. "Until we know who did what to the Explorer, promise me you won't start the engine without checking both places."

"I won't," I said. "So you think that was about us, not Darius?"

"Has to be. No one except Fraser knew we were picking Darius up," said Nate.

"But if it was done the way Colleen said...doesn't that sound improvised to you? And I keep going over it in my head. Whose chain have we yanked recently?"

"Let's go upstairs, sort through everything. You want dinner?" asked Nate.

"No, please. We had lunch late, and I had way too much of it. I want a hot shower, a glass of wine, and possibly some popcorn later to munch on."

"Sounds like a plan."

Forty-five minutes later, I had showered, washed my hair, applied a layer of orange body butter, and slipped into my pink plaid pajama shorts and tank. I pulled on a short robe and some fluffy socks and decided to let my hair dry naturally. Nate waited on the sofa in the office with two glasses and an open bottle of pinot noir.

"Guys have it so easy," I said.

"How's that?"

"It only takes you ten minutes to shower and change." I sat beside him.

"But then we have a long list of guy stuff we have to do that you ladies don't need to worry about."

"Like what?"

"Now I can't tell you that. That would be a violation of the guy code." He poured me a glass of wine.

"Thank you." I took the glass and a long sip.

Nate stood and walked to the case board. "I'll man the marker this evening. Obviously, we're looking for a woman."

"Possibly one with a connection to Olympia Price," I said.

"Possibly," said Nate. "But that's assuming Captain Price's motive is to protect the real murderer. I'd sure hate to believe that was the case. It could also be she pressured Sonny and Jenkins to make an arrest purely because she believed in Darius's guilt based on the murder weapon being found in the bag he discarded. Something this high profile, there'd be pressure to make a quick arrest."

"Or Captain Price has a connection to Trina Lynn, which clouds her judgement, or some reason to be predisposed to believe in Darius's guilt. There's a reason Sonny sent that message through Moon."

"Fair point," said Nate. "Sonny is wary of the special interest she's taken in the case, so we should be."

I took my wineglass and moved to my desk. "I'll see what I can find out about her."

Nate picked up the eraser. "And since we've established, based on the timeline and the combined accounts of the twins and Vicki Turpitt, that our killer is a woman, I'll get rid of some of the men on our case board." He erased Kevin Looney's name. "Poor Kevin didn't kill Trina, and I think we can rule out someone jealous of his affection for her, which takes him off the board altogether."

"Agreed." I opened a profile on Captain Olympia Price.

"And it wasn't our local anchorman, Grey Hamilton," said Nate. "But it could have been a woman who wanted Trina Lynn out of the way."

"So we still need to talk to him, see if he knows of any candidates. He probably has a stalker or two himself."

"And an ex-girlfriend or two." Nate studied the board.

"We can rule out Walker Nance. And honestly, I don't think it was Julia. Following up on her should be a low priority, I think."

"It's not Brantley Miller," said Nate. "A long-shot theory would be a twisted person who fancied themselves his avenger."

I looked up at him. "Depending on what his family situation was with the Millers, that could get pretty dark."

"Let's not go down that particular rabbit hole just yet," said Nate.

"We can come back to farfetched notions if none of the more likely narratives prove out."

"I'm erasing male family members," said Nate. "And August Lockwood, although I have to tell you, that doesn't sit right with me. Something about him...But Vicki was convincing when she said it was a woman who ran out of that alley."

All the photos of Trina Lynn on his walls. They were best friends, but even her mother said she wouldn't've been surprised to learn they were seeing each other.

Nate moved towards the sofa.

"Wait," I said.

Nate stopped, looked at me expectantly.

"Auggie and Trina's relationship was close," I said. "What if someone who has designs on Auggie misunderstood the situation? Thought he and Trina Lynn were lovers?"

"Could've been any of the members of his harem. Except Jaelyn White. She's black. Vicki was nearly certain the woman she saw was white, and the woman the twins saw—the same woman— was definitely white. Then again, all those girls were with Auggie the night of the murder, at the fire pit. His alibi alibis them as well."

"There's that." I bit my lip, chewed on it just a little. "But there's a pathology there. Something about him and those women is off."

"I'll give you that much. But right now my money is on one of Darius's ex-wives." Nate returned to the sofa and propped up his feet, commenced studying the case board.

I turned back to Captain Olympia Price. But on paper she was as upstanding as they come. She was married, with three grown children and two grandchildren. She and her husband had lived in the same West Ashley neighborhood for more than twenty-five years, and she'd worked at the Charleston Police Department for nearly that long. She volunteered with a long list of charitable organizations. And I could find no connection between her and anyone related to our case.

"Whatever is going on with Captain Price, we're not going to find it with a computer," I said.

"Why don't we walk through our current theory of the crime," said Nate. "I think that would be helpful."

"Okay," I said, "our perpetrator lured Trina Lynn to the alley on the pretext of giving her information regarding the petty officer's case. This person was not connected to that particular story, but could've had a connection to another story."

"This person knew Trina Lynn had a history with Darius," said Nate.

"Right. She waits for Trina Lynn in the alley, or perhaps Trina got there first. Either way, they met in the alley around 10:00. They argued. And the woman shot Trina. Then she ran out the alley on the Queen Street end, crossed Queen, and walked left towards East

Bay."

"She may have walked around a bit to see if anyone followed her. But pretty soon after that she must've headed down to White Point Garden. She was somewhere in that immediate area when Darius walked up and threw the bag in the trash can."

"Which had to have been pure luck—no one could've predicted he would even take a walk, much less discard a bag," I said.

"Right. But she's a fast thinker. She saw him discard the bag, sign an autograph, take a photo, and she waited for a moment when no one else was around, then she dug the bag out and put the gun inside," said Nate.

"And Margie Sue and Mary-Lou saw her, and at that point she had changed clothes, but it had to have been the same person."

"The shopping bag she had with her. She probably stashed that somewhere with the long skirt and big shirt, then just pulled on the skirt and switched the hoodie for the shirt," said Nate.

"But Mo and Jim still had to be close enough that she could catch up to them and follow them back to 86 Cannon," I said.

"Right. She waits until their backs are to her, digs out the bag, sticks the gun inside, and hurries to catch up to them," said Nate.

"As soon as she sees where they're staying, she calls the tip line and reports that she has witnessed Darius Baker dispose of a gun at White Point Garden, gives Mo Heedles's name—she probably overheard her telling Darius her name for the autograph."

"The police run ballistics on the gun. It's the murder weapon, but there are no prints on it, I'm guessing. Sonny knows the tip doesn't smell right, but his bosses' boss is sold," said Nate.

"The other thing we know about our culprit is that we have recently rattled them enough that they would try to blow us up," I said.

Nate rolled his lips in and out. "You know, you're right. And that rules out a lot of people right there. We haven't had enough time yet to rattle that many cages." He took the eraser to the case board and rubbed off everyone we hadn't had any contact with at all.

"My gut tells me this is one of Auggie's entourage. I'm going to vet those alibis some more," I said. "They saw me driving the Explorer. They thought that was my car. Whoever it was, it was me they were trying to kill. They saw me going in and out of Auggie's apartment twice in two days and saw me as a new threat on two fronts."

"I don't know...that feels thin to me," said Nate.

"You just don't know how devious women can be," I said.

"Is that a fact?"

"Not me, of course." I rolled my eyes at him. "I don't have a devious bone in my body. Well, except in the line of duty."

"I'll bear in mind you have those skills in your arsenal," said Nate.

"I'm going to start profiles on every one of Auggie's entourage—except Jaelyn. And I want to know more about Olympia Price."

"I'll verify arrivals for all of Darius's ex-wives," said Nate. "If one of them hired someone, the shooter has already left the country. That's going to be hard to prove. We need access to banking records to trace payments, that sort of thing. That's technology we don't have. We'd need someone in law enforcement to get a warrant."

"Let's put that in the contingency pile," I said. "For after we've eliminated all the other possibilities."

I moved back to the sofa, curled up beside him, and mulled our revised case board. We'd deleted most of the men, but added Auggie's women.

Suspect	Motives
Spouse of Lover/Wannabe - Julia Nance	Jealousy

- August Lockwood's admirers
  - Bailey Hart
  - Camille Shaw
  - Finn Weathers
  - Saige Martin
  - Yeats Collins

Family
- Georgia Causby	Unknown
- Laura Beth Causby	Unknown
- Sister-in-law	Unknown

Darius's Ex-Wives	Jealousy/Financial
- Arianna English	
- Vivianne Whitley	
- Lily McAdams	

"We still have way too many unknown motives on this case board," I said.

"All we can do is eliminate the knowns one by one."

"Julia Nance didn't know I was spying on her," I said. "We can strike her because she has no idea who we are. She certainly didn't try to kill us."

"Good point. I missed her."

"I hope it's not one of Darius's ex-wives," I said. "I like him. I think he sincerely believes none of them are capable of murder. For his sake, I want him to be right. But all that money...Darius has giraffe money. That kind of money changes people. It doesn't seem to have changed him though, not really."

An odd look passed across Nate's face.

"What are you thinking?" I asked.

"Huh? Oh...nothing. I like Darius too. You think Colleen has him slotted for the empty council seat?"

I scrutinized him. For the second time in the last few days, I had the feeling something was off with my husband. Something was bothering him, but he wasn't ready to talk about it just yet.

I said, "Of course she does. Otherwise she wouldn't have spent three nights at the county jail."

Nate looked towards the ceiling. "Do you hear that?"

"What?"

"Sounds like a helicopter," he said.

I listened. It was unmistakable. I shrugged. "Could be. It's after midnight. You ready for bed?"

"Why, Mrs. Andrews, I'm happy to escort you upstairs whenever you're ready and tuck you in."

TWENTY-SIX

Nate, Rhett, and I were in the middle of our morning run on the beach when Mamma called. We slowed to a walk so I could answer.

"Elizabeth, have you seen your father?" She was distraught.

"What do you mean?" I asked. "It's 5:30 in the morning. Isn't he at home?"

"I woke up and he was gone. There's no note. I have no idea what's happened to him. He wasn't feeling well yesterday. I told him it was because he was out in the night air riding around in the golf cart Thursday night like he didn't have a lick of sense. His temperature was back up. I'm afraid he's wandering around the town in a feverish state or something."

"Have you called Blake?"

"Of course. He hasn't seen him either. Neither has your sister."

"Mamma, try not to worry. He's got to be on the island somewhere. We'll find him. I'll call you back." I ended the call.

"Daddy—"

"I heard. You want to check in with Blake?"

I'd already tapped the line in my favorites list. "I am."

Blake answered on the first ring. "I'm just walking into the station. I'll get Sam and Rodney doing a grid search. Call me if you find him."

"We'll be right there," I said. "We can cover more territory if we divvy up the island into smaller chunks. We'll help."

"Makes sense."

We ran back to the house, hopped in my car and zipped over to the police station, speeding and running red lights. I had barely stopped the car before we hopped out and ran into the police station.

Blake stood by Nell's desk with Rodney Murphy and Sam Manigault. Rodney was talking, stopped in mid-sentence. Blake massaged his temples, his eyes closed. They all looked at us when we rushed in.

"Blake?" Just then I needed him to tell me Daddy was all right.

"He's at MUSC," said Blake.

"What? How?" The ferry was destroyed. Mamma had no idea where he was.

Rodney said, "Blake, again, I swear it never occurred to me that your mamma didn't know."

"He called 911 just before midnight. MUSC sent a helicopter."

Nate and I exchanged a glance.

"He went to the hospital in a helicopter without Mamma?" I said. "Why on earth would he do that? How could that even happen?"

"I don't know," said Blake. "We'll have to ask him."

We borrowed Darius's boat. Every other available boat that seated more than four people was in the rotation at the marina keeping people shuttled back and forth to the Isle of Palms Marina. Mamma, Nate and I, Blake, and Merry and Joe piled in. Blake drove the Chris Craft 36, which I might have enjoyed in other circumstances, to Ripley Light Marina off the Ashley River. I ordered an Uber to meet us and take us to the hospital. Poppy met us there.

Mamma inquired at the desk and learned that Daddy had been

admitted. We all went straight up to his room. Mamma pushed the door open and we all crowded in. He was sleeping. Tears slipped down Mamma's face.

She walked up to the left-hand side of the bed and laid her hand gently on his.

He opened his eyes. "Red bird," he said. "What are you doing here?" He blinked, looked around and saw the rest of us. He started to say something, then stopped and just laid there with his mouth open slightly.

"Frank," said Mamma. "Are you all right?"

"Yeah, uh...I didn't expect them to make such a fuss, really," he said.

"What happened? Why didn't you wake me up?" Mamma asked.

"Well, I woke up feeling hot," Daddy said. "I was afraid my fever had gone back up even more. But..." He gestured with both hands. "Well, you were mad at me to begin with. I just thought I'd have the doctor take my temperature and I'd be straight back home. I didn't expect to be drug across to the hospital in a helicopter."

"I don't understand," said Poppy. "Why did they bring you in the helicopter?"

"Dad," said Blake. "You called 911."

"Well, I thought it would ring over to the station, and Rodney would carry me over to Warren Harper's," said Daddy. "I felt a little disoriented, didn't want to drive."

"Dad, you know we're part of Charleston County's centralized 911 now," said Blake.

"Well, I forgot about that," said Daddy. "It was the middle of the night. I didn't want to disturb your mamma. I thought I'd be right back. But when Rodney came to get me, the helicopter was already on the way. He carried me over to the high school and they had me strapped down on a stretcher and up in the air before I could explain."

Blake closed his eyes, massaged his temples.

"The doctors here checked you over good, right?" I asked.

"Oh, yeah," he said. "They've run all kinds of tests."

"Why have they admitted you?" asked Mamma.

"Well, you know how I'm afraid of heights," said Daddy. "I really, really didn't want to get in that helicopter. I had some kind of anxiety attack, they think it was. But at the time, they thought it was my heart." Daddy chuckled. "They admitted me for observation."

For a minute we all just stared at him.

Mamma said, "So in the middle of the night, you woke up, didn't feel good, and instead of waking me up, you called 911."

"I didn't want to disturb you. You'd had a bad day. You'd just got to sleep good," said Daddy. "And you were still mad at me for going off in the golf cart."

"You scared me to death." Mamma's eyes were large. She was working on a good head of steam.

"Well, Carolyn, I was just trying to be considerate," said Daddy.

"But you're all right," Merry confirmed.

"I still have a fever, but the doctor said it's nothing to worry about," said Daddy.

"That's good," said Mamma. She brushed his hair back from his face. "Because when you get home, I'm am going to cheerfully kill you. And I would be sorely disappointed to be robbed of that pleasure."

TWENTY-SEVEN

Poppy dropped everyone but me off at the marina. I called an Uber and went to the airport to rent a car. By 7:30, I was headed out of the airport and back towards Charleston in a cream-colored Ford Edge. I drove back to the marina and waited for Nate to return in Darius's boat with our laptops and some basic equipment. We'd lost tens of thousands of dollars' worth of equipment in the back of the Explorer. It would take weeks—and lots of money—to replace it all. Just then I was pondering the deductible on our insurance.

It was almost 9:00 when Nate called and said he was pulling into the marina. I met him at the dock and helped move equipment to the back of the Edge.

"Maybe we should both stay in town today," said Nate. "I can work on my laptop from the passenger seat while you do your thing."

I tilted my head, flashed him a look that said, *Give me a break.*

"Okay, fine. I'm headed back to the house then." He kissed me goodbye. "Call me when you're ready for me to pick you up."

Auggie agreed to meet me in the clubhouse at Cooper River Farms. I had no desire whatsoever to go back to his apartment. His entourage might well all have some sort of pathological attachment to him. But in my personal experience, he invited attention from any woman handy. They could likely all benefit from the counsel of a high-dollar therapist. The question was, which one of them was a killer?

Architecturally, the clubhouse resembled a large farmhouse attached to a barn with a metal grain bin with huge windows in between the two. As I climbed the steps to the wide front porch, I scanned the area for any of Auggie's groupies. If they were there, they were well-hidden.

The main room of the clubhouse had soaring ceilings and exposed beams. Auggie waited in a leather chair facing the stone fireplace. I took a seat on the cream-colored sofa to his right.

"Thanks for seeing me again," I said.

His gaze seemed fixated on the fireplace. He looked up after a few seconds. "Have you found anything?"

"I'm not sure. I'm hoping you can help me sort it out," I said.

"I'll do my best." His eyes returned to the fireplace.

"The night Trina Lynn was killed, you were at the fire pit here, with your friends, right?"

"You know I was. Your husband has spoken to all of them."

"Right. It's not your alibi I'm questioning," I said.

He turned his head, looked at me directly, gave me a look that said, *What kind of bullshit is this?*

"You have a lot of girlfriends," I said.

"I have friends who are girls," he said tiredly, like maybe he had defended this before.

"Is that what happened to your long-term relationship? Your girlfriend didn't care for you spending so much time in the company of women?"

"That was part of it," said Auggie. "But we parted friends. It was actually Camille. We were engaged."

"Who broke it off?" I was pretty sure I knew the answer.

"I did," he said. "We want different things. It's good we

recognized it before we were married."

"Was Trina Lynn part of your...circle of friends?" I asked.

"Trina? No. She enjoyed her own company. And she spent time with Grey. And Walker. Her family."

"Did you spend a lot of time with her one on one?"

He lifted a shoulder. "I guess. We worked together. We discussed work. We were best friends."

"You have coffee with her alone, dinner, like that?"

"Sure. A couple times a week," he said.

"How did your other friends like that?"

He squinted at me. "I never asked."

"I have no doubt you were here the night Trina Lynn died." This was a lie. I thought it possible they had all collaborated on her death for some twisted reason. Not likely, but plausible. "But I need you to think back very carefully. I'm guessing an evening by the fire pit with your...group...that's something you do frequently."

"That's right."

"You're all relaxed, drinking beer. It's possible those evenings sort of blur together in your memories."

"It's possible, I guess, to some degree," he said. "What are you getting at?"

"Are you certain all six of those women—Bailey, Camille, Finn, Jaelyn, Saige and Yeats—were here this past Monday night? When you dashed out that list, could you have written all those names because they're all usually here, and not because of a specific memory of that particular night?"

He studied the ceiling. After a long moment he said, "Camille wasn't there. She said she had a headache and was going to bed early. I had forgotten about that. But seriously, Camille isn't capable of murder."

"What does Camille do for a living?" I already knew the answer to this, but I wanted him to help me convince himself.

"She's a production assistant at WCSC."

"She worked with you and Trina?"

"Yes."

"Who do you think will take Trina Lynn's place?"

Auggie turned to me, paled a bit. Very softly he said. "Likely Camille."

"So she stands to not only gain professionally, but also to take Trina's place at your side every day. Working together, having dinner, coffee...How did she take the breakup?"

"Not well at first, but I thought we were past all that. I can't believe she would..."

"I need some more time to look into this. It's possible she didn't. But if she did, I need proof."

He nodded. "Okay."

"Call her," I said. "Get her to come over here. Keep her here until I text you, can you do that?"

He licked his lips, nodded, his face grim. "All right."

TWENTY-EIGHT

With a quick look around to verify no one was around to see me, I took my pick set to Camille's lock. Standard equipment for many apartment complexes, it was an easy task. Camille's apartment was the same floorplan as Auggie's, but was decorated in soft blues and creams with a beach vibe. I started in her bathroom.

Medicine cabinets are often a treasure trove of information. Camille's told me she was on birth control, had allergies, and was likely being treated for either depression or bipolar disorder. The combination of Aripiprazole, Lexapro, Celexa, lithium, and Prozac could mean they were prescribed one at a time to try to combat depression. Or it could mean she was on a drug cocktail of some sort. I took photos of each bottle and moved on to the bathroom drawers.

The rest of the bathroom yielded nothing of interest, so I moved to the bedroom closet. It was a well-organized small walk-in, so well-organized it brought to mind my own closet. Sometimes tendencies were assets until they took over your life. I was self-aware enough to know I needed to watch myself. All the hat boxes and containers in Camille's closet were labeled except for one. I slid it from the bottom of the stack and opened the lid.

She and Auggie must've dated for several years. The photos were all of the two of them, sometimes with others, but they all reflected happy memories. I felt bad for her. She'd had a happy relationship. Did she hold Trina Lynn responsible for its demise?

I took a photo of the box and its contents, then took a deeper pass at the rest of the closet. She owned black clothing, but then again, so did I. Nothing else in the closet seemed out of the ordinary.

I moved to the bedroom and started with the nightstand. Thirty minutes later I had gone through every drawer in the bedroom and found nothing of note. I went back to the living room and settled in at Camille's desk. She didn't have the password to her laptop in the top drawer. I attached a small silver microcomputer via the USB port and launched a sequence to open the laptop. It took less than five minutes.

Nothing remarkable was in her email. I opened her photos and started scanning the electronic images. It didn't take long to figure out Camille had stalked Auggie and Trina Lynn. There were photos of them at work, closeups of their faces concentrating on something, laughing, perhaps arguing. Photos at dinner, in a bar, at a formal affair. Camille had clearly been obsessed with their relationship.

I checked the dates on a few of the photos. Some were older, up to two years ago. But some were much more recent.

I grabbed a hard drive from my bag and saved a sampling of the photos.

My phone dinged with a text from Auggie. *She's on her way back.*

I packed up my things and got out of there. Outside the door, I dashed for the stairs just as the elevator arrived.

TWENTY-NINE

I called Nate and told him what I'd found. "The only thing I wasn't able to patch together is how she knew about Darius's connection to Trina Lynn. But she's a journalist by trade. If she went digging into Trina Lynn, she would've found the marriage license."

"And then Darius turns up at the wrong place at the wrong time and she improvises," said Nate. "That fits. Are you ready for me to pick you up?"

"Not yet," I said. "We need to figure out how to get proof. Right now we don't have enough to exonerate Darius. I'm going to run by Carmella's, see if I can get a receipt for the cannoli. If we don't have proof it was Camille, if we can get Darius off the hook and try to get Sonny probable cause for a search warrant, he can likely find more in Camille's apartment than I was able to find today. Maybe some of those black clothes have gunshot residue, but I couldn't test them. The XCat was in the Explorer. That'll be an expensive toy to replace."

Nate was quiet for a few seconds. "We'll work it out. Promise me you won't stress over the money. The insurance will cover most of it. I have some money set aside. We'll be fine. I promise you."

"It's not just the equipment," I said. "It's that on top of everything else. We've got to have a new roof—"

"Liz, do you trust me?"

"Of course, you know I do—"

"This is not something you need to be worrying your pretty head over."

"Ooooh! Lookit. I am not a child—"

"Okay, I'm an idiot. That came out wrong. Everything's going to be all right. I promise you."

"I wish I could just turn off the part of me that can't stop adding up the cost of all this, but I can't."

"Stress never helped anything," said Nate. "Shall I pick you up in an hour?"

"I'll call you. I want to do a run by Olympia Price's neighborhood."

"Why?"

"I want to know why she tried to railroad Darius."

"We may never know that. It's in her head, whatever it is. She's a seasoned police captain. She's not going to confide that to you."

"I'm well aware of that." I might have been the teensiest bit testy on account of I felt like he was patronizing me on the money issue.

He sighed. "I know better than to try to dissuade you from doing whatever you have your mind set on. Just give me a thirty minutes' heads up and I'll pick you up at the marina in Charleston."

"Any news on a loaner ferry?"

"Yeah, Blake said they'd have that in place later this afternoon."

"All right. I'll call you."

I had lunch at Carmella's while the very cooperative lady behind the counter pulled the receipts from Sunday evening. There was a cash receipt for two cannoli at 10:15. Since no one was a hundred percent precise on the timeline, and there was nothing to tie Darius to the receipt, it didn't exonerate him by itself. But if the young lady who served him happened to recognize him, it would definitely help with reasonable doubt if it came down to it. She was due to come in at 3:00. I would pop back by for a cannolo and a chat.

Until then, I had a small slice of time on my hands and a nagging curiosity regarding Captain Olympia Price. It was a few minutes after one when I drove over to West Ashley. Captain Price lived in a large brick ranch on a shady corner lot in a well-established neighborhood. It had the feel of an old-fashioned community, as opposed to one of those with new houses, no trees, and people that moved in and out with a job change every few years.

On a Saturday, I expected someone of Captain Price's rank to be home. I parked down the street and pulled out my binoculars, hoping to get a look at her. I had no plans to break and enter her house. That would've been beyond reckless. I was pondering another way to get inside...a pretext, maybe...when she came out with a large cardboard box.

Trim, with a no-nonsense short haircut, she was attractive. I watched as she put the box in the back of a white Chevrolet Tahoe. I laid down the binoculars and picked up my phone. I zoomed in as far as I could and snapped her picture. She scanned the neighborhood, the way I sometimes do when I'm up to something I'd rather not be seen doing. What was that all about? A switch tripped on my internal alarm panel.

She closed the lift gate and went back inside. Why was she hell-bent on rushing to arrest Darius? Yes, the gun was compelling evidence, but there was a witness who'd not even been interviewed. Vicki Turpitt's account, when paired with that of the twins, made it virtually impossible for Trina Lynn's killer to have been a black man. Was Captain Price over-compensating, trying to avoid any appearance of favoritism because Darius was a celebrity? Was this woman just a garden variety racist? It was hard to imagine how she'd risen as far as she had in rank if that were the case.

She came back twice more with boxes and put them in the back of the car. Then she went back inside and came out with a purse. She climbed in, started the car, and backed out of her driveway.

Naturally, I followed.

I followed her all the way to the Salvation Army Family Store and donation center on Rivers Avenue in North Charleston. She dropped off all her boxes, got her receipt and left.

What was in those boxes? Was there not a closer place to her home to drop them off?

"You need me to stage a distraction?" Colleen appeared beside me in the passenger seat.

"Maybe," I said. "I'm not sure why, but my gut tells me it'd be a good idea to look in those boxes. I'm nosy like that. I'll holler if I need you." I climbed out of the car.

Two guys were collecting things at the donation center, both burly, with wide smiles and greying hair. I pulled out my ditzy blonde act. "Hey, y'all. My aunt just dropped off some things, and I'm afraid she donated my lime green cardigan by accident? Would it be all right if I had a look? Those are her boxes right there. I'm happy to pay for it."

They shrugged, looked at each other. "Sure," they said in unison.

I pulled on a pair of gloves. They looked at me sideways.

"I'm allergic to wool," I said. "I think she's got some wool things in here."

The two men went about their business.

In the third box I opened, I found a black warmup suit with a hoodie.

Surely it couldn't be *the* black warmup suit. Could it? *Sonavabitch.* My heart pounded in my ears. I tore open the last remaining box.

There was the white flouncy skirt and paisley jacket. I gasped, stared at it in disbelief for a moment. Why had I never considered it could be her? I felt sucker punched.

I stood back, photographed everything. Then I turned back to the men. "These were my mother's things. She passed away recently. I can't believe Aunt Jenny gave them away. Can I please have a copy of her receipt? I'll take it inside. I'd like to buy these things back. Please." I gave them my best distraught female look, which wasn't difficult in the circumstances.

"Okay, fine." The taller one pulled a yellow copy of a receipt from his book and handed it to me. "You need to talk to Carlene inside."

Carlene was understanding. I paid four times what they would've made off the items and took them outside to my car. I put them in the back and closed the lift gate.

"She's back," said Colleen.

I scanned the area. The white Tahoe was back at the donation intake canopy. Why on earth had she come back? Had she circled back, watched to see the boxes opened and processed into inventory? Once their contents were part of the store's inventory, there would've been no way to track where the items inside came from. Still...why hadn't she burned those things? She was a veteran detective.

Oh dear heaven. This was a trap.

She'd worked with Sonny for years. She knew exactly who I was. She'd watched this case carefully from the beginning to see if he reached out to me. She'd probably been watching *us*.

God's nightgown. The police captain had blown up our car.

The gentlemen were talking earnestly to Captain Price. One of them pointed to me. She turned to look.

"This isn't good," I said to Colleen.

"All the incriminating evidence is in the back of your car," said Colleen. "And she's a police captain. How do you want to play this?"

Olympia Price walked purposely in my direction. "Annie, I told you it's time we part with those things. Your mother wouldn't want you to hold on like this. The doctors agree."

She was speaking loudly, to be overheard. What was her plan?

"She's going to try to get you in her car," said Colleen. "Whatever you do, don't get in."

"Why, Aunt Jenny," I said, too loud, and too bright. "I'm so hurt you'd discard Mamma's things when you know how much they mean to me."

She was closing in. "Let's talk privately, in my car."

"I can't right now, Aunt Jenny. I have a doctor's appointment." I hopped in the car, closed the door, and quickly locked it.

She stood right outside my window, trying to kill me with her eyes. I was certain she had more concrete plans.

"*Drive,*" hollered Colleen. She disappeared.

I started the car, put it in reverse, and hit the gas hard. Then I did a quick three-point turn and headed out Credit Union Drive towards Rivers Avenue.

I glanced in the rearview.

Captain Price was in her Tahoe, but it wasn't moving.

Colleen had either swiped her keys or disabled the car.

My mind raced.

Nate.

Where was he?

At home.

He had to get out of the house.

I turned right on Rivers.

I couldn't put any tool we'd ever used past Captain Price. I couldn't call Nate on his phone or with mine. She could've installed software to let her listen to our calls. We were careful. It was unlikely. But I couldn't bet our lives on it.

She knew we were on to her anyway. That had been the whole point of this afternoon's charade.

Thank heaven we'd prepared for a situation just like this.

I hollered at Siri and voice texted Nate two words. *Take cover.* Colleen would buy us time.

THIRTY

I turned off my phone, grabbed a burner, my laptop, a ball cap, and a few other items from the back of the rental car, and left it at a laundromat in North Charleston. Scanning constantly for Price, I walked to a grocery store a couple blocks away and called a cab. The driver dropped me off at a Walmart in Summerville and I paid him in cash. Then I waited inside the Walmart for a few minutes before walking across the parking lot to a Panera Bread. I bought a drink and settled into a back booth.

The burner wasn't a smart phone. For the moment, I couldn't use any of the technology I'd come to rely on, because it could be traced. I had no way of tracking Nate, and it made me antsy. I calculated in my head how long it should take him to pick up our safe car and get to me. Probably a couple hours.

The 2009 Ford Expedition was registered to Starlight Enterprises, an LLC James Huger had helped us set up a while back. We'd met him while working a case around Christmas the year before. He was from Old Charleston money, and was well connected. If anyone checked into Starlight Enterprises, they'd find something akin to a Russian nesting doll—one company inside another, inside another, et cetera. Eventually, they would've led back to James Huger. The Expedition was parked in a lot James Huger owned in Charleston. He was a good friend to have.

At 5:15, Nate slid into the booth across from me. "Lockwood?" He wore a quizzical expression.

"Price."

"You can't be serious."

"Deadly so."

He glanced around the restaurant. "We'd best talk while we drive."

We'd stashed the thirty-four-foot Airstream trailer at a storage lot near Summerville. The Airstream was also registered to Starlight Enterprises, as was the twenty-seven acres of land near Cottageville, a small town in Colleton County nestled in the V between I-95 and I-26. It was heavily wooded, secluded, and offered easy access to both interstates, yet it was only an hour outside of Charleston.

It took us a little more than an hour to move the trailer and get everything set up. The shiny silver tube was our escape pod. Starlight Enterprises had installed water, sewer, and electricity on the land, so we had all the modern conveniences. The stove in the compact but modern kitchen ran on propane. We had two full tanks. The trailer was stocked with clothes, toiletries, non-perishable food, and wine—a bit like a condo deep in the woods.

"When's the last time you saw Colleen?" Nate asked when we were settled into the L-shaped cream leather built-in sofa inside the trailer. A dining-height table mounted to the floor provided workspace. We both opened our laptops.

"At the Salvation Army, with Olympia Price."

"Any idea what motive she would have to kill Trina Lynn?" asked Nate.

I shook my head. "Clearly I missed something on her profile. I need to get back online and figure this out."

"Satellite dish is all set." He opened his computer. "Shall we divide and conquer?"

"Let's. I'll dive deeper into her personal life."

"I'll cast a wider net on her career."

An hour later, I was feeling frustrated and hungry. "I think I'll make us some dinner. You hungry?"

"Sounds good." Nate studied the screen.

"Anything?" I asked.

"Not yet. Food may help us think better."

"I need some pasta." Noodles always helped my brain work better.

I made a simple fettuccine Alfredo and we moved to the banquette to eat. We talked little, each going back over everything we knew about Olympia Price.

"Her financials are rock solid," I said. "The house is paid for. Neither she nor her husband have any claims for collection or liens. He's a residential contractor. There's not a hint of scandal of any sort."

"And not a glimmer of corruption on the job."

"This has to be very personal." I twirled some noodles around my fork and delivered them to my mouth.

"You think she was protecting someone?" asked Nate.

"I think that has to be it. Someone with her career...it has to be family. My guess is one of her kids. But they all seem solid. Two of them, the girls, are married with children. They both live out of state, one in Georgia, one in North Carolina. The son—Mark—he's the youngest. Thirty-five. Works for Boeing. Something technology related. No red flags on his profile whatsoever. Not so much as a parking ticket."

"Hmm...I wonder if he's that much of an upstanding citizen, or if he's had a few parking tickets taken care of."

"I have no idea how to check on that. If we could talk to Sonny, he might have heard something," I said.

"I think we need to call him on one of the burners anyway,"

said Nate. "I know we said we were going to leave him alone, but after what happened today, I think we have to let him know what's going on. Blake too. Hell, she could try to get to us through anyone we're close to."

"Oh my God." Something grabbed at my chest from the inside. "I've been so wrapped up in figuring this thing out...why didn't I think of that?"

"This has all happened fast," said Nate.

I stood, went back to the sofa to get the burner phone. "I'm calling Blake now. Let's wait on Sonny."

Later, after Blake assured me he had everyone corralled at Mamma and Daddy's house and everyone was safe, I went back to Mark Price's profile.

And there it was. I sucked in a lungful of air.

"What?" Nate looked up from his laptop.

"The petty officer's girlfriend. Antonia. What did she say her ex-boyfriend's name was?"

"Mark Wentworth." Nate furrowed his brow. "Mark's a pretty common name. What are you thinking?"

"Mark Price's middle name is Wentworth. It was his grandmother's maiden name."

"That can't be a coincidence."

I logged in to Facebook using a fake profile I kept handy for fishing expeditions.

A few clicks later I was looking at Mark Wentworth's profile. "Looks like the all-American boy-next-door." Clean shaven, with close-cropped brown hair, and hazel eyes, he was smiling in most of the photos. He was a nice-looking guy. But so was Ted Bundy.

No middle name was noted. He had no friends with the last name Price. He wasn't Facebook friends with either of his sisters. I scrolled through his photos. He was into wilderness camping, off-road four wheelers—the kind some folks liked to get muddy—and fishing. My eyes gravitated to a photo of Mark with his arm around a beautiful Latina girl. "Look." I slid my laptop towards Nate. "Is this Antonia?"

"It is."

I spun my computer back around. "I need to find a photo of Mark Price." I searched Facebook for his sisters' profiles. It didn't take long to find a photo from a cookout from just this past weekend. One with the whole family smiling outside in what I'd bet was Captain Price's backyard.

"Oh my God."

Nate turned the computer back to him. "Mark Wentworth Price goes by the name Mark Wentworth. Antonia didn't mention that, or that he was related to Captain Price. I'd bet she didn't know. Otherwise she'd have really made a stink about the police not investigating her theory that Mark had killed her boyfriend. She wouldn't have left that out."

"Unless she knew and was afraid." I was thinking out loud. "But if that were it, she wouldn't have mentioned anything about her theory. She'd have kept quiet. I think we'll have to ask Mark himself why he doesn't use his last name."

"I'll call Antonia," said Nate. "I'm sure she'll be more than happy to tell us how to get in touch with him."

"Let's head into Summerville," I said.

When we were back in Summerville, away from our safe haven, Nate drove randomly through town while I used my iPhone to call Mark and set up a meet for the following night.

Then we called Sonny on his burner from ours and brought him up to speed. When we'd formulated a plan, I called him back from my iPhone and told him Nate and I were dropping the Baker/Causby case. I waxed poetic about how I was convinced now that Darius was guilty. I was betting Olympia Price had cloned at least one of the three of our phones, likely all of them. I didn't care if she believed what I told Sonny or not. But I needed her to think Sonny believed it. And I needed her to think she was outsmarting me when she showed up in Philadelphia Alley, like I knew she would.

THIRTY-ONE

I walked in through the Cumberland Street entrance to Philadelphia Alley, just like Margie Sue and Mary-Lou had Sunday night. Mark Wentworth Price had been eager to meet with me, just like Trina Lynn had been eager to meet with his mother. Trina Lynn had thought she was meeting a witness who would give her solid information proving her theory on the petty officer case was true. Mark thought he was being blackmailed.

He no doubt planned to leave me dead in the alley just like his mother had Trina Lynn. The only question in my mind was would he call his mother and ask for help, or would he try to handle this for himself, given that he appeared not to want to be associated with his family's last name. Whether he called her or she intercepted him after listening to our call, either way, I knew who I was meeting.

She waited for me in front of the brick church wall, right where Trina Lynn died.

"Clever of you to check those boxes," she said. "Too clever. But then, I expected you would do just that."

"I'm thinking maybe a hundred thousand dollars' worth of clever," I said. "But I was expecting Mark."

"Mark won't be coming this evening. He's been detained."

"Literally?" I asked. "Did you arrest him?"

"Don't be absurd."

"I figured it would be better to deal with him directly, him being the one who killed Petty Officer Fielding Davidson and all. Also, no offense, but his job pays much better. I'm thinking he has a hundred thousand to spare."

"Ah, so you're not so smart after all," she said. "Why would I pay you or allow him to, when I can just shoot you? You're as stupid as she was."

"She wanted money from you?" This shocked me.

"Of course she didn't want money from me." Her tone dismissed me as an idiot.

"What then?" I asked. "What did she want that would make you throw away a twenty-five-year career...a distinguished service record...why?" Of course I already knew the answer to this question.

"She didn't want anything." Her voice was harsh. "She would have taken everything."

"Ooooh," I said. "She wanted the story. She figured it all out, and she was going to put it on the news. Decorated police captain's son murdered a petty officer in cold blood."

"And what do you know about anything?" She sneered at me.

She wanted to know what all I knew. And most importantly, who all I'd told. She wouldn't kill me straightway after all.

"I know plenty. The only question that remains is, are you willing to pay for my silence?"

"Have you no decency?" she asked.

"Enough that I don't shoot people in alleys and try to blame an innocent man," I said.

She stilled. "I didn't plan to frame Darius. He was convenient."

"How could you? You've given your life to upholding the law."

She laughed harshly. "I have. And the law would have taken my family from me. Maybe someday you'll appreciate the importance of family loyalty. Very few people your age do."

"I'm plenty loyal to my family. None of them have killed anybody."

She stepped backward, as if I'd slapped her. "Mark wasn't in his right mind. Any jury would see that. That cheap hussy drove him wild running around. She apparently had a thing for men in uniform."

"I'm curious, did Petty Officer Davidson save that young girl from the sex trafficking ring before Mark killed him? Was Trina Lynn right? Or was that some other Good Samaritan?"

Her weary eyes glittered with hatred. "He did a good thing, saving that girl. I'm not saying he didn't."

"So, the petty officer stops on his way home from his girlfriend's house for pizza. He sees the attempted kidnapping going down, stops it...I'm guessing he took a few blows in the process. Maybe was beaten up pretty good. And Mark, who was stalking Antonia, had followed him from her apartment. He saw the whole thing. And it was his opportunity to get rid of his competition. Is that how it happened?

She stared at me hard. "I told you. That girl drove him a little crazy. She taunted him."

"If any jury would see that it was her fault, why not let Trina Lynn tell what she knew? Why not let a jury find Mark innocent?"

"You don't have children, do you?" she asked.

That was a gut punch. "No, I don't."

She nodded. "That's why you can't possibly understand. Mark would've never survived jail. He's not built for that. He's the son of a police captain. Everyone I've ever sent to jail and all their friends would've taken pleasure in torturing him and then killing him. I couldn't let that happen."

"And Trina Lynn was so close you had to kill her to save him." I tried to say it matter-of-factly, but it still sounded ludicrous.

"Like I said, you know nothing of what it is to have children."

"I know my parents would never kill anyone to protect me

from my own actions." I regretted the words as soon as they were out of my mouth. I didn't need to antagonize her.

"How dare you judge me!"

"And why, exactly, does Mark not use your last name? He *is* your biological son—yours and your husband's, right?"

"Of course he's our son. Our only son. Mark has some wrong ideas. He'd like to see the whole country dissolve into anarchy. It's a phase."

"So, to protect your only son, you murdered Trina Lynn...right in this very spot?" I said.

"I haven't decided yet whether I'm going to kill you as well, so choose your next words carefully—"

"Or you'll kill me exactly where you killed her?"

"I won't hesitate a moment to drop you right where you stand. Yes. Exactly where I dropped her."

From the roof of the adjacent building, floodlights lit the alley.

"Captain Price, lay down your weapon. Slowly." Sonny's voice.

Enraged and haughty, she looked into the lights. "Detective Ravenel, I don't know what you think you're doing, but I was about to arrest this young woman for the murder of Trina Lynn Causby. You'll find all the evidence you need in her possession."

"No, ma'am," said Sonny. "It's all been logged into evidence. Along with the photographs of you loading the boxes into your car and unloading them at the Salvation Army."

"Drop your weapon, ma'am." Jenkins. How many officers were up there with them?

Behind her, two uniformed officers approached, weapons drawn. I glanced over my shoulder. Two more approached from behind me.

Captain Price pulled a gun from under her jacket. She pointed it at my head.

"You're not getting away with this," she said.

I had my weapon, but if I moved, she'd shoot me, no doubt.

She was going to shoot me anyway.

Oh my God. This was it. Nate.

I could see it in her eyes. She was going to kill me. She was going to make them kill her.

"Drop it. Now," Sonny yelled. "Now."

A shot echoed down the alley.

Was I hit?

Captain Price dropped to the brick pathway.

THIRTY-TWO

The palm trees danced in the breeze, their fronds impossibly green against the Carolina blue sky. The heat and humidity abated overnight, with just a hint of fall in the air. Nate and I pulled into Mamma and Daddy's driveway in a shiny new silver Lincoln Navigator.

"I don't understand," I said again.

"I had time on my hands yesterday before everything went sideways. We needed a new car. If you'll recall, we've had very bad luck with the last three Explorers. I got a great deal."

"But these are so much more expensive. Why didn't you get a Tahoe, or...or a Subaru of some sort? I've never owned a car with a theme before. This car has a theme."

"I should never have told you that. I thought it was funny. It's a marketing thing. Look. We spend a lot of time in our cars. We depend on them to be reliable and to have enough room to carry all of our equipment—"

"And that's another thing...how in the world did you get so much of that replaced yesterday afternoon?"

"I simply had the time to knock a few things on our to-do list out. I was thinking it would take away some of your stress. And I have to tell you, this whole conversation feels like a distraction, so we don't talk about the fact you nearly died last night." He drew a deep breath, let it out slowly. "Sonny let that go too long."

I hadn't slept at all the night before. My nerves were still ragged. "I had a bad moment. One where I truly thought I'd never see you again."

"Never again," he said. "Never again will I agree to go unarmed to a scenario where your life is put in danger."

"You know why Sonny insisted on that," I said. "It's one thing for Sonny to shoot a captain during a sting. It's quite another, legally, if you do it. He was trying to protect you."

"And I need to protect you," he said.

"Listen, Mamma's going to come out here and drag us out of the car any minute now. Can we talk about this later?"

"Sure. Yeah. We'd best go inside."

We climbed out of the car. By the time we made it to the front porch, Daddy stood in the doorway. He looked me up and down. Then he turned to Nate. "Is this the new normal, son? My daughter having near death experiences?"

"*Frank.*" Mamma pushed him aside. "Come in the house, children, I've made pot roast."

Pot roast was Mamma's ultimate comfort food dish. She usually made it in cooler months. But that day, she knew I'd need comfort food. Perhaps she did too.

Merry and Joe and Blake and Poppy were in the foyer behind Mamma and Daddy. We walked through and I stopped to hug every one of the people I love most and thought I might never see again.

Mamma gentled us all to the table laden with melt-in-your-mouth pot roast and gravy, mashed potatoes, carrots, butter peas, fried okra, squash casserole, deviled eggs, and biscuits.

When we were all in our places, she prayed extra hard, and extra long. Then we all dug into the feast she'd prepared.

Blake reached for a normal tone, and almost found it. "Looks like Darius is a shoo-in for the vacant town council seat."

"He convinced me he's against development," I said. "He'll get my vote."

"Merry, when are you and Joe leaving for your trip again?" asked Poppy. "It just sounds amazing."

"In November," said Merry. "It's shoulder season in Patagonia then—spring. It won't be quite so crowded."

"So you'll be here for our anniversary?" asked Nate.

"Yeah," said Merry. "We'll be back in plenty of time. Are you planning a party?"

Nate turned to me. We hadn't discussed a party. But it sounded fun.

"I have a surprise planned," he said. "No one make plans for Christmas week this year. Actually...leave two weeks open. The Saturday before Christmas through the Saturday after New Year's. I'll plan this year's holiday celebration. If that's all right with you, Carolyn?" He looked at Mamma.

"You don't want me to plan Christmas?" She couldn't quite parse the idea.

"Every year you work so hard to make the holidays special. I'd consider it a favor if you'd let me do the heavy lifting this year. We'll celebrate Merry and Joe's wedding, our first anniversary, and the holidays. One big celebration. That sound okay?"

He looked at Mamma. We all knew this was her call.

"Well, if that's what you want." She gave him a bewildered look. "Frank's never planned a single thing his entire life."

"It's what I want," said Nate. "Thank you."

I looked at him sideways. What was he up to?

Colleen laughed her signature bray-snort laugh. She was perched on the sideboard watching us eat. "Fix me a plate, would you?"

If you tell me what's going on.

More bray-snorting ensued. "And spoil the surprise? Never in a million years."

Then tell me about Sara Catherine. I'd forgotten all about checking in on her. I'd wanted to reassure Mamma and Daddy she was fine.

"What about her?" Colleen asked.

Is she...okay? Is she happy with the Causbys? Does she need anything?

"Sara Catherine is well taken care of. She's fine. I watch after her."

You do? Why? How is she a part of your mission?

Colleen laughed again. "I can see down the road a little farther than you can. Someone has to look after things here after you've retired."

Retired? In case you haven't noticed, I'm nowhere close to retirement age.

"And she's only three," said Colleen. "Don't forget to fix me a plate. Don't skimp on the gravy now. And I want two biscuits."

AUTHOR'S NOTE

I've taken a slight liberty with time. Readers who live in Charleston County or visit frequently may notice this, so I wanted to explain. While this book will be released on September 3, 2019, the story takes place in the recent past, September 2015. This is only of note because Charleston is constantly changing. New inns and restaurants open and sometimes we lose those we love.

Because of the characters' personal timelines, I needed *Lowcountry Boomerang* to be set in 2015. This is all Calista McQueen's fault. Her story required *Lowcountry Bombshell* to take place in 2012, exactly fifty years after the death of Marilyn Monroe. And so the year of that book and all that come after was fixed.

That said, because readers like to know about restaurants and inns they can visit now, most of the locations in Charleston are portrayed in the book as they exist now. Cannon Street is not a one-way street any longer, though it was in 2015. The bed and breakfast, 86 Cannon, didn't actually open until 2017, as did Brown Fox Coffee in Mt. Pleasant.

The exception to this wrinkle in time is that St. Andrews Church in Mt. Pleasant, which stood whole in 2015, was ravaged by a fire April 22, 2018, and the main ministry building is now in the process of being rebuilt. The church is written into this story as it stood in 2015.

I hope you enjoy roaming the streets of Charleston with Liz as much as I do!

Susan M. Boyer

Susan M. Boyer is the author of the *USA Today* bestselling Liz Talbot mystery series. Her debut novel, *Lowcountry Boil*, won the Agatha Award for Best First Novel, the Daphne du Maurier Award for Excellence in Mystery/Suspense, and garnered several other award nominations, including the Macavity. The third in the series, *Lowcountry Boneyard*, was a Southern Independent Booksellers Alliance (SIBA) Okra Pick, a Daphne du Maurier Award finalist, and short-listed for the Pat Conroy Beach Music Mystery Prize. Susan loves beaches, Southern food, and small towns where everyone knows everyone, and everyone has crazy relatives. You'll find all of the above in her novels. She lives in Greenville, SC, with her husband and an inordinate number of houseplants.

The Liz Talbot Mystery Series
by Susan M. Boyer

LOWCOUNTRY BOIL (#1)
LOWCOUNTRY BOMBSHELL (#2)
LOWCOUNTRY BONEYARD (#3)
LOWCOUNTRY BORDELLO (#4)
LOWCOUNTRY BOOK CLUB (#5)
LOWCOUNTRY BONFIRE (#6)
LOWCOUNTRY BOOKSHOP (#7)
LOWCOUNTRY BOOMERANG (#8)
LOWCOUNTRY BOONDOGGLE (#9)

Henery Press Mystery Books

And finally, before you go...
Here are a few other mysteries
you might enjoy:

CIRCLE OF INFLUENCE

Annette Dashofy

A Zoe Chambers Mystery (#1)

Zoe Chambers, paramedic and deputy coroner in rural Pennsylvania's tight-knit Vance Township, has been privy to a number of local secrets over the years, some of them her own. But secrets become explosive when a dead body is found in the Township Board President's abandoned car.

As a January blizzard rages, Zoe and Police Chief Pete Adams launch a desperate search for the killer, even if it means uncovering secrets that could not only destroy Zoe and Pete, but also those closest to them.

Available at booksellers nationwide and online

Visit www.henerypress.com for details

LIVING THE VIDA LOLA

Melissa Bourbon

A Lola Cruz Mystery (#1)

Meet Lola Cruz, a fiery full-fledged PI at Camacho and Associates. Her first big case? A missing mother who may not want to be found. And to make her already busy life even more complicated, Lola's helping plan her cousin's quinceañera and battling her family and their old-fashioned views on women and careers. She's also reunited with the gorgeous Jack Callaghan, her high school crush whom she shamelessly tailed years ago and photographed doing the horizontal salsa with some other lucky girl.

Lola takes it all in stride, but when the subject of her search ends up dead, she has a lot more to worry about. Soon she finds herself wrapped up in the possibly shady practices of a tattoo parlor, local politics, and someone with serious—maybe deadly—road rage. But Lola is well-equipped to handle these challenges. She's a black-belt in kung fu, and her body isn't her only weapon. She's got smarts, sass, and more tenacity than her Mexican mafioso-wannabe grandfather. A few of her famous margaritas don't hurt, either.

Available at booksellers nationwide and online

Visit www.henerypress.com for details

STAGING IS MURDER

Grace Topping

A Laura Bishop Mystery (#1)

Laura Bishop just nabbed her first decorating commission—staging a 19th-century mansion that hasn't been updated for decades. But when a body falls from a laundry chute and lands at Laura's feet, replacing flowered wallpaper becomes the least of her duties.

To clear her assistant of the murder and save her fledgling business, Laura's determined to find the killer. Turns out it's not as easy as renovating a manor home, especially with two handsome men complicating her mission: the police detective on the case and the real estate agent trying to save the manse from foreclosure.

Worse still, the meddling of a horoscope-guided friend, a determined grandmother, and the local funeral director could get them all killed before Laura props the first pillow.

Available at booksellers nationwide and online

Visit www.henerypress.com for details

MURDER AT THE PALACE

Margaret Dumas

A Movie Palace Mystery (#1)

Welcome to the Palace movie theater! Now Showing: Philandering husbands, ghostly sidekicks, and a murder or two.

When Nora Paige's movie-star husband leaves her for his latest co-star, she flees Hollywood to take refuge in San Francisco at the Palace, a historic movie theater that shows the classic films she loves. There she finds a band of misfit film buffs who care about movies (almost) as much as she does.

She also finds some shady financial dealings and the body of a murdered stranger. Oh, and then there's Trixie, the lively ghost of a 1930's usherette who appears only to Nora and has a lot to catch up on. With the help of her new ghostly friend, can Nora catch the killer before there's another murder at the Palace?

Available at booksellers nationwide and online

Visit www.henerypress.com for details